I Guess
I'll Never Know

J.B. Millhollin

Grey Place Books—Mt. Juliet, TN
ISBN: 978-1-7358745-2-4
Library of Congress Control Number: *2022912794*
Title: *I Guess I'll Never Know*
Author: J.B. Millhollin
Digital distribution | 2022
Paperback | 2022

This is a work of fiction. The characters, names, incidents, places, and dialogue are products of the author's imagination, and are not to be construed as real.

Previous novels by JB Millhollin

Brakus
Brakus, Book 1
Everything he Touched, Book 2
With Nothing to Lose, Book 3

An Absence of Ethics
Forever Bound
Out of Reach
Redirect
Whisper of Hope

To Hide from a Northern Wind: Spencer Creek, Book 1
To Hide from a Northern Wind: Wilson County, Book 2
To Hide from a Northern Wind: Nashville Divided, Book 3
To Hide from a Northern Wind: River of Tears, Book 4

When Next We Meet

Coming Soon

Plausible Deception
The Reporter
An Unacceptable Conclusion
The Prosecutor
Life on Hold (Book 1)
Life Altered (Book 2)
My Turn

Chapter 1

First of all, to my family, friends and business acquaintances—I am so sorry I have to put you through this. It was not supposed to end this way. This was not supposed to be part of the story of either of our lives. It would have been so much easier for all of you, if I would have just walked into one of the many secluded woods in Tennessee and never walked out: or walked into a swiftly moving river: or thrown myself down an old abandoned mineshaft. Most likely, my body would never have been found. But I couldn't do that. I want you to bury me next to her. Handling my demise in this manner was really the only choice I had.

For those of you that *don't* know our story, I want you to understand. I want you to know how I came to the conclusion this was what was best for me. I want you to grasp what our relationship was all about and what you can have in your life with a little effort and a lot of love.

Our relationship was far from love at first sight for either of us. In fact, initially it was just the opposite. When we first met, I did not care for her—at all. Susan was with the DA's office and I was with the public defender's office. Every time we opposed each other in court, she beat me—*every single time.*

Nothing changed in our relationship when I found a new job and ended up doing the same thing she was doing, in the same office—prosecuting defendants. Even though we were just a room apart and cheering for the same team, nothing changed between us. Nothing changed, that is, until one day when I needed help concerning some difficult issues involving a case I was handling. She offered to work with me, to help me work through those issues—and that's when it all began.

Once I really got to know her and know her well, I asked her to marry me. From then on, nothing could keep us apart.

She was such an incredible individual in *so* many ways. I couldn't spend enough time with her. Whether working at the office, or just sitting, late at night, in front of the fireplace in our living room, I was always wanting more waking hours with her.

I am sorry we had no children. We tried. We would have, we just didn't have enough time. It was in the plans; we just simply didn't have enough time.

After we married, we loved living in Nashville. Our small apartment was expensive, but nice. However, when we bought the acreage, a home with a few acres out back, life changed. We spent hours each evening we were home, outside, just enjoying the outdoors either by ourselves or with our neighbors. We would often wake up on a Sunday morning, with perhaps a slight hangover, but laughing our way through the day about something someone said or did the previous night while we were all together.

I guess the low point, and for us it was only a slight bump in the road, was when she decided to run for the office of Davidson County District Attorney General, a decision she made, but with which I didn't concur. It was one of the few major decisions either of us ever made, without the approval of the spouse. She wanted to move up. I felt life was good right where we were. I didn't want the change, but she did. We never got a chance to figure out who might have been right and who might have been wrong.

We were just getting ready for the general election—she had won the primary with little difficulty. Susan left the house earlier than usual. She had a busy day and wanted to get an early start. I saw her when I arrived, but was absorbed in my own work all day. I left the office at my regular time, she said she was working late. She never made it past that last intersection near home. I unknowingly kissed her for the last time late that afternoon.

The only regret I really have now, is that her murder remains unsolved. They have had over three years, *three years*, to figure this all out. How complicated can it be? It's now a cold case. I continue to call, to ask the investigating officer what he has uncovered, but the answer is always the same.

After she died, I tried dating once or twice. But it always turned out the same. Once the date was over, I always found myself finishing off a bottle of wine, thinking of Susan and comparing her to the woman I was just with—a rather foolish game which Susan never lost.

I've had enough. I truly believe in an afterlife. Many don't, I do. I believe an afterlife, hopefully with her, will be immensely superior to the hell I am living now.

Please don't judge me harshly. Just bury me beside her. The space is there. Don't feel sorry for me, or for her. Instead, spend your time enjoying life with the one you love, each and every moment of each and every day. It's so short. It's so fragile. Find peace in what you do and with whom you love—never let it go. My best to all of you.

Chapter 2

“So, what did you do last night?”

“Why?”

“No particular reason. I was just interested in knowing what both you and Kim did last night. I didn’t mean to offend. And I didn’t call to argue. Even though I’m not living there with you right now, surely, we can civilly discuss what you and our daughter did last night, can’t we?”

“Come on, Andy. You don’t really care what either of us did last night. Now, why did you really call?”

“Jess, just humor me, will you? I got a little time here this morning, and I’d really like to discuss what the two of you did last night…and maybe discuss us too.”

“Whatever. Yeah, well we’re not discussing *us,* so forget about that. Me? I did nothing, absolutely nothing, which I also did frequently while living with you over the years. Kim had a date. She went out for a while—with Jack. They weren’t gone but an hour or so. They walked down and had ice cream, then came home.”

Andy Price put his feet up on his desk, leaned back and said, “You know anything about that kid? Is he okay? You know his family?”

“Yes, yes, I know his family. So do you. With all those many things you’re so wrapped up with at work, you just forgot. They live right down the street from us. Tall kid, skinny, but kind of cute. His dad runs that auto dealership down by…”

“Okay, okay I remember. How did the date go?”

“She said she had a good time, so I assume she did. She likes this kid. They haven’t discussed the future and probably won’t, but she does have a good time with him. They made plans to go to a movie Saturday night.”

“I would have liked to been there when she got home.”

“Maybe. But you would have *preferred* to be at work. You know that and so do I.”

"By the way, not to change the subject, but did you happen to see that article in the paper yesterday about that guy?"

She hesitated, then said, "Sure did."

"That had to tug at your heartstrings."

"Okay Andy, you ask me if I saw an article in the paper about *'that guy.'* What the hell is that supposed to mean? The paper is full of *'that guy'*. Who the hell are you talking about?"

"Sorry, sorry you're right. It was the article about the guy that killed himself. They published his suicide note. The one where his wife was that lawyer that got murdered about three years ago."

She hesitated. "Yes. I read it. Made me cry. I was surprised they published it. The whole thing was depressing and so sad."

"You know, they lived not far from us. If you continue on past our house on Cedar, our street, it goes right by their house. We really didn't live that far away from them."

"You weren't involved in that investigation, were you? That wasn't one of the five thousand cases you've worked on, is it?"

"Now come on babe, don't be that way. It's just a job. It's just…"

"It's just a job that's destroying our marriage, *that's all it is*—that's all it is."

"I hoped we could discuss that a little more in depth sometime today. I'd really like to come home instead of living in that two-room apartment. Could we discuss that whole job issue sometime tonight?"

"What's changed since the last time we discussed it?"

"Well, nothing, really. I have…"

"I've told you fifty goddamn times, Andy. I'm not living this way. You are gone all the time. You're gone all the *fricken time*. And unless something changes and changes quickly, I'm going to file. I can't live this way. I love you. Probably always will. But you spend 18 hours a day on the job and 6 hours with your family. That's not working and it's not *going* to work. *Period*! Now I have to go. I'll talk to you some other time. Let me know when you're ready to be part of this family. We can talk about it then."

"But, Jessica, I…"

As he hung up the phone, Garth Belding, walked by his desk and said, "I think you just got hung up on. You didn't finish your sentence, but one of the words you did finish was 'Jessica', which probably means another fight, and another quickly terminated phone call, right?"

"Yeah. Same old thing. She thinks I'm married to the job, not her."

"You are."

"You know, if you really were a *friend,* you'd keep your stupid opinions to yourself—quit being so judgmental. You always have been a judgmental jerk. By the way, you remember the murder of that attorney with the DA's office a few years back?"

"Yeah, I do. By the way, just to finish off that last topic of discussion, I'm probably also the best and only friend you've ever had. Just remember that, buddy You just remember all the things I've done for you over the years and that..."

"Oh, just shut the hell up, and move on. Answer the damn question."

"Yes, yes I remember her."

"You didn't work on that case, did you? I know I didn't."

"No. I think Harlan did."

"I wonder if anyone picked it up after he retired. He's been gone what about six months now?"

"Yes. I imagine by now it's just another cold case. I haven't talked to anyone that's worked on it since he retired. He was a good detective, and he wasn't able to uncover anything. I'm assuming you saw that article in the paper yesterday about her husband killing himself."

"Yes, I did. I have to admit, it brought a tear to my eye. That was a pretty compelling article. I didn't know those people lived out my way. They actually lived pretty close to where we do."

"You mean, pretty close to where '*you did live.*' 'You did live', would be the operative words here."

"Whatever. You really don't need to remind me."

"You having any success with getting her to let you move back in?"

"No. I'm afraid I'm going to have to change some things in my life this time, for her to reconsider."

"As maybe you should. You know..."

Andy stood. "Let me tell you what I *do* know—about you. What I *do* know, is that I'm not taking marital advice from someone that's already in his young life, been divorced twice. Now I need to go see Art."

A few minutes later he walked in the office of Arthur Stone, and as he did, he said, "Morning, Art, you got a few minutes?"

"About a few and no more. What do you want?"

Andy walked in and leaned his six-foot two inch, slightly overweight frame, against one of the two chairs sitting in front of the desk of his boss and said, "You remember three years ago or so, when that assistant DA was murdered?"

Art leaned back in his chair, and said, "You read that article in the paper?"

"I did, yes, I did. That note was tough to read. Right after that murder happened, he would call here almost every day and he continued to for months. But as time went by, the calls stopped coming in. I felt so sorry for him."
He hesitated. "But we can't make up the facts or make up the perps. We just couldn't figure out who did it, plain and simple. I think Harlan worked on that case day and night at first, then slowly started to back off a little because there was nothing left to investigate. Of course, he had other cases to work too, like we all do. But I know he was really frustrated."

"Art, I would like to take a shot at it."

"Really. Why?"

"It touched me. I'd really like to do some of my own investigating and see what I can turn up. I know Harlan is, or was, good at his job, but maybe a new set of eyes would help. Maybe a new approach would help."

"You going to do this on top of all you're working on now?"

"Yes."

"Good god, your wife will be calling me every day, instead of only once a week like she does now, or did. Why isn't she still calling? You two work things out?"

"Probably. At least to *her* satisfaction. I moved out."

"I'm sorry, Andy. Are one of you going to file?"

"No, not yet. We're just taking a time-out, as they say in grade school. I have no idea what we're going to do. But I do know I'll probably not tell her I'm taking on this case in addition to everything else I'm working on. I thought I'd just take a quick look at the paperwork, maybe ask a few questions. Do you have a problem with me working it?"

He studied Andy for only a moment, before he said, "No, I guess not. Certainly, solving it would be a positive for the department…and for the public. Go ahead. Don't spend a lot of time on it, but sure, take a look."

"Thanks. I suppose I best start with Harlan. I'll see what I can find out through him after I review the files. I mean, if it really looks like a complete dead end, I'll just stop and let the case die with her husband. But I would really like to take a look at the files, talk to Harlan and see where that takes me."

Later that night, as he put one of the Susan Jackson file's down and rubbed his tired eyes, he looked around one of the two rooms in which he now called home. What was left of a TV dinner, remained on the floor beside his chair. Sitting next to it, was a glass with the remains of a half-dozen ice cubes and just enough bourbon to cover the very bottom of the glass.

It was late…time to get some sleep before getting up tomorrow and following up a few ideas that came to mind after reviewing her file. He reached for his phone and punched in Jessica's number. It went straight to voicemail. He left no message. This was a routine that played out the same way, most every night of the week.

Andy terminated the call, walked in the second room of his two-room apartment, took off his shoes, then fell into bed with his clothes on. He was too tired to take them off, and it didn't matter to him whether they were wrinkled or not. As rushed as he normally was to get to the office each morning, he wouldn't need to take the time to put them on again. If they were wrinkled, so be it. Most likely no one at work would ever notice. The whole plan made perfect sense to him.

Chapter 3

our years earlier
Susan Jackson had tossed and turned, until she could take no more. She had been lying in bed for almost an hour as she tried to fall asleep *again,* figuring if she failed *this* time, she would try to gather up enough energy to get out of bed. Last night, initially, she had no problem falling asleep as soon as her head hit the pillow. Now, however, it was late enough in the early morning, there remained no other option but to get out of bed, perhaps briefly enjoy a few moments of early morning on the deck, get dressed and drive to work.

She slowly inched her way toward the edge of the bed, and once there, pushed off the sheets as she stood up. She didn't want to awaken Tom. She knew he had been up late working on a closing argument. She had gone to bed long before he had.

Susan felt around for her robe in the darkened room and finally found it near the end of the bed where she now remembered she left it.

She walked into the kitchen and fixed a cup of coffee. A quick look at her phone indicated a much warmer than normal, early November morning. Susan opened the double-doors to the deck, softly closed them behind her, and sat down in one of the two chairs.

The sun was just starting to push its way upward and into a beautiful light-blue sky. Toward the far end of their property, she could see a small herd of deer grazing, unaware of anything else in the world but each other,

Perfection. She smiled, as she used the only word that came to mind. A hot cup of coffee and a perfect late fall morning—what an incredible way to start the day. Just what she needed before she drove to the office and walked into the insanity of her *other* world.

She had been there no longer than fifteen minutes, when she heard the sound of sliding glass doors. As she turned, Tom said, "Morning. Wow, what a beautiful day."

He leaned down, kissed her, and as he did, he reached under her robe.

She grabbed his hand, and said, "Nope, not this morning. I have too much on my mind. Besides, last night should have been enough to keep you satisfied for a while, Romeo."

He smiled, sat down, and said, "You know, it's the nature of the beast to always be looking for just a little more."

As he sat, she smiled and said, "You're not telling me anything about you I don't already know. Did you see the deer? They've been there since I sat down, oblivious to the rest of the world. *That* would be a life I know nothing about and probably wouldn't enjoy."

"How long have you been up?"

"Fifteen, twenty minutes maybe. Did you finish getting ready for your hearing? I fell asleep before you got in bed."

"Yes, I'm ready. Hopefully, it'll be enough to convict. You coming over to watch or do you have too much going on?"

"I have way too much going on. That's why I tossed and turned all night. I need to learn how to quit taking my job to bed. Unfortunately, that doesn't work very well for me. I know it's the way it should be, but I just can't turn it all off that easily. By the way, how are you getting along at work? I know we discuss specifics every day. But what about your overall *job?* Are you enjoying it, or do you rue the day I ever talked you into leaving the dark side and coming to my side, the right side?"

He smiled, as he said, "It's taken a while, as you know. The mindset is so much different, but it's without doubt the best thing I ever did." He smiled, "Well, of course, other than marrying you. I can thank *you* for *that* life altering move too, I guess."

"As far as the job's concerned, you did me a favor. I love having you in the same office, despite the fact our paths don't cross much. It's comforting knowing you're close—that if I need to bend an ear, you're right there."

"What have you got going on today?"

"Well, along with all the other cases I'm trying to handle, yesterday Chuck said he's assigning a couple of new cases to me. I don't think they amount to much but, unfortunately, they'll probably take as much time to put together as a murder case does. I'm working pretty much at my max right now. I'm not sure I can handle many more cases and yet do them all justice. I need to discuss that with him today."

"What are the charges?"

"I think he said one was an assault, and the other was a burglary. Both involve repeaters. They've both been down this road a time or two."

"So, *do* you have more to do than you can handle?"

"Nope. It's getting close though. I'll talk to him today about it. I don't want to complain, but I also don't want to lose a case I should have won because I just have to much on my plate. What about you? What's going on with you?"

"Once I finish this case up today, I don't have too much that's pending. Maybe I could take one or two of your cases and at least get them ready for you to try."

"You have enough to do. I'll be fine. I may have to put in a few more hours, but I'll be fine."

He reached out and took her hand. "I know you'll be fine, but if I can help, you let me know. I have no way of knowing at any one point in time, exactly how heavy your workload is, but if I can help you, just know I'm willing."

"Well, I think that's the end of the deer. Looks like they're moving on."

He continued to watch the herd, but remained silent. As she started to rise, he said, "Hold on a minute. Do you still have a moment to talk about something? I mean, I know you take more time than I to get ready to go to work, and I don't really know what time you want to be in the office this morning. So, I'll keep this brief. But it seems now is as good as any to talk about what I what to ask you,"

She moved forward in her chair, as she said, "What's the problem? What's going on?"

"Now, I know you and I have talked about this before, but it's been a while. What are your thoughts about a baby? Are you ready yet?"

She smiled, pulled her hand away and sat back in her chair.

After a few moments of silence, he said, "Are you going to give me an answer, or just leave me guessing as to what your thoughts might be?"

She continued to look away, but she did finally say, "I'm just not ready, Tom. I'm sorry. I know how important that is to you, but I'm just not ready."

"Okay, okay I understand. And we can let it go for now, but I just want you to know, as I've said in the past, I'm ready any time you are."

"Oh, I know. You've made it perfectly clear. I'll let you know. I just need to settle into the job, get a little more organized, and..."

After a few seconds of silence, he said, "And what? What were you going to say?"

"I'm still...kicking around...running for..."

"Now wait...are you still considering running for the district attorney general's job? You aren't really still considering that are you?"

She smiled, stood and said, "I gotta go. I need to get ready for work. You coming along?"

She turned and walked away.

He stood and followed her, as he said, "Hey, are you *really* still considering running for his job? I thought you had already made that decision. I thought you had given up on the idea of running. You know how much work that is? We'll *never* see each other." He reached out and grabbed her robe, turned her around and said, "Are you really still thinking about running?"

She smiled and kissed him. "I don't know, maybe, might be. It's still months away yet. I have time to figure that all out. Don't worry about it."

She turned and as she walked away, she said, "I'll make you my first deputy. We'll make love in the district attorney's office if I win."

As he followed her, he said, "Is that supposed to be a positive? Is that supposed to be something that excites me? *You really think that's a positive?* Well, it isn't. That's just not a turn-on for me. You won't have time for that anyway. Would you rather do *that*...than have children? Hey, talk to..."

Susan turned on the water for her shower. She could no longer hear him. She smiled. It was time to plant the seed and let him slowly accept it. She was still weighing her options, but right now, unless someone or something changed her mind, her plan was to run for the office.

She had concluded that if she did decide to run, knowing Tom as she did, he would become as much involved and wrapped up in the idea of winning, as she did. At least, that was *her* assessment of his mindset if she did decide to run. Hopefully she had him figured out, because, unless something happened to change her mind, she was most all of ninety-nine percent certain she was going to run

.

Chapter 4

"Morning, Amy."

"Morning, Susan. Hey, you're almost late. That's way unusual for you. Where have you been?"

"For some reason, it just took a little longer for me to get ready. What do I have this morning, other than my meeting with Chuck in a few minutes?"

Amy, after following Susan into her office, said, "Wow, you look great. I wish I had a figure like yours. You still work out?"

"Oh, a little now and then—when I have time. Now, who's coming in? What's your schedule showing? I want to make sure it's consistent with mine."

"Let me look."

As Susan was reviewing phone messages from the preview day, Amy walked back in, and said, "Nothing's changed from what I gave you midafternoon yesterday. I have a block of time set off for you to see Chuck first, then, later this morning, the cop that handled one of the new cases assigned to you—State vs. Wagner—is coming in to discuss it with you."

"Everything this afternoon remains unchanged from what you've already told me about?"

"Yes."

"Okay, let me look over a few things before I go see Chuck. So, I don't lose track of time, let me know when it's nine, and I'll run down to see him."

An hour later, Amy notified Susan it was time for her meeting. As she walked in his office, she said, "Morning, Chuck."

He stood as he said, "Morning, Susan. Have a chair. You have time to talk a minute or two about those two new cases I assigned you?"

"I do yes. But, Chuck, you know, as concerns those new cases, to be honest, I already have a pretty full schedule right now. With those cases you gave me last week, I have more than enough to do already, without adding on."

He smiled and said, "I'll never give you more than you can handle. Neither of these should press you for time."

"Tell me about them."

"Both cases were cases Jack Morgan was supposed to handle. But, of course, he's moved on, so I had to reassign them. State vs. Wagner involves an assault. The defendant beat the hell out of guy in the bathroom of one of the downtown bars. Really, the only issue is the reluctant witnesses. There were quite a few guys in the bathroom, but none of them, other than one individual, want to testify against him. They're all afraid of him. You'll just have to talk to each one of them and see what they might agree to do."

"What about the victim?"

"He'll testify against Wagner. There's no doubt about that."

"What's the defendant's attorney say about his position?"

"He says these two have had issues in the past, and the complaining witness is just getting back at him for those prior issues. He says the complaining witness was so drunk he didn't even know where he was, let alone know who used him as a punching bag."

"The guy got any priors?"

"Yes. He's a mean, vindictive son-of-a-bitch. We need to convict him. He's wiggled his way out of bad situations in the past— situations which he created. We need to put him away."

"What's the second case?"

"State verses Hepner. It's a burglary. He wasn't caught at the scene. But there was a witness and he will testify it was him. He was employed there and he had cash on him when arrested. But his wife will testify he was home all night."

"Is he a problem beyond this charge?"

"Drugs are his problem. From what I understand, he's fine as long as he's not using, but when he's using, he's an animal. He has a couple of prior robbery convictions, the last of which involved a knife. He just needs to dry out in prison for a couple of years, and maybe he'll be alright. He needs to be convicted, just like the first one I told you about, which is why I'm assigning both of these cases to you. I know you'll get the job done."

"Got it. They've both been set for trial, right?"

"Yes, but you should have plenty of time to prepare."

"I'll talk to the officers. If I uncover any issues, I'll let you know." She stood. "Is that it Chuck?"

He smiled, and said, "Short and sweet. Right to the point. You never change, which is why I'm glad you're on our side. One question."

"What's that?"

"Are you going to run?"

"For your job?"

"Yes."

"I don't know. I've tossed it around, but I don't know. Anything else."

"You'd be a great district attorney general Susan you really would."

She turned to walk away and as she did, she said, "Yeah I would, but so would plenty of others. I'll let you know."

An hour later, officer Jack Thompson walked in her office.

Susan stood and said, "Officer Thompson, nice to meet you. Have a seat. You're here concerning State vs. Wagner, correct?"

As he sat, he said, "Yes."

"I understand this man has been in trouble before."

"He's been involved in a number of other situations involving minor assault, but nothing that really hurt anyone—until now."

"Will the complaining witness verify he was the one that did this?"

"Yes. But everyone else is too afraid of him to come forward. No one else will work with us to convict him."

"Does he deny it?"

"Yes. The guy is nuts. He is a problem about every other night. He's either creating a disturbance pushing someone around, or verbally abusing the patrons of whichever bar he's in. We've been called out a number of times concerning him. This is really the first time we got him where we want him. We need a conviction."

"So, we only have two witnesses—the defendant and the victim?"

"There were others in that bathroom, but they're too afraid to testify against him—except..."

"Except who, except what?"

"There is one guy that was in there at the time, but he was in one of the stalls and *said* he never saw anything. I might be able to get him to testify. I know he saw what happened, but let me work on him a little."

"Just let me know. Anything else?"

"Nope. That's it."

She stood. "Call me if anything else comes up. I'll let you know if they want to take your deposition and when the case is set for trial."

"Thanks."

As he left her office, Susan walked out behind him and said, "Amy, see if you can find George Black, Officer George Black. Tell him I want to see him when he gets a moment and to bring his file on Sam Hepner."

Early that afternoon, Amy informed her Officer Black was waiting to see her in the reception area. She told her to send him right in.

Susan stood as he entered the room. "Good afternoon, George. Did you bring your file on Hepner with you?"

"I did, I sure did. I got it right here."

She sat as he handed her the file. "Have a seat. Let's discuss the case for a moment if you have time."

"Sure. I have the time."

As she looked through the pages of the file folder, she said, "So he broke into a store, after hours, where he was employed, is that correct?"

"Yes. He knew there was money available, and he needed it to buy drugs."

"Did you find anything else on his person, other than the money?"

"No."

"Did he deny it was him?"

"Yes. But we have a witness that saw someone leave the building after hours. He ran right past his car. It wasn't that difficult to identify him."

She leaned back in her chair and said, "If it's so open and shut, why is he denying it?"

"He just says it wasn't him, His wife says he was home all night. He says the eyewitness is mistaken." He hesitated for a moment, and looked away.

She waited. It was obvious there was something he wanted to say.

As he reengaged, he said, "This dude is a pretty good guy when he's not on drugs. But I know him, I know his past. I've picked him up before for petty issues. When he's on drugs he is absolutely crazy. He's unlike anyone I've ever seen. He'll do anything—absolutely anything. He needs to dry out and prison is where he needs to do it."

She smiled, and said, "Then that's where we need to make sure he goes. Leave your file. Let me look it over. I'll let you know if they want to take your depo and when it's set for trial. Thanks for coming in."

Susan never arrived home until a little after seven. She dropped her purse on one of the chairs in the living room, and walked straight to the built-in bar, where she poured herself a glass of merlot.

As she turned around, Tom walked in from the deck, and said, "You were busy today. I tried to get in to see you a couple of times but you were with someone."

She kissed him as she walked by and said, "It was a hell of a long day. You fixing something for supper?"

He smiled and followed her out on the deck. "It was still warm enough to grill out so it's steaks and corn on the cob. I was just waiting for you to get home."

She dropped down into one of the deck chairs, took a deep breath, and said, "Home. Thank God. Days like today are what make this job so tough. If there wasn't so much self-satisfaction in what I do, I'd move on in the blink of an eye."

As he placed the steaks on the grill, Tom said, "Did you end up with two more cases?"

"Yes, I did. I had a visit with Chuck first, and then talked to both officers, along with everything else I needed to do today. I *should* be there at the office as we speak…I *shouldn't* be here, drinking wine, and eating steak. I need to go back tonight and…"

Tom leaned down, kissed her, and said, "You should be right here, that's where you should be. Now relax. Let me fix supper. Have another glass of wine and just enjoy the view, enjoy your husband, the smell of steaks on the grill, your life with a man that…"

"Chuck asked me if I was going to run for his office."

"You're kidding. What did…"

"I don't know what to do. On the one hand, I could…

She noticed Tom tried to comment a couple of times, but as she started to argue both sides of the issue with herself, he finally just smiled at her, walked to the grill and flipped the steaks.

Chapter 5

Susan was in her office the next morning long before Amy arrived. She couldn't sleep and left the house as soon as she was dressed. By the time her secretary arrived, she was working on her third active file.

She heard her walk through the outer office door, pull all the files, and straighten up her work area, as she always did before checking with Susan to further coordinate the day's activities.

"Morning. How long have you been here? Did you just stay all night?"

As Susan continued to review a deposition she had taken weeks ago, she smiled, and said, "I got here about an hour ago. And no, I didn't stay all night but I should have. I'm on my second pot of coffee. How was your evening?"

"Oh, good…just pretty good. Pretty much good, anyway. How 'bout you?"

Susan looked up. She leaned back in her chair and said, "Hmm, it doesn't look like it went so good from here. Now, again, how was your evening?"

"Good. Just about like I had planned, I guess." She started to back away from Susan's desk.

"Wait a minute. Sit down."

Amy stopped, but never moved.

"Amy, sit down…*now*."

She did as she was told.

"What's with the bruise?"

"Nothing. I fell."

"Bullshit. Were you and Derrick at it again?"

Amy looked down for a moment. When she reengaged, she smiled, and said, "Yes. But you should see him. I'm picture-perfect compared to him."

"What the hell happened?"

"Really, nothing. He just got mad about some new clothes I brought home and started giving me a bunch of shit about it. Before long he was in my face. That's not a good thing for me. I get a little crazy when that happens, as I've told you before."

"What about the mark, Amy?"

"Oh, he shoved me. I got up and hit him right in the nose." She smiled. "I might have broken it, I'm not sure. I know when he kissed me goodbye this morning, I made sure I was at a good angle to push his nose a little and he grimaced, so I think I broke it. Oh, he slapped me pretty hard on the side of my face and it bruised me, but I'm good—I'm okay. Besides a little pain never hurt anyone, right?"

"I'm not sure I can agree with you on that, but let's move on. How many times has it been that you've come to work this way? Why don't you get rid of him?"

"Because I love him. But the bastard's not going to get away with anything. He's not going to shove me around, or verbally abuse me or I'm going to beat the living hell out of him." She smiled. "And to be perfectly honest…I think the guy likes it. But that doesn't matter to me one way or the other. No one, and I mean no one, is going to take advantage of me or push me around. They do, they're going to hear from me one way or the other."

"How do all your rules concerning inflicting pain pertain to a boss…a boss like me? I mean, I'm really not a fighter. I know we've discussed various issues you were having at home, but I had no idea your relationship with him was quite like this."

She stood. "I need to clean up a couple of issues before your first appointment. I just don't like people taking advantage of me…or pushing me around…or making fun of my weight. No big deal. *You* never do that. You're the best."

Later in the morning, while Susan was reviewing a file concerning a trial later in the month and still evaluating Amy's remarks, she walked in and said, "There's a Larry Whitacre here to see you. He said you told him to stop by sometime. He said you needed to see him on the Wagner assault case. He wondered if now was a good time."

"Well, he remembered part of the conversation anyway. I actually told him to make an appointment and *then* come see me. But, send him in. I'll see him now."

She stood as he walked in.

"Morning, Mr. Whitacre, nice to see you."

She extended her hand, which the witness ignored. As he sat, he said, "What do you need from me? Why did you want to see me?"

She sat as she said, "I'll make this brief. Did you witness an assault in a downtown bar bathroom involving Jim Wagner?"

He stood up.

"Sit down, Mr. Whitacre."

He turned to leave her office.

"If you don't sit down, you'll be in jail before the day's over. I don't mind talking to you behind bars. I have no doubt an officer can find something wrong with what you're doing—whether it's drugs or jaywalking. Now sit down until both of us have finished this conversation."

He stopped, thought for a moment, then sat back down.

"Now, what about that fight? You know, he almost killed that guy."

"Doesn't affect me."

"I know that. I understand that. But it *could* have been *you*. It could have been anyone in that bar, or any other bar Wagner just happens to be in any night of the week. You know the guy's trouble. I have no doubt you've seen him do this before. This isn't the first time, and it won't be the last. We need to get him out of the bars and into prison. Now tell me about the evening."

He thought for a moment, then said, "Before we get to that, tell me this. What if he's not convicted? What if I testify and he's not convicted? What the hell do you think happens to me?"

"Listen. All I can tell you is that if you do testify, and if the complaining witness testifies, the chance of him being convicted is damn near a hundred percent. I really believe your testimony is all we need to put him away. Now tell me what you saw that night."

He looked down for a moment as he reviewed his options, which Susan had intentionally limited.

When he looked up, he said, "He walked in the bathroom, walked up to the guy and just beat the living hell out of him. I don't know what happened outside the bathroom between them. All I know is what I seen, and that's what I seen."

"Okay, good, good, that's exactly want I want you to say at the time of trial. I want you to simply say there was no doubt it was him, and he's the one that beat the hell out of that poor guy. Can you do that for me?"

He said nothing, continuing to stare at Susan.

"Can you do that for me—for that poor guy he beat up?"

He whispered, "If he gets off, he'll kill me."

"Then we need to make sure he doesn't. Now I'll have you served with a subpoena, you just be sure and honor it, okay?"

Again, he said nothing.

"Larry, are you okay with that?"

Finally, he whispered, "Yes. Maybe. I don't know. What should I do between now and then? Will he know I'm going to testify against him?"

"No. I am going to use you on rebuttal. He's going to get up on the stand and lie his ass off. When he does, I'll have you testify he's lying. He'll never know what hit him. Just continue to appear as though you have nothing to do with the trial, and you should be fine. He'll never know otherwise. The only thing you'll have to worry about is if we *don't* convict, which we will."

She stood. "Think about it. I really need you to testify. Stay in touch. If anything changes on my end, I'll let you know."

Amy walked in after he left. "Whoa, he was a tough looking customer. I listened the best I could to make sure he didn't hurt you."

"I'm thinking based on your statements this morning, he's the kind of man you enjoy. He should have been a real turn-on for you."

Amy smiled and said, "He kinda was, but he was just a little to grody for me. I like bad boys that clean up, at least a little. You need anything from me or you got all the files you need?"

"Bring in the other new file. I think I have this Wagner case ready to try now that I've talked to Whitacre. Get the defendant's wife in that new break-in case, on the phone for me. I need to talk to her for a minute."

Susan just stood to go get another cup of coffee, when Amy opened her office door and said, "Ms. Hepner is on line one. Good luck."

"Will she be hard to deal with?"

Amy smiled. "Good luck."

"Hello, this is Assistant District Attorney General Jackson. Is this Ms. Hepner?"

"Hell yes, it is. You knew that when you picked up the phone. What do you want? And make it quick. I got kids to take care of."

"Ma'am, I just wanted to visit with you a moment about your husband and his involvement in the break-in involving Carver Electronics. Can you talk about that with me for a moment?"

"What do you want to talk about?"

"Well, as I understand the conversation you had with law enforcement, you told them your husband was home the night it happened, is that correct?"

"Yes, that's what I told them because that's the truth. Now, is that it?"

"Ma'am, we have an eyewitness who saw him running from the building at or about the time the business was robbed."

"Well then you don't need me, do you?"

"We could still use your testimony to further corroborate it was your husband. You know how much help he could get in jail—with his drug issues? It could benefit you and the kids the rest of your lives."

"Yeah, and who's going to pay the bills while he's gone? I can't. I have to take care of our children. I don't got time to work. We would starve to death without his income, even though it's not that much. Now, we got anything else we need to discuss?"

"Would you at least *consider* helping us? We really could use your testimony at the time of trial or your assistance in getting him just to plead guilty. As I said, in the long run, it could be the best thing that ever happened to you, to your family."

"You wouldn't know what's best for me or my family if it jumped up and bit you in the ass. No, I won't help. I've talked long enough. I'm done."

She terminated the call.

Amy walked in as Susan looked up. "Did that not go well?"

"That went about as bad as a phone call could go. I'm thinking we got about all the witnesses lined up we're going to get as concerns the Hepner case. We're going to need to try the case *without* any cooperation from his wife. Because she made that it crystal clear we are *never* going to try the case *with* it."

Chapter 6

"**S**o, yesterday you got everything organized—all the witnesses lined up as concerns both those new trials?"

Susan was ready to walk out the door, but Amy had stopped her to briefly discuss the status of both new cases.

"Yes. Why don't you call the secretaries for the defendant's attorneys in both cases and just ask if they could find out whether their attorney wants to take depositions. They probably will since the state would be paying the bill. Both of the defendants are indigent."

"Okay. I'll check on that and let you know. Now…"

"I'm in a hurry. I don't want to be late. What?"

"So, you're going to see a former lover and have coffee with him, and…"

"Oh, don't be so dramatic. There's no more 'and' about it. He's *not* …a former lover. I wasn't *formerly*…in …love with…oh, never mind. Yes, I *am* going to have coffee with a *friend* and that's it. Nothing else…other than…that. Now go back to work. Get something done before I return."

As she walked out the door, Amy said, "I'll want to hear all about this 'meeting' when you get back."

"Yeah, whatever."

Susan waited in a small coffee bar a block away from her office. It had been a while since she had seen him. In fact, she hadn't seen him since she told him they couldn't see each other again. He hadn't taken it well. But he asked to meet her today and, because of the way their relationship ended, she felt she at least owed him that.

She could feel the chill of a cold late November wind as it blew Greg Long through the front door of the small coffee shop. He gave her a brief waive and a smile as they set his full cup down on the counter. Tall, good-looking, and with a walk that exuded self-confidence, he picked up the cup and walked toward her table.

"Hi. So good to see you, Susan."

She stood and hugged him, noticing that cologne which she had purchased for him and, at least while they were a couple, he had used every day thereafter.

As they sat, he said, "How are you? You look great. That new guy must be good for you. Or…maybe it's just the overall concept of marriage. Maybe that's why you look so good—marriage just suits you."

"You always did know just what to say. You always did know how to sweep them off their feet. How are you? By the way, you too look great—looks like you're still working out."

"Yes, I am."

He continued to stare at her, to the point it was making her somewhat uncomfortable. Finally, he said, "So, how's work? How's prosecuting all the evil in this world suiting you?"

During the next thirty minutes, they discussed work along with work-related issues, for about as long as Susan had planned on being away from the office. It was nearly time for her to tell him she needed to return to work.

"I saw that quick peak at your watch. I figured you wouldn't have much time to spend with me, but I did want to see you."

She smiled, as she said, "No, no, I've still got some time set off for…I mean, I'm not ready to leave yet. Sorry. I didn't mean to have it appear as though our time together today was limited. It's been a while. I'm glad you called. It's just a habit—looking at the time is just a habit for me, as well as, unfortunately, it is for many others. But, tell me something. Why did you want to see me? Was there a specific reason, or…"?

He smiled. "Nope. No specific reason. I missed seeing you. That's it. I wanted to see you, to have a cup of coffee with you and visit with you. I was just wondering how everything was going. We were together a long time before…"

"I know. I understand. And again, I'm sorry it all turned out as it did. I really am."

"So, tell me about your life—about your life with Tom. Are you happy? Is he a good roommate? Children in mind?"

Susan smiled. "I guess the answer is yes, yes, and yes. After Tom was hired and when we both started to have feelings for each other, I was somewhat concerned about being able to work together in the same office. But it's worked out well. He's happy with his job as am

I. We don't really cross paths much. He's got his cases, I have mine. Everything considered, life is good. What about you? Still breaking up all those marriages?"

He laughed, and said, "I'm not sure that's exactly how I would describe my life's work. I'm still specializing in legally *dissolving* marriages, but I don't think I would quite describe it as 'breaking up all those marriages.' Maybe, just picking up the pieces after they've already been broken would be more appropriate."

"As you know, I tried that for a while. I'm still relieved I found out in time there were other aspects of the practice of law I would like, as opposed to that one area—domestic law—that I hated. I know there's a place in the practice for what you do, but I don't know how you do it day in and day out."

"You moved...I think. I think someone said maybe you moved to a different home. Is that right?"

"Yes. We got out of the downtown turmoil and now have a home and a few acres with it. That's worked out really well for us. We can leave all the hustle and bustle of Nashville behind when, at the end of the day, we shut down the office and go home. That was definitely one of the best moves I've ever made."

She looked at her watch. "I really need to go."

"I understand. I'm sorry, I didn't mean to interfere with your daily activities. I just really wanted to..."

She stood as she said, "No, no—not a problem. I've been wanting to catch up for quite some time. I'm really glad you called. I have been wanting to sit down and visit with you anyway. But I just wasn't sure whether...well, to be honest, whether you would want to hear from me, or whether you'd even return a call from me. That's why I was really glad when I noticed you called."

He stood and said, "Would you mind if we did this again...maybe in a month or so? No timetable, or anything like that, but maybe just get together and talk about life, along with what each of us are doing? Would that be an inconvenience or distasteful for you?"

"No, no certainly not. Tell you what. This time I'll give you a call. It will probably be a month or six weeks or two weeks—who knows. I'll just give you a call and if you're available we'll get together here."

He hugged her and whispered, "Thanks, Susan. Take care."

She had just finished returning her fourth call, when Amy walked into her office, and sat down.

"What?"

"So, what happened?"

"To whom? What are you talking about?"

"Your new lover. That guy you just got back from meeting. How did that go for you?"

Susan leaned back and said, "You know, that's how rumors get started. What you're doing right now is how viscous, outlandish rumors get started. You didn't mention to anyone I was going to have coffee with him, did you?"

"Are you kidding? Come on now, you know better than that. Absolutely not." She smiled and said, "Now give it up lady. What happened? Who was he? What was he to you?"

"Okay, this is going to be short and very dull. I was dating him when I met Tom at a party. Greg and I had talked of marriage, but not very seriously. We had just discussed it. I left him for Tom. There were some things about Greg that bothered me and Tom came along at the right time. That's about it."

"There must have been a few things you *did* like too. How long were you two together?"

"About a year. Yes, there were. He was a really good lawyer. I learned from him. He was a good conversationalist…a good…kisser too. Just a pretty good guy all the way around,"

"How did he take it when you ended everything?"

"Not too well. I heard from him almost every day right after I told him we were through. He had a little bit of a temper. There were times I really had to calm him down. But then, hearing from him became less frequent and I heard through mutual friends he was dating someone else. Not that I really cared at that point, but I did want him to be happy. I heard from him about once a week, just to visit, until about three or four months ago, when I quit hearing from him altogether. Then, the other day, he contacted me and wanted to meet just to catch up."

"So how did today work out?"

"Fine. We got along like we always did. He never made it uncomfortable. In fact, we agreed to meet in the future, maybe once a month, to just discuss our lives, and touch base. There is no romance involved anymore. We're just friends."

“Maybe.”

“Maybe what?”

“Maybe just friends. Maybe just friends from *your* point of view, probably not from his. I would venture to say he’s a lot more interested in you than just a friend.”

“Well, I’m not at all interested in him. If I get that vibe from him, that will be the end of meeting for coffee. I really enjoy hearing what’s going on from other lawyers involved in his area of law. It makes me feel so much better that I’m doing what I’m doing. Nope, you’re wrong. I could tell today he had accepted his life…*and* he had accepted mine.”

Amy stood. “Could be. Just be careful with him. It sounds to me like he’s got something else in mind other than just being your friend.”

“Sounds to me like you’re full of shit. Now move on. I still need to send out all those letters you typed up today. Quit assessing my relationship with my friends and move on.”

As she turned to walk out the door, Amy said, “Just sayin’, Susan, just sayin’…”

Chapter 7

They had planned very little for Sunday and so far, with few exceptions, that was exactly what both of them had done—very little.

Susan had spent the morning cleaning up around the house, while Tom had worked on a small portion of the fence separating their home from the neighbors. Both had agreed that after they had taken care of their own respective jobs, since it was to be another warm November day, they would meet on the deck in the early afternoon. So far, all had gone as planned. Just before 1:00 p.m., Susan concluded her obligations for the day were completed, and stretched out on one of the loungers with a new book. Tom walked through the double-glass doors shortly thereafter, with a book under one arm and two drinks in hand.

Once each had settled in and both started reading, Tom said, "Oh, I meant to say something yesterday, but I forgot. When I stopped by your office to see if we had plans for this weekend, Amy said you were out. When I pressed her, she said you were meeting with an old friend. She said she didn't know his name—just that you were meeting with him. Who was that? Was it someone I know?"

"Hmm. She didn't mention you were looking for me."

"I really wasn't *looking* for you. I just…I told her not to worry about it. I had nothing important to discuss with you—I just wanted to see you."

She hesitated for a moment, then said, "Well, as a matter of fact, I got a call from Greg and he wanted to meet me for coffee."

He put his book down, and said, "Greg Long?"

"Yes, Greg Long."

"What did he want?"

"Just to touch base with me I guess, and see how I was doing. He never really gave me a specific reason why he wanted to get together."

"So, you're starting to see old lovers now, huh? You marry me, but now after a marriage of very short duration, you're starting to see old lovers again? Hmm. I always knew life with you would be interesting, but I never figured it would be interesting in *this* respect."

"Oh relax—quit being so dramatic. He just wanted to see how we were getting along and discuss the practice of law, that's all."

"Is he in a relationship?"

"Never asked. Didn't care."

"Is he still interested in you?"

"Never asked. Didn't care."

Tom opened his book, as he said, "You still have feelings for him? Are you still wondering *what if?*"

She put her book down, turned toward him and said, "Now listen, Tom. We've been down this road before with the same guy. I picked *you* because you were best for me and I loved the hell out of you. There were a number of reasons for that. You were a much better conversationalist, he's never been a very good lawyer, and…a…. well, there were other reasons too. There's only one man in my life, and I can tell you without doubt, there will never ever be another. Now, any questions?"

"No, no I think that covered it. Tell me the next time he calls though, would you?"

"Will that help calm your concerns about me leaving you for him? Will that do the job?"

"Yup."

"Well, then by good golly, that's just what I'll do. Can we move on now—maybe just read, get a little sun and enjoy the day before the madness starts over again tomorrow?"

He stood, walked the few feet that separated them, leaned down and kissed her. "I love you. Always will. In spite of all your former lovers."

She smiled. "Go back to your book, buddy. We're good, you and I, and as far as I'm concerned, that's never going to change."

"What did you do over the weekend?"

"Very little. In fact, yesterday afternoon, Tom and I did absolutely nothing but relax out on the deck and read."

"Yeah, we didn't do much either."

"Oh, by the way, Tom told me you mentioned something about me having coffee with an old friend. He quizzed me about who it was and I, of course, told him the truth. That led to a spirited conversation for the next few minutes."

"I'm sorry, I'm really sorry, I didn't know what to tell him."

"Not a problem. There are no secrets between us. To be honest, I think it was probably good we had the discussion. I've felt for quite some time he wondered about Greg and about how I still felt about him. We had a good conversation and I think it eased his mind."

"You going to see this Greg again or should I just ignore him the next time he calls?"

"I'll probably see him again. It's not a big deal, and he really is still a friend of mine. Would you get either Corey Abbott or Teresa Wisner on the phone? I want to talk to both of them about those two new cases I have. By the way, did you talk to either of them or their secretaries about depositions?"

"No. Neither returned my call."

A few minutes later, Amy informed Susan, Corey was on line one.

"Hi Corey, how are you?"

"Good, Susan. Been a while."

"Yes, it has. I won't bother you but a moment, but have you had a chance to talk to your client, Wagner?"

"Yes, I have. In fact, I've talked to him a number of times."

"Any thoughts of resolving the case, or are we just going to need to try it?"

"He'll plead to a simple misdemeanor, if that will work—just pay a small fine and be on his way."

"That's not going to work for us. Not with this guy. I see we have a trial date in a few months. You want to depose anyone?"

"Yes. The victim is the only one though. You know, you don't have much evidence. You only got the victim."

"Well, I got people who said they saw them walk in the bathroom about the same time. But other than that, you're correct. Doesn't matter though. Whatever we have is what we're going to stand on. We're not pleading this down. The guy has been a continual problem for law enforcement, and if we have an opportunity to put him away, we're going to take it. I'll put Amy back on and you two can figure out dates to depose the victim."

A few minutes later, Amy came in her office, and gave her the dates Corey had available. As she started to return to her desk, Susan told her to get Teresa Wisner on the phone.

"Hi, Teresa. How's the practice? You been at it now, about a year? How's it all coming together for you?"

"Good, Susan, good. Yes, it's been about a year and I love it."

"I'm hearing good things about you. Keep up the good work. Now, what about this burglary case—this Hepner case. What's your position on that case?"

"We'll need to try it. He swears it wasn't him, and his wife is backing him up. She says he was home all night."

"Yeah, I talked to her. I'm really glad you are handling her and not me. What about depositions? Again, do you want to depose anyone?"

"Probably that one witness. I need to know exactly what he did see, how far away he was and things of that nature."

"Okay, that works for me. I'll transfer you to Amy and you two can set something up. It'll need to be at least a month away. I am booked solid between now and then. If you change your mind concerning a plea let me know, and I'll be glad to discuss it with you."

Later, Amy walked in Susan's office, and said, "Here's the dates for depos concerning Hepner."

"Thanks. It appears to me I have a full calendar as far out as the end of the year."

"Yes, you are busy. Any chance of getting either of these two cases resolved, or do you just need to try them?"

"I'll have to try them both. I'm not going to reduce the charges to the extent they want me to, and to be honest, I understand why both attorneys want to try their case. They have a chance of getting both those guys off. I'll have to try them."

"From what I've read, it appears to me you should be able to get a conviction on both."

"We'll see. You know how juries are. We'll just have to see."

Chapter 8

They had both just finished a late supper and subsequently found their way to the two overstuffed chairs sitting in front of their fireplace.

Susan needed to review a file she brought home from the office while Tom penciled out an opening statement he would need for a trial scheduled to begin the following Monday.

After he had been working on his statement for nearly a half-hour, Tom put his pen down, rubbed his eyes, looked up at her, and said, "What do you have scheduled for tomorrow?"

"Nothing special as far as I'm concerned. I need to meet with Brian tomorrow morning. He said he wanted to see me about something."

"Brian...?"

"Sorry. There are two of them aren't there. Brian Jenkins."

"Any particular reason, or does he just want to visit?"

"I'm not sure. He's one of just a few in our office I really don't know very well. He's got a little seniority, and I respect that. So, when he said he wanted to see me, I didn't question him. I just asked when."

"Morning, Amy. How was your evening—and your weekend for that matter?"

"Good. Didn't do much. I haven't looked at the schedule. Anything special for the week?"

"I got that suppression hearing on Friday, and a meeting with Brian today, in his office. But other than that, it looks pretty average."

"When do you see Brian? I don't show him on your calendar."

She looked at her watch and said, "In just a few minutes."

"Hi, Brian."

He stood. "Morning. How are you, Susan?"

"Good."

"You got a minute to talk?"

"Sure, sure, what's going on?"

"You want to close the door?"

"Certainly."

Susan closed the door behind her.

As he was sitting down, he said, "How long have you been here now? I can't remember exactly when you started."

Even seated, it wasn't difficult to tell how large a man Brian really was. He was tall, overweight, and, most likely physically intimidating to most jurors.

"Just going on five years." She hesitated, then said, "How long have you been here? I know you've been here longer than most of the rest of the lawyers in the office but when did you start here?"

He smiled. "It's been a while. I've been here about ten years now."

"I'll bet you've seen it all during those ten years."

"I have. I think I've tried every kind of case there is. Of course, now, I try only high-profile cases, but in the beginning, I tried them all. I've tried everything from dog bite cases to murder."

"You must like it here. If you've been here that long, you must like what you do."

"I do. I wouldn't even consider a change in occupation. I've had opportunities—in fact many of them. But I like what I do and I like the people I work with. Anymore, it's hard to find anyone anywhere, that can say that. So many people hate getting up in the morning and going to work. As you know, I'm here all day, most of each week. I don't see much of the family unless we go on vacation or I'm just physically unable to get to the office, in which case I'm on the phone numerous times a day with my secretary."

"I'm pretty much the same way, Brian. I wouldn't want to work anywhere else, or with any other group of people."

"Well, I know you have a lot going on, as do I, but I just wanted to visit a moment. There's a rumor going around that you're thinking about running for Chuck's job. Is that accurate? Are you considering running for the district attorney general's position?"

She hesitated. Now she knew why he wanted to see her. It had nothing to do with any of her current cases, or her personal life.

"Well, I don't…I really hadn't thought to much about it. I will tell you I have considered it, but I am not sure what I'm going to do. I've heard you might be running. Is that correct?"

"Yes. That's the reason I wanted to speak with you today. I was really surprised when I heard you were interested in the job. I don't think there's ever been a woman district attorney general elected in Davidson County."

She smiled and said, "Then winning would make me the first."

"Yes, I guess it would. Aren't you a Democrat?"

"I am."

"I heard you were. I'm a registered Republican, which means, if we both won our primaries, we would move on to the general election against each other."

"Yes, *if* I decide to run and *if* we both won our respective primary, that's true."

"Well, as you know, I've been here a long time. I've thought about running in the past, but I just felt I needed a little more experience. I've got that now, and I really figured I would run this time around."

"You sound like the logical candidate. Is Chuck going to support you?"

"Actually, that's the main reason for wanting to talk to you. He said he would if no one else from the office ran. If someone else runs, he said he would most likely remain neutral. Of course, his endorsement would carry a lot of weight. Without someone *else* from the office running, he would swing all his support to that one person, and it would most likely be the difference between winning and losing."

"I agree."

There was an uncomfortable silence, while neither said a word, until he said, "Have you talked to anyone about managing or handling a campaign for you?"

"Oh, I just tossed it around, but nothing of any consequence."

"Did you talk to Sally McHorton about being your campaign manager?"

Susan hesitated. "Where did that come from? Why would you specifically ask about her?"

Brian smiled. "Big city, small town. Word gets around quickly in Nashville. There aren't many secrets here."

"Well, I…yes…I talked to her, but I've made no plans. I was just asking her about the process."

"She's kind of a woman's liber isn't she?"

"That's 'kind of a' worn-out, over-used term anymore but to be honest, we're *all* woman libers today. That's no longer an exception anymore, Brian, it's an established way of life."

He smiled and leaned forward. "Okay, let me get to the point so we can both get back to putting the bad guys in jail. I really want to run. I think I'm ready for the position. I've got the experience, I think Chuck will back me, and I think I'm ready to manage the office. Now, certainly someone running from this office against me, wouldn't help. But I think experience is a critical factor, and while I admire your tenacity and high expectations, I would think a few more years in the position you now have, before you run, would serve you well."

"So, why are we having this discussion? You want to know if I'm intending on running—is that why we're having this talk?"

"Pretty much."

She stood. "Well, we might as well end the conversation right now then. I don't know. I have no idea whether I'm running or not. I've had a few people inquire, both within and outside the office, but I don't know and won't know for a while yet."

"I understand. Now, don't get me wrong. I don't care if you run. I guess I was just concerned about Chuck's endorsement if both of us end up running against each other. If it seems like I was pushing you for a decision, or in some way trying to change your mind if you have decided to run, I didn't mean it that way."

"She smiled and said, "I understand. When I decide what I'm going to do, one way or the other, I'll let you know. It's a little early yet. I'm just not certain."

"Thanks. I would really appreciate that,"

"Certainly, Brian. Thanks for being as candid as you have been."

Later, that evening, as they finished up the dinner dishes, Tom said, "Hey, you never did tell me what Brian wanted to see you about. Did you see him? What did he want?"

"Sorry. With everything else that went on today, I just forgot to mention it, I guess. He wanted to talk about the election."

"The district attorney general election?"

"Yup."

"What about it? Just the fact that you're considering running?"

"Well, first and foremost, he wanted me to know he was going to run and that he was basically best-suited for the job. That's the first thing he made clear. But he went on to talk about getting Chuck's endorsement. He emphasized it was really important to whoever got it. He was quick to point out that, at this point, he was getting it. But if we both ran, Chuck would most likely not endorse either of us, which would help neither of us."

"Is that all he wanted—just to discuss the election?"

"Pretty much. He wanted to know if I had talked to Sally. I told her I had but not to employ her—just to talk in generalities about the election. He called her a 'woman's liber', That's the first time I've really heard that term used in quite a while. But anyway, that's what he wanted."

"Have you made a decision yet?"

She smiled and put her arms around him. "Nope. But when I do, you'll be the first to know, buddy, the very first."

She kissed him, then said, "Let's sit in front of the fireplace for a while before bed. You want a cup of coffee?"

"I do. You make the coffee; I'll make the fire."

Chapter 9

"Morning Amy."

"Hey, boss, where have you been?"

"I'm not *that* late, am I? We had…I didn't leave home until…there were some things going on at home and I just couldn't get away until a little later. Hell, I'm only about a half-hour late anyway."

Amy smiled as she said, "I don't suppose you want to discuss those 'things' going on at home that resulted in you getting here later than usual, do you? I wonder if a couple of those 'things' that caused you to be late might have been your husband and the bedroom?"

"Don't be silly. It had nothing to…never mind. What's going on? I don't think I have a very heavy schedule today, do I?"

"No. You did, however, already get a call from a Sally McHorton. She said to have you call her when you arrived. Who's she? That name isn't familiar."

"She is involved in politics. She advises. She manages campaigns."

"Political campaigns?"

"Yes. Could you get me a cup of coffee while I go through the phone messages that I didn't get a chance to return yesterday?"

As Amy brought her a cup, she said, "Why are you talking to her? Are you really thinking about running for Chuck's job?"

"I am…sort of, yes."

"You know, normally, someone either runs for office or they don't. There's no place in politics for 'sort of.' Are you going to run, or aren't you?"

"I honestly don't know. Tom isn't wild about the idea at all. And after my discussion with Brian yesterday, he wasn't very encouraging either, since he's running for the same office."

"So, what. Run against him."

"He's a lot more experienced than I am. He would probably have Chuck's endorsement too. I just don't think…I don't know what I'm going to do. That's one of the reasons I called her. She's a pro at what she does. I want her insight before I go a step further. She's also a friend and I know I can trust her judgement."

"When do you need to know what you're going to do?"

"The primary is in May, so I have some time to consider my options. But I need to decide fairly soon whether I'm going to run, so I can file, start campaigning and start collecting donations. It's not a cheap process, that I *do* know. And of course, both Brian and I will be waiting to see who Chuck supports, if anyone. Without a doubt, that is a major factor. He is pretty sure Chuck is supporting him. He may be right, but I'm not sure that's going to be the deciding factor for me. Get the Wagner assault file for me. I need to call that witness—I think Whitacre is his name. I need to make sure he's going to testify. The trial date isn't that far away."

A few minutes later, Amy let Susan know he was on line one.

"Larry, this is Susan Jackson, how are you?"

"I'm fine, I'm doing fine. What do you want?"

"Larry, the trial for Wagner is coming up before long. Have you given any additional thought to testifying?"

"Some."

"Have you come to any conclusions yet?"

"I'm just not sure what to do."

"I understand. Does Wagner have a lot of friends? Is he part of a gang?"

"He has no friends. No, he's not part of a gang. No one can get along with him."

"So, he's the only one you need to worry about as concerns retribution if you do testify, right?"

"That's pretty much right, yes. If he's convicted, I should be fine. If he's not, I'm in a world of shit."

"Well, I'm telling you if you testify, he *will* be convicted. So, your odds of having a problem with him are extremely slight. And if by chance he's convicted, but out of jail pending sentencing, we will protect you the best we can until he's sentenced. So, you should have nothing to worry about either way."

He hesitated. "Let me think about it. I still got some time, right?"

"Yes. I'll contact you a couple of weeks prior to the trial date."

She terminated the call shortly thereafter.

"Amy, get that cop on the phone—the one that's involved in the Wagner case. I think Jack Thompson is his name."

A few minutes later, Amy informed her Jack was on line two.

"Hi, Jack. You have a moment to talk?"

"I do, yes. I'm just getting ready to go, but what do you need?"

"I haven't served a subpoena on Larry Whitacre yet. I just talked to him. He's still not sure whether he wants to testify. I told him I could almost insure him Wagner would be convicted if he did. I think he's about there, but I want you to serve a subpoena on him just in case. I want to use him on rebuttal. I have no doubt they'll call Wagner to the stand. They about have to. We'll use Larry then. I haven't disclosed him as someone who might testify for the prosecution because up until now, he said he wouldn't help us."

"Are you getting the subpoena ready? If you have it ready for me, I'll just swing by and pick it up sometime today."

"I'll make sure it's ready by noon, if that works for you."

"I'll make it work. When is the trial date?"

"I can't tell you right off the top of my head. I'll let you know in plenty of time. Let me ask you something. Wagner must have put up bail money. I see he's out. You know who put it up?"

"No idea. He's got a few relatives around here, I know that. Maybe they pooled their money and got him released."

She hesitated for a moment, then said, "If he's convicted, but released on bail previously set, we'll need to protect Larry from the date of the conviction until Wagner is sentenced. I have no doubt with his record, he'll be sentenced to prison. I'll argue against leaving him out of jail, prior to sentencing, but you know what the judge will do and so do I."

"We'll take care of the witness the best we can. I'll pick up the subpoena early this afternoon."

"Thanks, Jack."

Susan walked into the kitchen and said, "Well, have you got supper ready or do I need to go have a drink, after a really, really long day? Which is it?"

He turned around, and said, "It's going to be a few more minutes. Where you been? Hell, it's almost seven-thirty. I've been home for two hours."

She kissed him, smiled and said, "Life in the real world is a little more complicated than in the world you live in. Did you do anything today or just loaf? I was really busy. After Amy went home, the first time I looked at my watch it was seven."

He already had a drink in hand. Susan poured herself a short glass of wine, and they walked in the den.

"You know, sometimes you can really be a smartass. I worked today…I really did. So, what happened today that took so much of *your* time?"

"She laughed and said, "I was only teasing you—hoping for some kind of reaction, which I got. Oh, I did a little of everything, I guess. I did get behind schedule when I returned Sally McHorton's call. She talked forever."

"You talked to her today?"

"Yes. I talked and talked and talked to her. The call must have lasted 45 minutes."

"Are you going to run?"

"Maybe. She says she's already talked to a number of people who say they'll support me. They like the idea of a woman DA. I've never had a problem with Brian, but apparently a lot of people have. At least that's what they're telling Sally. She wants to meet with me in the next few days."

"When does she need to know what you're going to do?"

"As soon as possible. The primary isn't far off, and she wants to start getting commitments, both personal and financial, from people she thinks would support me."

He turned away, and remained silent.

She leaned forward in her chair, and said softly, "Tom, you know I can't do this without you, without your support."

He said nothing.

"Tom, look at me."

He turned toward her and said, "I know that…and as I've said before, you know it's up to you. This decision is up to you and only you."

"Okay, what's your concern? I know you don't want me to run, but why? You've been reluctant from the first day I told you I was considering it, but why?"

"Time, Susan, time. Look at your watch. You getting home this late isn't unusual. What the hell's going to happen if you get that job. Will you be getting home at ten—going to work at five—working all weekends and all holidays? That's what's bothering me."

She remained silent as she considered his concerns. Finally, she said, "I understand. I don't have to run. You know that. I'll do whatever you think I should do. If you don't want me to run, I won't."

He provided no response.

"You know, I might not even win. Brian could beat me. Or someone in the primary could beat me. I don't have all that much experience yet. I'm qualified but I don't have those years of experience Brian and many others do have. So, I may not win at either level."

"Okay, now look. You know for a fact I'll support you in whatever you decide to do. I'm just saying I'm concerned about the time issue—about our time together. And if we do decide to have children…I just don't want to lose you to the job."

She set her glass down, walked to the couch and sat down in his lap. "You know, nothing is ever going to come between you and I—nothing is ever going to affect what we have. If I run, if it consumes me and affects our relationship in any way, I'll quit so quick I'll make Brian's head spin. I'll never, ever do anything to affect the relationship between my man and me."

He smiled. "*Your man and you—whatever.* Okay, I'll hold you to that. Let's see how everything progresses and figure it out from there. We'll handle it like we do everything else—get all the facts, make a decision."

"Sounds fair to me. Now, the decision *we're* making right now, is that *we* both go eat. Because *we* are really, really hungry."

Chapter 10

She rotated her chair and looked out the window. A short weekend had turned into a long Monday morning, and it was only a few minutes past eight. She had been in the office since six a.m.

There was so much to consider. Her trial schedule was full—she really needed to focus fully on work. But the election was an issue which just kept sneaking into her uppermost thoughts. She hadn't really expressed her true feelings when the conversation with Tom turned to whether or not she would run.

She wanted to run—she wanted that job as much as she had ever wanted anything in her life. But she knew she needed to be careful. She needed Tom, his approval, his help, his wisdom. They would need to discuss all the ramifications before she committed. Hopefully she would be able to offset all his negativity with a positive response. If she couldn't—if she couldn't…

"Morning, boss. Are you here already?"

Susan never turned around, as she said, "Yes. I've been here forever. And it'll probably seem like forever before I leave tonight. How was your weekend?"

"Not the best," she said softly.

Susan swiveled around in her chair. She gasped as she looked at Amy, now seated in front of her desk.

She had scratch marks on her face, and her eye was swollen shut, while the skin around it was just starting to turn an ugly black and blue. Along with all the obvious marks, her left arm was encased in a cast.

"What the hell happened? Were you in a car accident? Are you hurt anywhere else? Did you need me? Why didn't you call. I would have…"

"No, no nothing like that at all. Derrick and I didn't agree on a few things and let's just say the conversation ended in an unfortunate manner."

"He did this to you?"

"Yes."

"What happened? How the hell did it all come to this?"

"We started arguing as soon as I walked in the door Friday night after work. Of course, he isn't working now. He was laid off earlier in the week, so now he's either at a job interview or home. He had been home all afternoon and for *most* of the afternoon had been drinking. When I came home, he was ready to argue and we did that for a couple of hours."

"That's already a recipe for disaster. What happened then?"

"We quit for a while. We just stayed away from each other. But then, we started arguing about supper. By that time, I had consumed the amount of vodka I know I shouldn't go beyond. I just figured what the hell…what difference could one more drink possibly make at that point in time, one way or the other."

"Oh yeah, that was certainly sound logic."

"Believe me, there was no logic involved in the whole evening. Once I had that third drink, things really got bad. I served him a plate of food, and right after that he really got mad it me for something I said, I guess—I can't remember. But he dumped his food in the garbage."

"Don't you remember everything that happened?"

"Oh, I remember *most* of it—I think. So then, he made a comment about the fact that I was gaining weight and he had taken all he was going to take from a fat pig. I swung at him and missed. He slapped me; I think. Then I scratched his face, pretty bad really, and he hit me with a frying pan in my arm—broke it."

She hesitated. "Then I grabbed something, and hit him right in the balls. He doubled over, and I knew he was done. I left. I drove myself to the emergency room. They wanted to know what happened. I told them I fell down. They didn't believe me—I didn't care. I've slept in my car since then."

"My god, Amy that's awful. Why didn't you just get out when it first started?"

"I…will…never, ever, back down from someone like him. He's a bully. He started the argument. He tried to do all he could to hurt me any way he could. They're all the same—they hit you, you hit back, only harder. I believe in that, and I will *never* back off. The only problem with that philosophy is sometimes you end up…getting hurt…and with maybe a…broken arm, which…I…have today."

"How you going to do your work? Can you work with one arm?"

"Don't worry. I'll have everything you need today, ready today. That will not be a problem."

"What about the future, Amy? What are you going to do about your relationship, your marriage?"

She looked down, collected her thoughts and said, "I'm not really sure. Now that I'm sober and thinking right again, I really don't want to leave him. I still love him. But regardless of how much I love him, if the son-of-a-bitch comes after me with a knife, I'll use a gun. I can't change that thought process just because I may have come out of the last few days a little worse off than he did."

She looked up and said, "I'll call him later today."

"I got a good divorce lawyer for you to call if you need one. As you know, I can't represent you. By the way, through the next few years, continue to remind me I don't really want to be on the wrong side of you. Do that for me will you?"

Amy smiled and said, "Don't worry about that. We are good together and I don't anticipate that ever changing." She stood. "I'm going to work. If I have a problem getting things done, I'll let you know, but I don't anticipate their being any issues at my desk."

As she walked out, Susan said, "When you have a moment, get the attorney for Hepner on the phone for me—Teresa Wisner."

A few minutes later, Amy informed her Teresa was on the line.

"Hi Teresa, Susan Jackson. Do you have a moment to talk?"

"Certainly. I assume you want to discuss Hepner, is that correct?"

"Yes. Is the trial still on, or does he want to discuss a plea?"

"I've asked him that same question a number of times, but he continues to insist he didn't do anything wrong. Of course, that wife of his continues to tell me he was home all night. So as of right now, he won't even consider a plea—to anything."

"I assumed that. The reason I really called was to ask you if his wife was going to testify on his behalf. Is that her intention at this point in time?"

"I think so."

"Okay. I briefly talked to her on the phone right after this happened to see if she was going to testify for him, or let him handle the problem himself. She made it clear in no uncertain terms he was home all night. She didn't really say what she would do at the time of trial, but she made it clear she was his alibi, so I assumed she would testify. I wanted to factor in her testimony when I was thinking about offering a plea deal. But if you say he isn't even interested in talking, I guess I don't have to worry about that issue."

"He told me the last time I talked to him he wasn't interested—that he was just plain not guilty. I'll let you know if that changes, but for now we are preparing for trial."

"He doesn't have much of a record so that is a nonfactor in any type of discussion we might have in resolving this. I assume that's why the judge released him with such a low bond. So, that would certainly work favorably for him. Just let me know if he changes his mind. Don't wait until it's time to start the trial, because as you know in prior dealings with me, that's to late—I don't bargain then."

"I understand. I'll call you if anything changes."

Late in the day, Amy walked in her office with a number of files and laid them on her desk.

"How you feeling? Were you able to get everything I needed finished up?"

"I was, yes. As you know I had to work through the noon hour, but I got it all done."

"How's the arm?"

She sat down. "It hurts."

"I see a few more bruises are showing up as time goes by. That must have been a real dozy of a fight. I guess I should be happy you're here at all."

"That's not the first time with him, as you know. But it was the worst it's ever been."

"Have you talked to him today?"

"Yes, a couple of times. He thinks he might have a new job lined up. He was in a good mood."

"Is he walking upright, or still bent over?"

She laughed and said, "He just told me not to touch him when I got home."

Susan leaned forward and said, "Are you two really staying together after all that happened last night? I'd be afraid he would attack me while I'm sleeping. Isn't it time you both just moved on?"

"I love him. We both got it out of our system last night…I think. He knows if he starts something, I'm going to finish it. That's how it ended last night. He started it, I kicked him in the balls. I ended it, just like I always do. I'll see you in the morning."

"I hope so."

Chapter 11

Susan had been seated for over fifteen minutes, waiting for her friend to arrive. She had finished one cup of coffee and just ordered another, when she saw Dorothy walk through the coffeeshop door.

She waived. Dorothy saw her, smiled and walked through the maze of small tables scattered here and about the coffeeshop.

As she reached Susan's table, she embraced Dorothy and said, "My gosh, how long's it been, Dorothy? I don't think I've seen you since…well since…"

As Dorothy took off her coat, and signaled for a cup of coffee, they both sat down as she said, "My it's a cold November day out there. Now, I think the last time I saw you…I think you were just getting ready to graduate from law school. So that's been what…about…?"

"It's been at least five years. I've been with the district attorney's office for five years, and I know I haven't seen you since I went to work there."

Susan couldn't help but notice the bags under Dorothy's eyes. Her clothes were loosely fitting, as if she had borrowed them from another woman to wear today. Unfortunately, if she had borrowed them, whoever she borrowed them from was much larger than Dorothy.

"So, how do you like working there?"

"Good. I like it. I'm thinking about making a move in the future, but no plans yet. I do enjoy working with the people I work with. What about you, Dorothy? Are you working?"

"No, no, not me. I've got those three kids you know, and they take most all my time. I don't know if you knew I had that third one. I think you knew I had Charlie, and John, but Caleb, he's only about six months old. So, taking care of all three of them keeps me pretty busy."

"I can imagine it does. What about Gabe? You married Gabe Longmire, right? Is he able to help you at all?"

"Not really. Oh, when he's not working, he can, and lately that's been quite a bit. He lost his job about a month ago. He just started a new one working maintenance with one of the hotels here, downtown, and I think he's going to really like it. But we haven't had a lot of income the past month because he hasn't been working. He's been home. *That's* been interesting to say the least. He's working now, which is best for all five of us. Did I hear you just moved?"

"Yes, we did. Tom and I moved out of the downtown area and bought a small acreage. It's not that far away from downtown, and we love it. It's nice to go home and really get away from the hustle and bustle of the city. What about you? As I recall, you were living south of town, is that correct?"

"I was yes—still am. Same place we've been living since we got married. It's a little small for us now, what with this last kid, but we're doing fine, just fine. Who's that guy you married? Did he graduate from high school with us?"

"No, no, he's not from here. Tom moved here about ten years ago. He came to work for the district attorney's office not so long ago, we fell in love and got married. Best guy ever. We have a fantastic relationship. I don't know what I'd do without him."

Susan noticed Dorothy's hand appeared to be shaking. She wouldn't ask. She would let her tell her own story in her own time—as she wished.

"How long have you two been married now?"

"Oh, I don't know. We got married a few months before Charley was born, I guess. You apparently remember my husband from high school. You remember he was a couple of years older than us?"

"Certainly, I remember. He treated you well. He was a good guy."

Dorothy briefly looked away, and when she reengaged, she said, "Yeah, well that's changed a little. It's nothing I want to discuss, but our relationship has changed. What about kids? You haven't had a kid you haven't told me about, have you?"

Susan smiled and said, "Nope. And really, I doubt that happens anytime soon. Tom and I are happy the way things are. Maybe, once we are really settled, you know, with our jobs, with each other, we might talk about children, but it's too soon—to soon for both of us."

"I wish one of us would have thought that through a little better—you know, like you and Tom obviously have. We had one right after we were married, and two since. But we really didn't even have time to get to know each other before we had a child screaming for something to eat. It wasn't…it wasn't the direction I had planned for my life, but it is what…it…is, I guess. You mentioned maybe you might be changing jobs. What are thinking about changing to?"

"Oh, I've been considering running for the position of Davidson County District Attorney General. But I'm not sure just yet what I'm going to do."

"Wow, that's impressive. When is the election? When would you run?"

"The primaries are in May and the election is in August. I've been thinking about it for a while, but I'm just not sure what to do."

"Well, if you decide to run, you will sure get our votes, you know that. If I can help, you just let me know. Course, we couldn't help financially, but maybe I could hand out stuff, or knock-on doors. But I'd probably have to take the kids with me."

"I understand. I'll let you know if we need some help if I do decide to run." She carefully considered her next question, but concluded it needed to be asked. "How are you and Gabe getting along?"

Dorothy hesitated, looked down for a moment, then as she looked up at Susan, she said, "We'll be fine. We've had a tough go of it lately. Three kids, no income, hasn't helped any. But we seem to have weathered the storm, as they say. I think…I think we're closer than we've ever been."

"Good, Dorothy, I hope so. I really do."

"You know, you're lucky. Well, maybe not lucky, maybe you're just smarter than I am. But somehow, you've managed to have it all. You got a good man. You haven't started a family yet. You got a good income, both of you, and you're not locked into, well maybe 'locked into' isn't the best term, but you're not tied down in a relationship you couldn't get out of if you wanted to. You're a lucky woman, Susan, you really are. I hope you know that."

They talked in generalities for a few more minutes, until Dorothy said she needed to pick up the children from a friend that was watching them while she had coffee with Susan.

Later that evening, as she walked through the door, Tom yelled, "Hey, come on in here. I just started a fire. I got an extra glass and the bottle of wine is with me. Where have you been?"

She walked in the den as she said, "I 've been at the office."

"You were gone during the afternoon for a while though, right? I walked down to your office a couple of times, but you were gone both times."

As she sat down near him, she took a drink, and said, "I had an old friend call me up. She wanted to meet for coffee. I haven't seen her in years, so I told her I'd meet her. I was gone for over an hour."

"How was she?"

"Fine, she was fine. Right now, it seems she may be living under some difficult conditions, but she's getting along okay."

"What kind of conditions?"

"Oh, her husband's been laid off and they haven't had any income for a while. But he just found a job so maybe that will help resolve that issue for them, although I don't think they are or ever will be well off financially. They have three young children. The clothes she was wearing didn't appear…she's just under a lot of pressure right now."

"I'm sure she was glad to see you."

"I'm really not sure she was. In fact, I'm not sure why she wanted to see me in the first place, to be honest. She seemed strange to me. She certainly wasn't the girl I knew in high school. And she shook, her hands shook. She just didn't seem quite right. I'm not sure how to explain that, but she just seemed a little off to me."

Susan took another drink, then said, "It was a difficult hour. I wonder if she needs help…" She turned toward Tom, smiled and said, "I'm sure she's fine. People change. She's changed. Enough about me—tell me all about your day."

Chapter 12

Tom peaked around Susan's doorframe, and said, "You got a minute?"

"For you, sure. Come on in."

He walked in and closed the door behind him.

He then walked around her desk, as she said, "Wait a minute. What are you doing? Tom, now Tom…"

He leaned down and kissed her as he simultaneously placed a hand on her breast.

She stood up immediately, pulled away, and whispered, "Stop that. Now, you go sit down. We've been through this before. Move away, you… sex…enthusiast…" She pointed toward a chair, and said, "Now go. Sit. Sit."

He stood upright, smiled at her, then walked around the end of her desk, taking a seat.

"Sorry. But I needed a little more than a kiss this morning. Now I'm good. I just wanted to see you for a moment…and of course touch you for a moment. I'm okay now. How's the morning going for you?"

She sat, as she said, "You know, someday someone's going to catch us Tom and I don't want what they saw making its way around the office. You know that. Now, please respect my thoughts about that. *Okay?* We've been through this…"

"I'm sorry. It won't happen again, at least not before next week…or so. Maybe. You mentioned before we left home Chuck messaged that he needed to see you. For most of us peons, being summoned to the boss's office is normally not a good sign."

"I don't really know what he wants. He told Amy, even before I got here this morning, to have me stop by sometime today. That's what I'll do as soon as *the fondler* gets out of my office and goes back to his own desk."

"Okay, okay, I'm out of here." He stood as he smiled and said, "Let me know if he wants anything of substance. I have a relatively boring day ahead of me, and I might need something to stimulate it. You didn't do much to assist in that respect, so maybe some news of significance involving his office will excite me."

"Whatever. Now, go, go on back to work."

As soon as he walked out the door, she told Amy she was going to see Chuck and would be back shortly.

As she walked through his door, she smiled and said, "Morning, Chuck. You wanted to see me?"

"Yes, if you have a little extra time."

"I do." She sat, and said, "Is there a problem?"

"No, no not at all. I was just checking in with you. We haven't sat down and talked in quite a while. I see you're on the schedule to start that Wagner assault trial next week. Everything ready to go?"

"Yeah, I guess so. Not a lot of witnesses or evidence, but we'll go with what we got and see what happens."

"Is your schedule full?"

"It is, yes. It's about as much of a load as I've carried since I started working here. But do you have something you want me to do—to work on? I'll fit it in if you do."

"No, however, that is one of the reasons I wanted to see you— because of that type of work ethic, that energy that you normally exhibit." He hesitated, for a second, cleared his throat, and said, "Have you come to a decision about running for my job?"

"No, not really. I'm just trying to sort out the pros and cons of both scenarios—running versus just continuing to do what I'm doing, which I love."

"It's probably time for you to make a decision, even if it's kept quiet until you get all your ducks in order."

"Yeah, you're probably right. In fact, I have no doubt you're right, but it's such a big move for me. I've never been involved with politics in any respect. It's pretty obvious your position is as much politics as it is practicing law."

"Want my two cents worth?"

"Certainly."

He leaned forward in his chair, and said, "Throw your hat in the ring. Run for the job. Don't even think twice."

"Really. That's what you think I should do? You know Brian is running too, don't you? He's not made it a secret. I suppose someone else could throw their name in too. I'm a woman—I'm not sure that's a positive."

He leaned back in his chair, smiled and said, "Being a woman is far from the negative issue it used to be. And you're right, there may be someone besides you two that might run, but both of you would have a leg up over an outsider."

He looked away for a moment, then turned toward her, smiled and said, "You know, Susan, you have it all. You're attractive, which doesn't necessarily help, but it doesn't hurt. You're smart. You're aggressive. Your record of convictions is as good as it gets. You're honest. Your work ethic is incredible. In addition to all those qualities, you have absolutely no ghosts in the closet. At least, none that have surfaced while you've been here. You are a perfect candidate for the job."

She hesitated.

"Yeah, I know. You want to know whether I'm supporting you or Brian. He's definitely qualified too. To be honest, at this point, I really can't support either of you. As time goes on, I'll probably back one of you or the other. I won't take long to decide, but for now, I'm staying neutral. In fact, I would be an idiot to support you and then have you not even run for the job now, wouldn't I?"

"I guess you would. Yes, indeed you would."

He stood. "That's all I wanted to discuss with you. If I were you, I'd call whoever your campaign manager is and tell her to get the ball rolling—that you're all in. You deserve the job."

She stood, shook his hand, and said, "That's just what I'm going to do. Thank you for the vote of confidence, Chuck. I needed that."

As soon as she reached her office, she punched in Sally's number.

"Hi, Susan."

"Sally, how's your day going?"

"It would go a whole lot better if you were to tell me you've finally made up your mind and you're going to run."

"Nothing like getting right to the point."

"You made up your mind?"

"No. We need to talk again."

"When and where."

"Let's meet here at my office. I still have lots of questions to ask and you seem to be the only one with all the answers."

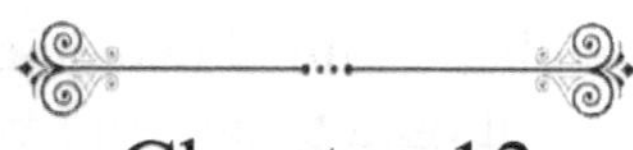

Chapter 13

"**A**re you working late tonight?

"Actually, Amy, I'm meeting with Sally McHorton, here, in about fifteen minutes. We need to discuss this election issue and try to come to a conclusion concerning what I'm going to do."

"You still haven't decided?"

"No."

"You know, that's not like you. Normally, once you've considered all the variables in any situation, you make your mind up immediately."

"Sure do."

"But not this time?"

"Nope, not this time. There is a variable or two that still has me confused. I need to discuss everything with Sally—see if she can help clear my mind. Hopefully, she'll help me come to a conclusion concerning whether or not I'm running and get that decision out of the way."

"What exactly is it that concerns you? What's the factor that is confusing to you? I might be all you need to help you come to a conclusion."

Susan smiled. "Oh, I'm sure you could help. But I need to discuss this one, with her—with the expert in this field. You need to go home and try to stay out of another brawl with your husband. Why don't you go ahead and leave? I'll fill you in on what happened at our little meeting for two when you get here in the morning."

"Okay, but you know I can evaluate and discuss with the best of them. You know that I…"

They both heard the outer office door open and close. Amy went to investigate and came back shortly. "Sally is here. You want me to send her on back?"

"I do. yes."

"Are you sure you…"

"Thanks, Amy. I'll tell you all about it tomorrow and you can offer your thoughts then."

"Oh sure, after you've already decided. Whatever. I'll see you in the morning."

Susan stood as Sally walked through her office door.

"Sally. Nice to see you. Have a chair."

They shook hands and, as they did, she felt those same butterflies in her stomach she always felt just before she gave her closing statement in front of a jury.

"Well, have you decided yet, or do you still want to talk about it?"

"We need to talk. I'm just not sure this is what I want to do."

Sally smiled and said, "I understand. Obviously, this is one of those times in life you really need to be sure of what you decide. You certainly aren't taking it lightly—nor can you. You can't change your mind when you do commit. Once the decision is made, you need to be all in. So, if you have doubts, and those doubts continue to linger, we need to quit right now—save you the money and save all the time and energy. This could very well be a life-altering decision. You need to be fully committed if you're going to move on."

"I'm not—at least I'm not at this time. There are a couple of major reasons. One is because I hate to lose, and to be honest, I'm not that positive I'm going to win if I *do* run—or if I even have a good chance at winning."

"You have never been involved in any type of politics, have you?"

"Nope, never."

"It's a world of its own, Susan. I've been involved one way or another since I graduated from Vanderbilt twenty years ago. It's a crazy world in and of itself. But it's also extremely rewarding, especially if you're on the winning team. I can certainly understand your apprehension in that respect."

"What complicates it somewhat is that I have never been down this road before and, to be honest, I have a great job now. I really enjoy what I do. I'm not sure how I'll get along in a new role—in a completely different role within the practice of law."

"I can ease your mind concerning that issue. You'll get along fine, Susan. You're smart, you're savvy, you work well with people…I've done my own research. You would handle your new position very well. That's really not a concern of mine at all."

Susan leaned back in her chair and frowned as she said, "You've done your research, huh? So, why don't you just tell me what your research has disclosed about me running for this office."

"Well, as I'm sure you are aware, during the course of each day and night, I talk to many, many people, men and woman, both influential about the city and just your common everyday citizen. While in those discussions, I might happen to ask them how they feel about a woman for the DA's office. I have not received one negative comment about it."

"Certainly, that's helpful."

"I've also had a chance to discuss, with selected women around the city, the issue of possible campaign contributions to a campaign to elect a woman to the office. I already have a considerable amount of money committed if you run. I know money will not be an issue at all."

"Well, I have to admit that's impressive. Are there any major issues you anticipate?"

"Will Chuck endorse you?"

"I don't know. And from my discussions with him, he isn't sure either. Another issue is that I believe there's another man from this office that might run against me."

"Wouldn't be Brian Jenkins, would it?"

"How did you know?"

"You should know by now I really get around. By the way, I don't think he can beat you."

"I'm afraid he will if Chuck endorses him. Since you get around like you do, have you heard about others that might be running for the office?"

"Yes. There are three or four other men that are considering running. I know them all. I really don't think you'll need to worry about any of them."

"Are any of them running as a democrat?"

"Yes, a couple. Of course, I assume you already know that running as a democrat probably already gives you a leg up in Nashville, don't you?"

"I figured it probably did."

"What has Chuck said about endorsing you or anyone else?"

"He said he would endorse me if Brian didn't run. He wasn't so clear about what he would do if Brian ran. He might not endorse either of us. How will that affect the race if it comes down to both Brian and me, and Chuck doesn't endorse either of us."

"I think you'll beat the shit out of him, that's what I think."

Susan said nothing more as she looked away.

Sally waited for her to respond. When none was forthcoming, she said, "What's the real problem here, Susan? You have been all over the board—you've asked questions that were right on point, and my responses have all been favorable. I really think, based on all the factors I normally look at before I take anyone on as a client, that you can beat anyone that runs. Your reputation is impeccable. You have good friends and business ties that will help in your campaign. You got me, and I'm pretty damn good at what I do. It's clear to me you want the job. You got the drive to do what needs to be done to win. What the hell is in your way? What is it that's holding you back? You said you had a couple of issues about running. We've discussed one of them. What's the other?"

She turned toward Sally and said, "Tom."

"What about Tom? Doesn't he want you to run?"

"Let's just say he's a little reluctant."

"About what?"

"He's afraid it will take up more time than I devote to the job now, which is significant. I think he's afraid it might affect our relationship. He's worried about that and, to be honest, so am I."

Sally smiled. "You're lucky. You're lucky you both care enough about each other for it to make a difference concerning whether or not you take what amounts to a huge step in your life. I can only tell you that you're not unconditionally married to the job, even if you do win. If it starts to get in the way, quit. If it starts affecting your marriage and it's not proceeding in a manner that suits you or Tom, quit. It's that simple. With your background and your history in the practice of law, I would guess you could get a job with just about any law firm you wish. You're not married to the position; you're married to Tom."

"I understand. It's just tough knowing what to do. I'm not sure he's really behind me in this. He says he is, but I'm just...not sure...if he is."

She stood. "I can't help you there, Susan. All I can do is hold your hand and guide you through the process—hopefully a winning one. You have a great chance to win, I can tell you that. But I don't give out marital advice. I don't advise people what their odds of keeping their marriage together might be. I can only help you get the job. The rest of your life is your business."

"I know, I know, and I understand that, but you asked what the problem was—now you know."

"You need to come to conclusion. We need to file your paperwork so you're ready to roll in the primaries. I need to either help you, or I need to help another individual that also wants to run and wants to hire me. I haven't told you who it is and won't. But they want my services if I'm available. I'm not available, if you want me. You have a much better chance of winning than he does. Just let me know how you want to proceed in the next few days."

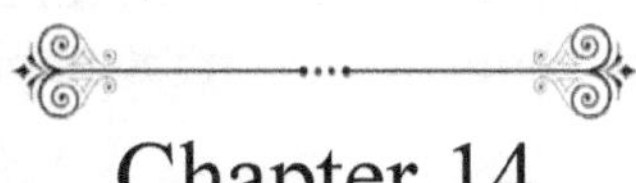

Chapter 14

They sat quietly in front of the fire, both concentrating on the book they were reading—at least, that was what Susan made it appear as though she was doing. The fire warmed her. It was a chilly late January evening and the rest of the house, while comfortable, was not warm enough. It only just took the edge off. Certainly, if the chill was the only thing on her mind, she could sit quietly, reading her book and not worry about the conversation that needed to take place tonight. It couldn't wait another day.

Tom lowered his book, and said, "So…did you meet with Sally again this afternoon?"

She hesitated for a moment, then said, "Yes, I did. I guess I forgot to tell you about the meeting. With so much to talk about involving everything else that went on today, I guess it just slipped my mind. Yes, I did meet with her."

"You want to talk about it?"

"Oh…I don't know. Guess it's up to you. Maybe you just want to wait and talk about it tomorrow…or maybe the next day, maybe?"

"Why put it off? What did she say?"

Susan put her book down, looked at him, and said, "Tom, I just…I'm just not sure what to do…"

He closed his book, placed it on the end table, and said, "Okay, we're going to get this issue out of the way tonight, right now, one way or the other. It's been the elephant in the room for long enough. Now, what did she say?"

"Okay, okay I agree. To sum it all up, once again she said she thought I could win. She said she continues to talk to a number of people whom she considered important in the election process, and they all feel I have a good chance. I'm a little young maybe, but my credentials speak for themselves."

Tom looked away, as he considered, then processed her answers.

"What about campaign contributions and the overall cost to us? Can we afford this?"

"She told me she already had people ready to start contributing to the campaign. She said money wouldn't be an issue."

"Was she concerned about what might happen if Chuck doesn't endorse you?"

"No."

"Okay, let's change the course of this conversation. What *was* she concerned about?"

"The biggest concerns she had was that I wasn't going to run."

"She thinks you'll win?"

"Yes, she continues to believe I can win."

He looked away, watching the fire, clearly deep in thought.

After a few moments of silence, he turned toward her, and said, "What do *you* think?"

"Tom, I am concerned about us—about you and I. I'm concerned about the same thing you are—that there just won't be enough hours in the day. Not having the job before, I do know one thing—it takes a lot of time. But to be honest, I don't think Chuck spends as much time in the office as I do. The job is really more one of administration than actually court room activity. But not having that kind of responsibility, or being involved in that kind of situation day after day, I absolutely have no idea how the change might affect our relationship."

"You know, I've given it a lot of thought too. I know it's what you want. I know there may not be another time this opportunity presents itself again."

He hesitated. Then he started to smile as he said, "I really think you should run. I have faith in our marriage. I have faith in you and I. I really think you should run."

She stood, walked to where he was seated and sat down in his lap.

She kissed him, and said, "You need to know that nothing, and I mean nothing, is ever going to get in the way of our marriage. I love you more than life itself. If the campaign is getting way out of hand concerning our time together, I will withdraw as a candidate, If I win the job and it appears it is somehow affecting our marriage, I will resign in the blink of an eye. Nothing, Tom, and I mean this with all my heart—nothing will ever get in the way of you and I."

He smiled. "Should I start making posters for our car. I'm a hell of a sign maker. What do you want me to do?"

"Take me upstairs. Let's do what we do so well."

"I really can't carry you up those steps, but I can follow close behind."

"Lead the way. I'll be up after I take care of the fire."

The next morning, Amy was already working when Susan walked in the office door.

"Where you been? I've already had about a half dozen calls for you."

"Sorry. I just got up late. I had a late night and just slept in a little later than usual, I guess." She reached her desk as she said, "Anything going on? Is my first appointment still not until ten?"

Amy followed her into Susan's office and said, "Yes, that's your first appointment. Ok, what happened? What happened at the meeting you had with Sally?'

"It was a long, long meeting, but pretty productive."

"That's nice to know, *but what happened—what's the verdict*? Yea or nay? Running or not running? I thought about it all night and almost called you, but I didn't want to bother."

"She's filing the paperwork this morning. We're going to give it a go, I guess."

Amy smiled and walked toward Susan, as she said, "Thank God. I really didn't know what you were going to do. You need a hug."

They embraced, as Susan said, "It's a whole new day today, that's for sure. I have no idea what I'm doing or what I'm supposed to do. Sally said she would lead me through it step-by-step."

As Amy walked back toward the doorway, she said, "Okay, so what's the next step?'

"It all starts tonight. She's having a meeting in her building. She's invited a number of people she knows who are going to contribute to the campaign and support me. She wants me to meet them. I want you and your husband to be there if you're not busy—not to contribute, but just to meet the people that are supporting me, so you'll know them if they call or stop in. Can you be there?"

"Wouldn't miss it. You going to tell Chuck today?"

"Yes. I'm actually going to do that in about five minutes."

"You going to tell Brian?"

"Nope. He can find out about it right along with everyone else. Oh, and the press will be there tonight too. Oh, and she's going to have me give a talk, which I am a little uncomfortable with, but I'll do it."

"You better get used to that. You win this race you're going to be speaking in front of the camaras frequently. You might as well start getting used to it right now. Because you *are* going to win. I have absolutely no doubt about that."

She unfastened her bra and let it drop on the floor, on top of all her other clothes that had gone before it.

She turned to look at Tom—he was under the sheet, which he had pulled up to his waist. His arms were folded as he leaned back against the headboard, and he had a grin from ear to ear.

She never even looked for a nightgown. As she started walking to her side of the bed, she said, "Don't even think about it. The day has been way to long, and I'm way to tired."

"You look like you're ready to drop. Just hit the light and crawl in beside me. I, like you, am way too tired to even think about sex."

She turned off the light, and crawled in bed, moving close to him. As she turned away, he moved up behind her, putting his arm over her, holding her body near him.

"You know, I've never been so proud of anyone in my life, as I was of you tonight."

"Really? I didn't do much."

"You stood out."

"What do you mean? I don't understand."

"You were in a class all by yourself tonight. I watched how people watched you. You controlled the room. You are a born politician if you ask me."

"That's nice of you to say, but I felt like a fish out of water."

"Your speech was perfect. You were absolutely beautiful in that dress. You... controlled... the room."

"Thanks, I think. Love you."

"I was so proud. You know, I have no idea what I would do without you. I'm really glad you decided to run. I'll be right there with you all the way. I can make signs you know. Really, I can do a sign for our car if you want me to."

She failed to respond.

He moved in closer as he whispered, "You want me to make signs for you? I am really good at it."

She said nothing. He could tell somewhere between how proud he was of her, and his comments about his sign-making skills, she had fallen asleep.

He smiled, held her close and closed his eyes.

63

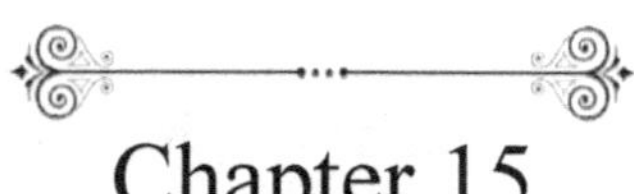

Chapter 15

Susan had been waiting in the judge's outer office for in excess of thirty minutes. She had been informed by Corey Abbott, attorney for Sam Wagner, that he had been held up in court elsewhere and would be about a half-hour late.

Unfortunately, that information had been passed on to her *after* she arrived for the defendant's pre-trial conference, rather than before. As a result, instead of being able to use those thirty minutes to her advantage, she sat here, doing nothing but thinking about all the things she might have accomplished if she had been told he would be late *before* she left her office. Forty-five minutes after the hearing was to begin, he walked in the outer chamber's door and sat down a seat away from her.

He looked at her, and said, "Sorry I'm late, but it was unavoidable."

"You always were and it always was."

He studied her for a minute, then smiled and said, "Come on, let's don't start this trial off on a bad note."

She smiled and said, "Just kidding." She paused, then said, "Well, not really. You always were detained, and you were never, ever, on time. Other than that, you're basically a great guy. Now, you ready to plead this guy and move on too other, much more important cases?"

"I don't think so. How you been?"

"Good, Corey. It's been a while. On occasion, I've wondered if you were still around, or, you know, whether one of your female friends had killed you off during one of your many arguments."

"Not yet, anyway. Nope, I'm still around."

"How's Rita, or whatever her name is. It is Rita, right?"

"Oh, she's okay, I think. I'm just pretty sure she is. And yes, it is, or I mean was, Rita."

"Not with her anymore?"

"Not really."

"Is it an on-again off-again relationship?"

"No, it's pretty much an 'off again' thing. Has been for over a year."

"Oh. Sorry. I didn't know."

"This is a first, you know—you and I against each other."

"I didn't know you were doing this kind of work—criminal defense work."

"Yeah, well the domestic relations work I was doing didn't work out so well."

"Couldn't make a living?"

"To be honest, I couldn't win a case. I just wasn't very good at it."

He hesitated for a moment, then said, "How about your life? Who you with now?"

"The same guy I was with after I left you."

"Really?"

"Yes, really. We've been married a while now."

"Is he a lawyer?"

"Yes. In fact, he's in the same office I'm in."

He smiled. "I get it. A little office romance turned into marriage. Happens all the time. It's nothing to be ashamed of."

"Actually, that's *not* how it happened, but I'm also not going into how it *did* happen. Who's your current woman, Corey? I know you got one. You always did."

"It's not important. You wouldn't know her. You and this guy happy? I mean is everything okay?"

"Why do you ask?"

"Just curious."

She smiled. "You know, some things never change."

"He hesitated for a moment, then said, "I still miss our talks. I really do."

"Your problem, Corey, is that you always enjoyed talking to many of us...*women*. There wasn't one you didn't enjoy talking to."

"I've changed, Susan. I'm really looking to settle down, maybe have a few kids, and..."

The judge's court reporter walked into the room and said, "The judge will see both of you now. Go on in."

As Susan walked through the door, the judge stood and said, "Morning Susan, how are you? How's everything in the DA's office?"

Susan shook his hand, and said, "Good, Judge. Not much has changed since the last time I tried a case in your court."

As the judge sat down, he said, "There's a rumor going around about you running for Chuck's job. Any truth to it?"

Susan sat down, smiled and said, "There may be, Judge, there may be."

"You would fill Chuck's shoes just fine. Now, sir, I guess I haven't seen you in my courtroom before. Your name is Corey…"

"Yes, sir, Corey Abbott."

"Have you done a lot of this type of work? If so, it must have been done outside of Davidson County."

"I've done some, Your Honor, but not a lot. I've done a lot of domestic work until recently. I got a little fed up with that area of law and thought I'd try criminal law for a while—just see if I liked it more than all that domestic strife."

"I wish you luck, Mr. Abbott. I'm not sure this is much different than what you were doing, but we'll see. So…we got a deal on this case or are we going to try it?"

Susan looked at Corey, then at the judge, smiled and said, "I think you'll find that Corey is reluctant to agree on anything, whether it involves this case or any other aspect of life. I don't believe we're going to be able to resolve this, Your Honor. I'm quite sure we'll need to try it."

The judge looked at Corey and said, "Is she correct?"

"About which part?"

"About not being able to resolve this."

"Probably, Judge. I'll discuss it again with my client, but the last I knew he didn't want to plead to anything."

Corey thought for a moment, then turned toward Susan and said, "Do you have any more evidence than what you've already disclosed?"

"Not yet, no. But would it matter? I mean you and I never were able to agree on *anything*. Would it really matter if there was another witness or two?

She turned toward the judge and said, "I have no doubt we'll need to try this."

"I get the feeling there's a little past history involving the two of you and your involvement with each other than meets the eye. Am I missing something here?"

Susan smiled, looked at Corey and said, "In another life, Corey and I were involved. That was, however, another time, long ago, and long over. No, Judge, you're not missing anything."

Corey moved forward in his chair, looked at Susan and said, "It doesn't have to be over, you know. We could talk about that later, and see…"

"Corey, don't even *consider* going there."

"Judge, there's no involvement of any kind concerning the two of us. The state's ready to proceed."

The judge smiled, and said, "Well, I guess that's that. I see there are no pretrial motions on file. I'll just plan on seeing the two of you in the courtroom a few weeks from today."

Both Corey and Susan stood and left the judge's chambers together. closing the door behind them as they did.

Corey said, "Would you like to get a cup of coffee?"

Susan stopped, turned to look at him, and said, "What's going on with you? I haven't heard from you since we broke up. What's changed that I don't know about?"

"I… I saw you today, and I just realized I made a mistake. You have some time to talk?"

"No, *and* I won't have time to talk in the future—at least about you and I. Remember, I told you after that one incident, you would never lay a hand on me again. You haven't and you won't. No need to talk."

"I lost my temper—once, just once during the whole time we dated."

"Wrong! You lost your temper to the extent you *hit* me only once. You lost your temper a lot of times. Doesn't matter anyway. I'm happily married. I hope one day you are too, Corey. Now I gotta go. See you in court, counselor."

Later that night, as they sat in front of the fire, enjoying the last few sips of wine in the bottom of their glasses, Susan said, "That pretrial was interesting today."

Tom said, "Oh, my gosh, with all I had going on today, I forgot about that. How was your old friend and lover, Corey?"

She gave him a stare, but said nothing.

"Okay, okay, how was the pretrial?"

"It was fine. I knew Corey would never come to an agreement with me on anything. He never was able to resolve anything in his life. I didn't expect this case to be any different. We're set for trial in a few weeks."

"Did you have a chance to visit with him out of the presence of the judge?"

"Unfortunately, yes. In fact, he wanted to go get a cup of coffee with me after the hearing was over."

"You're kidding. What did you say?"

"I basically told him *when hell freezes over*. Those days are long gone. I told him I was happily married and was staying that way."

"It's been a while since we really talked about him. He's into criminal defense work now?"

"I guess."

"Weren't you two involved for quite some time? It's been a while since we discussed him, but I'm thinking you were with him maybe a year or more?"

"It was about that long, yes. It lasted until I just got sick of arguing with him at home and then going to work and arguing with the attorney on the other side of a case I was trying in the courtroom. He always did have a hell of a temper. When he hit me, once was all it took. As you know, I left him that same night and never looked back."

"But didn't he harass you for a while after that. I can't accurately remember the stories about all your men—just too many."

"Bullshit, there weren't that many. But yes, he continued to harass me, until one day I had a cop friend of mine call him and tell him if he called me again, he would arrest his ass, throw him in jail and throw away the key. Apparently, the cop was believable. I never heard from him again."

He smiled and said, "And then you met me."

"Yes, Tom, then I met you, and those days with that jerk were finally over. To be honest, I was really thankful that I got out of my relationship with him physically unharmed. When he lost his temper, he was uncontrollable. Absolutely, uncontrollable."

Chapter 16

Susan had tried her best to sleep throughout the night. She was unsuccessful. She had concluded this was most likely just the beginning of many restless nights until the primary election was behind her.

As she sat at her desk, she reconsidered that conclusion—that portion of her conclusion in that this was, most likely, just the start of many sleepless nights before the primary. Those *sleepless nights* most likely would *not end* once the primary election was over. In fact, assuming she won, the general election would be held not long after that, and she wondered if she would sleep *at all* if she had persevered in the primary

Then, if she won that one, she would have the job to handle, a job which she really had no idea if she was qualified to perform—a job which was different in so many ways from the one she now had. That would cause her to lose sleep too, and then… and then…

She put her pen down, leaned back and smiled. *And then,* she would perform the duties of the job she had wanted since she became a practicing attorney—and she would enjoy every minute of it, sleep or no sleep.

Susan leaned forward, picked up her pen and started to review another file, as she had been doing since a little before five. It was quiet…peaceful. She had taken advantage of the early morning peace to review all of the cases that were close to trial.

The two cases that loomed in her immediate future—State vs. Wagner and State vs. Hepner—were the files she focused on. She was almost ready to try both. She needed to talk to each attorney one more time, just to make sure there remained no opportunity to resolve either case. Assuming there wasn't, she would then talk to the officers one more time before they selected a jury. Both cases appeared to her to be winnable without much additional attention.

About an hour later, she was just opening a new file when she heard the outer office door open and close. Susan moved the file aside and waited.

A few seconds later, Amy sat down and said, "How long have you been here?"

"To long."

"Did you get caught up?"

Susan said, "Just about." She hesitated, then started to smile.

"What?"

"Oh nothing, nothing."

"No, tell me. What are you smiling about?"

"I was just thinking how good you look—no bruises, no cuts, no broken bones. You look almost normal. It must have been a good night."

"It was. It was a good night in our house." She hesitated for a moment then said, "You know, I never had an opportunity to talk to you yesterday. You were always either in court or on the phone. I walked out the office door last night after I had waited a half-hour to visit with you and you were still on the phone."

Susan leaned forward, as she said, "What happened? Did he hurt you again?"

"No, no nothing like that at all. I just wanted to tell you how proud I was of you the other night. You were so good at that party. You looked great and gave a great speech. I was just proud to tell those people that I worked for you. I mean, you really had them eating out of your hand. Everyone was so excited about you running and that speech you gave was so professional. I was just proud I could call you my boss, that's all. I just wanted you to know."

Susan smiled and said, "Thanks, Amy. Those are kind words. It was a good start, that's for sure. I just hope it continues as upbeat and positive as it was that night."

"Where do you go from here? What's next?"

"I have no idea. That's what I'm paying Sally to do—to keep me informed and moving in the right direction."

"You know, she called three times yesterday. I told her after the second time I would have you call her when you got in, but she called again anyway. I doubt, with all the messages you had, you even saw hers."

"I didn't. In fact, I didn't look through any of them until this morning. I didn't get out of here until around seven. I went through them this morning and noticed she had called all those times. If she calls today just make sure I get to talk to her. By the way…"

The phone rang. Susan looked at caller ID, and said, "That's her. I'll talk to her now and just get it over with for the day."

Amy walked out of her office, as Susan said, "Morning. How's it all looking today?"

"Just as good as it did yesterday. You're hard to run down. Can you have that secretary of yours contact you immediately when I need to talk to you? In fact, give me your private cell number. I needed to talk to you all day yesterday and couldn't reach you. That was just a little frustrating."

"What do you need? I was in court most of the day. I didn't get out of here until after seven."

"Why didn't you call me last night when you got home? You know, we must stay in close contact, Susan, we…"

"Okay, okay I get it, I understand. I'll try to do better. Now, what's going on?"

"Well I just wanted you to know you really did well the other night. You really wowed them. We picked up a lot more money through the course of the evening. Your campaign, at least through the primary, is pretty much already paid for."

"Wow! That's great news."

"Well, then there's the general election. We will get some money from the Democratic Party, but I think I can raise the balance of what we need if you get by the primary. Speaking of the primary, I now know your two opponents."

"Who are they?"

"A couple of guys I've never heard of. I got their names at the office. I can't remember either of their names off the top of my head. One of them is just out of law school—he won't be a problem. The other one has run for the job three times and lost every time. He's also about seventy years old. The others that were considering running, all pulled out of the race when they heard you were running."

"Hmm. I'm not really sure why they would do that. I wouldn't think I would pose much of a challenge."

"You have no idea how highly you're regarded in the legal community, Susan. You've built a great reputation in a short time."

"So, what's next?"

"I'll start putting together an agenda. You and I are going to basically live together for the next few months, so you might as well get used to it. We have a lot to do, a lot of people to talk to, in a short period of time. You might as well tell your boss that I'm going to need a lot of your time from now on and to just get used to it."

"I understand. But you need to understand I have a job to do here too. I'll give you all the time I can, but I still have a job, and if I lose the primary or the general election, I still want to come to work here each and every morning."

"I get it, I get it. Don't worry. I'm not going to put you in that kind of situation. I understand. Listen, I gotta go. I'll circle 'round and touch base with you later this week. I should have a full schedule for you to look over and determine if you have any conflicts. Most of your speaking engagements will be at night, and…"

"I really need to go. Talk to you later."

Susan terminated the call. She didn't need to terminate it, but she had heard all she needed to hear. Sally made it sound overwhelming. Susan had a thousand things to do today. Listening to her go on and on for the next two hours was not on that list.

She walked through the door a little before eight. She hung up her coat and walked in the living room, where Tom was sitting near the fireplace, watching TV. As she walked in, he stood, and said as he walked by, "Good to see you. I have the grill all warmed up. I'll let you know a few minutes before they're ready."

He walked through the door and out onto the porch with steaks in hand. She sat down for a moment, just long enough to mentally firm up her position, then followed him to the deck.

"Hey, no kiss…no 'How'd your day go?' No hug? Nothing? Is everything okay?"

He never turned around as he continued to move the steaks around, and said, "Yeah, sure everything's great. I won't be long."

She walked up behind him and turned him around.

"What's wrong? This isn't you at all. What's going on?"

"Let's talk about it at supper. It's no big deal." He tried to turn away, but she wouldn't let him.

"Let's talk right now. What's going on?"

"You know I haven't seen you for most of three days. Is this the way it's going to be? Am I going to go days in a row without seeing you? Just be upfront with me and tell me, so I know what to expect."

She looked down for a moment, before she looked at him and said, "First of all, I'm sorry it's been that way lately. But secondly, yes, it's probably going to be this way until the primary. And if I win that, until the general. And if I win that, *then* it really might slow down. But until then it's going to be tough."

He turned toward the grill and flipped the steaks.

"Look at me, Tom. Now listen. I will forget this whole election thing in the blink of an eye, with no second thoughts whatsoever, if you want me to. My marriage is way, way more important than this job. Now, we have been through this and through it. I *thought* we had come to a conclusion."

He moved the steaks away from the heat, took a deep breath, then looked at her and said, "I'm sorry. I shouldn't have said anything. This is just the first time I have ever felt our marriage was second to anything." He kissed her, smiled and said, "I'm fine. I was just feeling sorry for myself. I missed you, and I, to be honest, felt a little lost without you."

"Again, I'll give it all up in the blink of an eye if you want me to—and never look back. You mean more to me than anything, anything in the world, and I mean that."

He smiled, moved the steaks back over the heat, and said, "Go inside. It's chilly out here. I shouldn't have ever brought the subject up. In reality, I'll be more upset than Sally if you don't follow all this through. In time, I'll learn to accept life with a little less of you in it. It's really going to be difficult, but I do want you to run, I want you to win. So, let's talk about all that when I bring in these steaks in about…oh, about fifteen minutes."

"Are we okay?"

"Yes, hon, we're fine. I just needed to know what to expect. Now I feel I have a better idea concerning where we are at, and what's coming down the road before the election. It's going to take a little time to accept the changes in both our lives, but I'll learn to live with it. Thanks for talking it through with me. See you in a few minutes."

Susan walked back through the sliding glass doors, and as she shut them, she continued to consider Tom's comments. That talk was inevitable. She knew it would come as soon as their time apart started to increase. She knew it would come; she just didn't think it would be this soon. He got it off his chest, and she told him exactly how she felt. What she told him was from the heart. She would never, ever let *anything* come between her and the man she loved. Unfortunately, if that meant staying completely out of politics, then so be it.

Chapter 17

Susan opened the Wagner assault file, and started to carefully review the facts one more time. The trial was scheduled to start in a few weeks, and she wasn't actually as concerned about the facts, as she was about the attorney. Corey Abbott was unpredictable. She knew him all too well. He would do absolutely anything to get what he wanted. While they were together, he had proven that time after time. If he didn't get his way, he would made sure and make life a living hell for whoever happened to be nearby. He was definitely someone to watch closely. She wouldn't be surprised at *anything* he did in an effort to win the case.

As she finished a quick review of the file, Amy walked in her office and said, "Chuck just contacted me and wanted to know if you were busy. I told him you weren't right now, but you had appointments all day starting in about a half-hour. He said he'd be right down."

"Just send him in when he gets here. I haven't talked to him in a while. We need to catch up."

A few minutes later, he walked through her door.

She stood as he walked in.

"Sit, sit Susan." He sat as she did. "How are you? You've been busy. I've been trying to touch base with you for a week."

"Yes, it's been a busy couple of weeks. I've been meaning to stop down and see you too, but just haven't felt I could take the time. I'm glad you stopped in. I've got a hell of a schedule coming up, but I did want to tell you the news."

"I already heard. It's all over the office—actually all over town." He smiled. "I just want you to know how pleased I am that you have decided to run. You and I have talked about it enough times, and I had no doubt you knew that was what I really wanted you to do. I am really glad you finally made a decision and glad you decided the way you did. Have you started to campaign yet?"

"Yes. There is, however, one thing I wanted to ask you. I assume if I lose the election, my job here is still secure. Is that correct?"

"Certainly. I want you in this office in whatever capacity it might be. Your job is still yours if you lose. I'm thinking you've got a pretty good shot at winning both the primary and the general elections. I can support you in the primary, and I will. But of course, the general election might be a different story. We'll just have to wait and see about that. If someone else runs against you from this office in the general election, I would most likely not support either. That all remains to be seen."

"I understand. I just wanted to make sure I still had a job here if I lost either election."

He stood. "As far as I'm concerned you can work here as long as I have anything to say about it. I can't speak for my successor, but who knows—maybe my successor will be you, so there won't be any of those types of decisions to make. Again, I'm really glad you decided to run. Let me know if there's anything I can do to help you get ready or further support you in any manner."

He walked out of the room and as he did, Susan thought now would be a good time to discuss Chuck's involvement in the election with Sally. His support would be invaluable. He was highly thought of and had retained the office through a number of elections.

Just as she was about to tell Amy to contact Sally, Amy told her Corey Abbott was on line one.

"And speak of the devil," she said softly. Should she take it now, or put it off and call him back later? No reason to put him off—she would be dreading making the return call until she made it.

"Hi Corey, what's going on?"

"Morning, Susan. I see you finally took the leap. Congratulations. Hopefully you'll win both elections and we'll finally have someone in charge of the district attorney's office we can trust."

"Oh really. I didn't know you had trust issues with this office. In fact, I thought you only just started representing defendants in criminal cases."

"Well, I did just start on a full-time basis, but I've had a few cases with your office over the years, not with you, but with your office, and I felt the people I dealt with were real jerks. That's one of the reasons I went to the civil side and got out of criminal law—your people were just too tough and stubborn to deal with."

"Sorry to hear that. What can I do for you?"

"By the way, if you become district attorney general, maybe there's a position there for me—in your office. You think we could work together?"

She leaned back in her chair, and said, "Doubt it."

He laughed, and said, "Keep me in mind if you do win both elections. You already know I'm a hard worker, and I…well, let's just say you know me pretty well and leave it at that. Keep me in mind if you win."

"Corey, what do you want? I got a million things going on today."

"I just wanted to talk to you about the Wagner case for a moment."

"What about it?"

"How about pleading him down to a misdemeanor—maybe just simple assault. Then let him pay a fine and be on his way."

"I thought we had been all through that. No. I'm not reducing the charge. He's bad news. He's either going to plead as charged, or we're going to try him."

He hesitated, took a deep breath, and said, "You know, he's got a big family. And part of that family's got a lot of money. Right now, I have the opportunity to do some good for this kid, and perhaps start representing everyone else in their family. It's really a bid deal for me, Susan. I need a little help from you. If I can't get this resolved in this manner, or some variation of it, I may lose their business altogether. Now, what can you do for me?"

She sat up. "Corey, I'm sorry you're in that position. But I can't give this kid a break just because you need a favor. And by the way, you know better than trying to make that kind of deal with me, of all people. Just plead him. Maybe the judge will give him a break."

He remained silent for a few moments, then said, "Is there nothing we can do to plead this down to something else? Is there nothing you will do to help this kid out in some way? He really needs the break and…"

"No. No, Corey, I can't do anything. If he won't plead, we try it,"

Again he hesitated before he said, "You know, you always were a bitch—from day one. Okay, I'll try the case, and I'll beat your fucking ass into the ground. Thanks for nothing."

They had discussed both of their days in detail. Each had filled their wine glasses more than once. A late evening supper was nearly ready, as they watched the flames in the fireplace begin to die down.

Tom stood and said, "You want to eat?"

She hesitated, drank what was left in her wine glass, and said, "I had a tough conversation today."

"What do you mean? Tough how?"

"Promise me you'll do nothing about this when I tell you. This is *my* problem. I haven't said anything to anyone about it and probably won't."

"Well, okay, sure. if that's what you want."

"I got a call from Corey Abbott."

He sat back down, as he said, "This sounds bad already."

"He wanted me to reduce the charge in that Wagner case I told you about. I told him in no uncertain terms I wasn't going to do that."

"Bet he didn't take that well. At least based on what you've told me about him, that would not be unexpected."

"No, it didn't go well at all. He told me he was about to get all the family's business, which was a big deal for him, and he needed a break. I told him there would be no break for this kid—that I was going to try him on what he had been charged with and he needed to plead him or try the case."

"What'd he say?"

"He went nuts."

Tom leaned forward in his chair, as he said, "Should we tell Chuck, or report him to the police, or should we…"

"No, no, let's just see what happens. I know full well he'll deny what he said, and it will all come down to a one-on-one type of situation. You know those types of comments—one-on-one—are always tough to prove. I know him. I know I need to watch out for him and I will. But the conversation was a little disconcerting."

"I'm sure it was. Are you sure you…?"

"I got this handled, Tom. I debated about even telling you, but in the end, I just really felt you should know. Now, you've been told, you're aware of the conversation, and that's all I wanted. I'll handle it from here on."

Later that night, as she again considered the call, she decided she would just take it day-by-day with Corey. She already knew what he was capable of doing.

But this was the last straw with him. If he confronted her again in that manner, she would inform the authorities *and* the bar association. They could take it from there.

Chapter 18

The next morning, as she sat in her office, she was still considering whether or not she was moving in the right direction concerning Corey. She wasn't sure just simply forgetting their last conversation was the best option.

But, on the other hand, before yesterday, other than the one hearing they had together, they had not had any contact whatsoever since they were a couple. Maybe after yesterday, other than their time before a judge, a situation necessitating contact would not present itself again. Maybe after the phone call yesterday, he understood her position when it came to their relationship. However, just in case, she concluded she would turn over any other cases she might have with him in the future, to someone else in the office.

As she continued to process the issue, Amy came through her office door and said, "You want to talk to Brian? He's here. I told him you were getting ready for a hearing, but he'd like to talk to you if you have a moment."

"Yeah, sure, send him in."

As Brian walked through her office door with a big smile on his face, he extended his hand, as he said, "Well, I think congratulations are in order. I heard not long ago you were running for the office. You haven't said much about it. I just assumed you were still considering all your options. Congratulations."

She stood, shook his hand and said, "Yes, I have decided to run. I held off coming to a conclusion for a long time, but it was time to make a decision. Running was what I decided to do. Congratulations to you too. Big move for both of us."

"Are you in a hurry? Are you going to a hearing?"

"I am, but I have a little time. Sit, sit. Did you get someone to help you through the election maze or are you just going to do it yourself?"

"I'm just going to handle it myself, at least through the primary. If I get through it, I'll hire someone. I don't really have the money to hire anyone now anyway. Besides that, the competition isn't that tough as concerns the primary. I'll just wait and see who my competition is and who Chuck supports before I figure out what I'm going to do for the general election."

"Do you know anyone who's running against you yet."

"Yes. So far, it's a couple of guys that have absolutely no experience in prosecuting. One of them is a defense attorney and the other one primarily handles domestic issues. To be honest, I don't think either one of them has a chance in the primary, especially if Chuck provides me with a little support."

"Well, you know he'll do that. You should be in good shape. I don't know a lot about the two guys running against me, but Sally seems to know all about them, and doesn't think they should provide much of a problem."

"I heard you hired McHorton, is that correct?"

"I did, yes. Actually, she came to me initially. I hadn't even thought about a manager, but she came to the office one day and said she would like to handle my campaign, if I was going to run. She and I hit it off right off the bat, and so, yes, she's handling whatever I do."

"So, you're thinking you'll probably win your primary, and if I win, it will be you and I in the general?"

"That's the way, at this point, it looks to me. You know as well as I, there have certainly been bigger upsets than one of those two guys beating me in the primary. But if I was wagering on the outcome, I would say in the general election, it's going to come down to either you or me. I assume if you beat me, I can still work here, for you, after the election is over?"

He smiled and said, "Absolutely. And I assume the same is true for me working for you?"

"Definitely."

Brian remained silent for a moment, before he said, "You know, I've dreamed about having Chuck's job ever since I started working here. That's been a while ago…that's been years ago."

"So have I."

"Chuck's recommendation will probably seal the deal for one of us."

"I guess I haven't thought that far ahead. I'm just trying to get through today. Sally is handling all the possibilities and probabilities for me right now concerning who's vote I need and who's recommendation I need. I'm really glad I have her to take that load off my shoulders. Just like today, I have a thousand things going on. I don't have time to worry about an election."

He stood. "I'll let you go and quit bothering you. But I'm just saying, if Chuck recommends one or the other of us, that person's going to win. At least that's my view."

"You know, he may not choose sides at all. I would not be surprised if he just stayed in the middle of the road and let the voters decide without a recommendation from him."

"I really think the voters have a right to know who he thinks is best suited for the job. He may not look at it that way, but that's the way I look at it. I'll get out of here so you can go to your hearing. Again, congratulations."

"Thanks, Brian."

As he walked out, Amy messaged her Sally was on line one.

"Damn good thing I'm ready for this hearing," she whispered to herself.

"Hi Sally. What's going on?"

"I just wanted to touch base with you. I've had a chance to do a little research concerning both the guys running against you. Based on what I've learned, you should have absolutely no problem getting through the primary. Neither of them appears as though they will be an issue, not only based on their background, but based on a few people whose opinions I value."

"That's good to hear. Brian was just in to see me."

"Brain Jenkins?"

"Yes. He's running in the Republican primary. He's pretty sure he'll prevail. Of course, I never have seen him when he thought he was ever going to lose at anything. He's always sure he'll win, and most of the time he does. I could tell today he figured his primary would not be a problem. I got the idea he wasn't much concerned about me either. It was hard to tell because believing he will win, at anything, is just a part of his DNA, no matter the situation. But I just felt he was pretty confident. Of course, if we do run against each other, the issue of Chuck's position remains a major factor."

"Let's take all of these issues one at a time. Let's get by the primary first. I have a schedule ready for you and I'll fax it over. It sets out, at least for the time being, your speaking engagements I have you lined up to do in addition to all your fundraisers. Look it over and if you have a conflict let me know right away. I've already committed to all the events on the list, hoping they would work for you."

"Thanks, Sally. I'll look it over."

"You know, you ate almost nothing for supper."

They both sat before the fireplace and a fire Tom had started long before she arrived home.

She nodded her head and took another sip of wine.

"You didn't say much either. You were pretty quiet, talking to me only when I asked you a question. I thought I'd give you some time to decompress before I tried talking with you about anything important. But you're…you're just really quiet. Something happen at work today…or somewhere else today…or. do you and I have a problem?"

She smiled as she said, "Sorry. Long day at work."

"You want to talk about it, or just let it go?"

She looked down, and said, "Well, first I had to prepare for that hearing, that suppression hearing, which I eventually lost. Then there was Brian. He came in and was really upbeat about his chances of winning his primary and ultimately beating me. Then came Sally. She sent me a campaign schedule which I didn't even bring home. I knew you would pass out if you saw it. I have no doubt, if I run against Brian, he feels Chuck is going to support him. And to be honest, if he does, I'm probably done."

He stood up and walked to the couch, sitting down next to her. He put his arm around her, and pulled her close.

"One day at a time, Susan. We'll get through this. You had a busy day. You lost a hearing, but you haven't lost the war—you'll still get your shot to convict at the time of the trial. You knew Sally was going to have a horrendous schedule for you, but you can go through the list and pick and choose all you want. You're not tied down to any of those events…yet. And you have no idea what Chuck's going to do. He could just as easily support you. You're a little discouraged about matters that may or may not even happen…and about matters you still have some control over."

He hugged her, and pulled her even closer, as he said, "Everything's going to be fine. It's all going just as planned."

She snuggled up next to him, and said, softly, "You always know what to say. You're the best, Tom. I don't know what I would ever do without you."

Chapter 19

Susan walked in Tom's office and stopped in front of his desk. He was on his phone and indicated to her he would be but one more minute.

As he terminated the call, he said, "You got your jacket on for what reason? Where are you going?"

"I told you earlier in the week I was meeting Greg today for coffee. Let's see. I think you and I are too close. I mean, has it actually reached the point between us where I have to tell you *and* remember for you too?"

"Whatever. How long are you going to be gone?"

"Not long."

"And tell me again why you're meeting with him."

"I told him we should stay in touch, and that's what we're doing. I really want to question him a little about his job and exactly what it is he likes about it. Maybe I'll switch to the other side, you never know."

"Yeah, when hell freezes over. When are you coming back?'

"Probably an hour or so. I'm sure it won't be any longer than that."

"Okay. Keep bundled up. That wind is cold even for March."

They were to meet at the same coffee house where they met the last time they were together. As she walked through the door, she saw him wave from a small table near the far wall.

She got a cup of coffee, and as she approached, he stood.

He pulled her chair out for her. "Susan, you really do look great. Life must be agreeing with you."

As she sat, she smiled, and said, "It is. Life is just pretty good right now—busy, but good."

During the next half-hour, they discussed everything but business including family, old friends, mutual friends and current events. As her time grew short, she said, "Before I need to go back to the office,

I want to get serious for a moment. I want to talk about your practice and how you feel about working on your own, versus what I do—for the government. How is your practice doing? You still like what you do on a daily basis?"

"I do, yes. It's hectic, and it can be a roller coaster ride from hell at times, but I do enjoy it. There's nothing else I would rather do."

"How's the money, Greg? Is that also part of that 'roller coaster ride from hell?' Is it worth your time?"

"Yes. Of course, you need to carefully pick and choose who your next clients are going to be, but it can be very, very lucrative if you're good at what you do, *and* you can be somewhat selective concerning who you represent."

"So, for instance…"

"Hold it. Hold on. Why the in-depth questions about my practice? You interested in changing horses here? You interested in a civil practice rather than what you're doing? I thought you were happy with your job and who you work with. What's changed?"

"No, no I'm not *unhappy* at all. I just want to know what it's like in your world. To be honest, since the last time I talked to you, I've checked with some of my former classmates concerning their practice. Most of them make it sound more interesting and lucrative than what I'm doing."

"Hmm. I'm not sure if I had a choice to make between your situation right now and mine, I would take mine."

"Really? Why?"

"Well, for one thing, the uncertainty of my job is an ongoing concern. I never know who is and who isn't going to walk through my door on a daily basis. You, on the other hand, don't have to worry about that. Benefits are also an issue. You have many benefits that I don't have, unless I pay to get them. Self-satisfaction is also an issue. After you convict someone that's been a threat to society, the self- satisfaction and pride in what you just did, has to be incredible."

"You have a good practice. I would think you shouldn't have to worry about being busy or about a good paycheck each month."

"You get to work with witnesses that are cops. Sometimes I work with people that are, well, let's just say less than reputable. Sometimes I can't choose who my clients are—the money is just too good."

"Certainly, you would have had and still do have the opportunity to take a government job, or a job with a corporation. But you're still doing what you're doing. Any particular reason?"

"I don't really want a boss. That's one thing about this job. You can be your own boss, where with yours, you have Chuck that determines what you work on every day."

Susan looked away for a moment, then said, "So, all in all, factoring in what we've just discussed, you would prefer your job over mine?"

"I really can't say that for sure. I think I'm pretty much where I should be, but you…you should stay right where you are. You're really good at what you do. Besides that, knowing you as I do, you're much better suited for putting the bad guys away, than you are dealing with people like I, on occasion, have to deal with, just to make sure I have enough to pay the expenses for the month. I wouldn't even consider switching jobs if I were you. By the way, I hear you made a big decision not long ago."

"Yes, I did."

"How's everything look? You certainly should beat the two you're up against in the primary,"

"Yes, I have a good chance against both of them, but I just don't know about the general election. We'll just have to see who I'm running against and go from there. I'm sure Brian is running, and he'll be tough to beat."

Greg leaned forward, and said, "Not to change the subject, but what about us?"

"What 'us?' Is there an 'us?' I don't think so, other than 'us' as just good friends."

"What about one more chance? You want to try you and me once more and make it work this time?"

She stood. "I better go. No, Greg, I don't think that's going to happen."

He stood. "Ok, now be specific. I really want an answer. What's he got that I don't?"

"Me."

He smiled. "Okay, okay I get it. But I'm telling you, I'm not going to quit. If you two have issues, I'm going to be standing right there. I still love you Susan and I'm just not ready to say it's really over, no matter how long it's been."

"Greg, I love discussing business with you, but as far as you and I are concerned we are done."

"We'll see."

He grabbed her arms and pulled her near, kissing her on the check.

"Keep me informed concerning the elections. I want to contribute something to your campaign too. Who should I talk to?"

"I'll send you the information. Thanks, Greg. I really appreciate you explaining the pros and cons of your practice. I already knew most of them but you did confirm one thing—I'm well suited for what I do, and I don't need a change."

"I assume I can call you sometime soon and we can get together for coffee again? Is that all right with you?"

"Yes…sure. Give me a call when you're ready, but let's wait until after the primary."

As she walked away, he said, "If you want to get together sooner, just let me know. For you, I'm always available."

A few minutes later, she walked through the reception area and into her office, with Amy close behind.

"Where you been? You've had a million calls, half of them from Sally."

"Oh, I had an out of the office meeting. No big deal. You got my phone messages?"

As she handed them to Susan, she said, "Were you out with that Greg or whatever his name is?"

"As a matter of fact, I was. How'd you know that? I didn't think I told you where I was going. You're not following me now, are you?"

"Nope. Certainly not. But Tom has stopped by two or three times wondering if you were back. He told me you were meeting with an old friend, and when I asked him if it was that Greg guy, he told me it was. Now, Susan if you want my opinion, you've got a good man, and…"

"Don't need your opinion."

Amy walked up to the front of her desk, and said, "Look Susan, you need to rethink what you're…"

"No, I don't. I'm thinking just fine, thank you. He's just a friend and nothing more. Now go back to work.'"

"Okay, don't say I didn't warn you. As I said, Sally called maybe three or four times while you were gone. You might want to call her back first."

"Get her on the phone right now. I spent more time in conference with *my friend,* than I figured I would. We have a lot to do before we close the office for the day."

Chapter 20

Three sat quietly in one of the courthouse conference rooms directly across the hallway from the courtroom. They had concluded picking a jury, opening statements were now over, and one of the officers had already testified.

Officer Jack Thompson said, "You're calling me next right?"

"Yes. By the way, I thought your partner did a good job. He wasn't at the scene as long as you were and never talked to the defendant, but he did a good job setting the scene for what's to follow."

Susan glanced at the victim, John Ward. He was slight in stature, and as he sat quietly, he shook. He was visibly shaking in fear.

"John, how are you doing? Are you doing okay?"

He hesitated for a moment, then said, "I'm fine. I'm a little nervous as you might have noticed, but I'm fine. Just go through the process one more time for me, will you? How much more do I have to do?"

"Well, Jack is going to testify as to what he saw that night when he arrived at the bar. Then you're going to get up on the stand and tell the jurors what this guy did to you. Now again, you haven't heard from him while the case has been pending, correct?"

"Yes, that's correct. He's stayed away from me. But if I testify against him, I may hear from him if he's out of jail waiting to be sentenced or whatever they do with them between the time they are convicted and the time they go to jail."

"We'll just try to put him behind bars immediately if he's convicted."

"That didn't go so well when he was first charged. I know the officer at the time thought he would remain behind bars until the case was tried, but he got out on bond."

"Yes, that didn't work the way I thought it would, but you also heard nothing from him. So, it worked out fine."

"I guess."

There was a knock on the door. The court attendant indicated the judge was ready to begin. All three walked across the hall and took their seats. Susan glanced at the defense table and Corey Abbott, who smiled and nodded. She never acknowledged him. Susan was not apprehensive about trying the case, but she was concerned about trying it against Corey. Their relationship had clearly become toxic.

Once Officer Thompson had been sworn in and all the basic foundational questions had been asked and answered, Susan was ready to question the officer about the specifics of the incident.

"So, tell us officer, why were you there, in that bar, that night?"

"We received a call from the bar owner, concerned about a fight two guys were involved in. He said someone was hurt pretty badly, and they needed us. I went there with the officer that just finished testifying."

"When you arrived, what did you observe?"

"I located the bar owner. He told me the one that was injured was lying on the floor near the bathroom door and they were waiting for an ambulance."

"What did you do then?"

"I walked over to the injured party, a Mr. John Ward, and asked him how he was."

"What did you observe while talking with him?"

"He was beat up pretty good. It appeared his nose was broken, he had cuts on his face, and he told me he wasn't sure he could stand."

"Did he tell you what happened?"

Corey stood, and said, "Objection. The complaining witness is here. Let him testify as to his injuries and what happened. The officer testified as to what he observed and that's enough."

"Sustained."

"Nothing further, Your Honor."

"Any questions for this witness, Mr. Abbott?"

"Yes, Your Honor, just one. Did he tell you who did this to him?"

"Not right away. He did later."

"Did you ask him?"

"Yes, but he wouldn't respond."

"Nothing further."

"The state would call John Ward to come forward and take the stand."

Once all the foundational questions had been asked and answered, Susan was ready for the facts.

"Now sir, were you in the Landmark Bar on the date in question?"

"Yes."

"And while there, did you have any interaction with the defendant in this case, Sam Wagner?"

"I did, yes."

"Tell us about it. First of all, did you know the defendant prior to that night?"

"No."

"Okay, now tell us about your contact with him."

"I walked up to the bar, which was crowded that night, and moved in between a couple of guys to order a drink. One of them was Jim Wagner."

"Go on. What happened then?"

"He told me to get in line behind him. There was enough room for all of us. I just told him I wasn't going to do that. I was there and I was going to stay there."

"Had you observed him earlier in the evening?"

"No."

"Never met him before?"

"No"

"What happened then?"

"Nothing. I got my beer and went back to my table."

"When did you see him or talk to him again?"

"When I walked in the bathroom."

"Tell us what happened."

"I was in there using the urinal. The defendant was standing behind me. He said...he said something like...'You worthless piece of shit, when I tell you to do something after this, you do it, or I'll by god kill you.'"

"Were there others in the bathroom with you?"

"Yes. But they all got out of there when they heard him say that."

"What happened next?"

"Once I finished, I turned around and he hit me. I never had a chance to stop him. I didn't know that was what he was going to do, so I never even had a chance to try to defend myself. Then while lying on the ground, he kicked me three or four times."

"The man that did this—is he here in the courtroom?"

"Yes."

"Point him out."

The witness pointed at the defendant, and said, "That's him. He's the one."

"Any doubt in your mind?"

"Not really."

"Were you injured?"

"Yes, I had a couple of broken ribs and my nose was broken. Hurt like hell."

"Were you hospitalized?"

"No, but I was taken to the emergency room. They looked me over, taped me up and sent me home. To be honest, I felt lucky. I thought he was going to kill me."

"Nothing further, Your Honor."

"Cross, Mr. Abbott?"

Corey stood. "Yes, Your Honor. Now sir, it was by your own admission, dark in that bathroom, wasn't it?"

"Yes."

"And when you turned around, someone hit you immediately didn't they?"

"Yes."

"The blow knocked you down, and it had to have stunned you, correct?"

"Well, yes it did. He hit me hard and I was bleeding…my face was bleeding."

"There were other people in the bathroom at the time, but none of them have testified on your behalf, have they?"

"No."

"So, you were stunned with a blow to the face, lying on the ground, and you think it was the defendant that did it, is that about right?"

"I guess so."

"Nothing further, You Honor."

"Redirect?"

"Yes. Now, Mr. Ward, are you sure it was the defendant that hit you?"

"I'm sure. I'm just pretty sure, yes."

"You looked right at him. Was it light enough to see? I mean I realize it was dark, but you could still see who it was that hit you, correct?"

"Pretty much, yes."

Susan looked through her notes for a second, before she said, "Nothing further."

"Any additional cross, Mr. Abbott?"

"No, Your Honor."

"The State rests."

"Your Honor, on behalf of the defendant, we would like to make a motion out of the presence of the jury."

"Mr. Bailiff, would you escort the jury out of the courtroom. If they are needed again, you can bring them back when I tell you too."

The jury was escorted out of the courtroom, and the judge looked at Corey as he said, "Please proceed."

"Your Honor, on behalf of the defendant in this case, we would move for a judgement of acquittal. The state has not carried its burden of proof. Clearly the victim really isn't sure of anything, and he certainly isn't sure enough that it was the defendant that did this to him, to warrant a conviction. There is a vast absence of evidence in this case and not enough to warrant a guilty verdict. We would ask for a judgement of acquittal and dismissal of all charges, which is warranted because of the State's complete lack of evidence—it's simply not enough to warrant a conviction under any circumstances."

"Response on behalf of the state?"

"Yes, Your Honor." Susan stood. "Judge, I realize the evidence is not substantial, but it's enough. We have a witness who said he was beaten, and we have evidence from law enforcement to substantiate that fact. In addition, we have a complaining witness who has identified his assailant. Certainly, it's not perfect. His testimony is not perfect, but it's enough to convict unless refuted. The evidence is enough to generate a jury question, and certainly enough to move beyond a judgement of acquittal. If the defendant didn't do this, let him get up there and say so."

She sat down, and held her breath.

"Folks I'm going to take a look at a couple of cases and do a little research concerning the issue now before the court. Let's just adjourn until tomorrow morning at nine. Bailiff, let the jury go for tonight, and have them back here at nine tomorrow morning. Court is adjourned for the day."

Chapter 21

"SO, exactly what's going to happen today?"

Susan sat in a conference room the following morning with John Ward, waiting for the judge to order their appearance in the courtroom.

"Well, the first major issue will be whether or not the judge sustains their motion to dismiss the case. If he does that, we are done. If it goes our way, it will be up to the defense to present a case. I assume the only person they will have testify is the defendant. At least that was what the defendant's attorney told me one day while he and I were on speaking terms."

"You seem to have a problem with him."

"Let's just say we don't care for each other and leave it at that."

A knock on the door was their indication the judge was ready to open court.

Once they took their seats, the judge walked in the courtroom, sat down and said, "First of all, as concerns the defendant's motion for judgement of acquittal, I have had a chance to review a number of cases concerning the issue. I have concluded that while the prosecution's case isn't the most compelling I've ever heard, it's also not the weakest. I'm going to allow the trial to proceed, and once it's over we may perhaps address the issue again, depending on what other evidence is presented. Mr. Bailiff please bring the jury in. Mr. Abbott, I believe the ball is in your court. Please proceed."

As the jury filed back into the courtroom, Corey stood and said, "But Your Honor, I don't mean to be argumentative, but what they presented to the court did not even come close to establishing their burden of proof. I don't understand. There wasn't enough evidence to even begin to…"

The judge slammed his gavel down on the sounding block, and said, "Call your witness, Mr. Abbott."

"Yes sir. We call the defendant to the stand to be sworn and testify."

Jim Wagner had done little to physically prepare for trial. He looked disheveled. His hair was long and greasy, his clothes looked like he had slept in them, and he walked with a swagger that smacked of superiority.

Once he was situated and the questions concerning foundation had been asked and answered, his attorney said, "Now, can you give us a timeline concerning where you were the night in question—say from about 4 p.m. until ten that night?"

"Certainly. I got off work around five, then hit a couple of different bars before I ended up at the Landmark around seven. I stayed there until about nine, at which time I went home."

"So, you're saying whatever happened at that bar after nine, you couldn't have been a part of because you weren't there?"

"Correct."

"While you were there, did you have contact in some form or fashion with the complaining witness in this case?"

"Yes, I did."

"Tell us what happened."

"He tried to push in ahead of me while I was getting something to drink at the bar. I told him to stop. He paid no attention to me. He kept moving forward, out of line and finally he got what he wanted. That's the only time I saw him."

"Did you use the bathroom while there?"

"No."

"You never used the bathroom, you never saw the complaining witness again, and you never struck him, is that correct?"

"That is exactly right."

Susan caught a glimpse of movement behind her. She turned to see a half-row of well-dressed people, hanging on every word the defendant said. That, she concluded, must be the family that Corey was trying to impress. They hadn't been there yesterday. They must have just shown up to watch Sam testify, most likely not having time to waste on the other witnesses that had already testified.

"Nothing further, Your Honor."

"Cross-examine, Ms. Jackson?"

"So, as I understand your position, Mr. Wagner, you were there that night, you saw the Mr. Ward, but nothing happened involving the two of you, is that correct?"

"Yup, that's right."

Susan couldn't help but notice how sure he was, how convincing he was—how full of confidence, and…how full of himself.

"You weren't in the bathroom, as Mr. Ward said you were?"

"Nope."

"Are you saying the victim is lying about the entire incident, Mr. Wagner?"

"Nope. Not really." He smiled. "The blow to his head just confused him a little—he's got me mixed up with someone else. Someone must have hit him pretty hard, because he's all mixed up in the head."

"You been in trouble before?"

"Like what do you mean? My parents been mad at me once or twice if that's what you're askin'."

"Ever been charged with anything before?"

Corey stood and said, "Objection, Your Honor,"

"Overruled. I'm going to let him answer,"

"I been charged, but they was all dismissed as they should have been."

She could see this was going nowhere fast. The witness clearly thought he had her right where he wanted her, and to be honest, he did. She would need to wait until rebuttal to make her case. This guy was to experienced—way to savvy to convict himself.

"Nothing further, Your Honor."

"Any additional testimony from the defense?"

Corey stood and said, "None, Your Honor. The defense rests. At this time, we would like to renew our motion…"

"Hold on there, Mr. Abbott. Does the state wish to offer any evidence in rebuttal?"

Susan stood and said, "We would, Your Honor."

Corey sat down as Susan said, "We would call Larry Whitacre to the stand to be sworn."

Everyone stared at the new witness walking toward the witness chair whom no one but Susan knew anything about.

Once he was seated, Susan said, "State your name for the record."

"Larry Whitacre."

"Mr. Whitacre where are you from?"

"Here in Nashville."

"Do you know the defendant and the victim involved in this trial?"

"Not really. I mean, I know their faces from seeing them around, and seeing them at the bars that I frequent. But that's the only way I know them."

"When was the last time you saw both the victim and the defendant?"

"That night this incident happened. The night the victim was struck. That night in the bar—at the Land mark."

Corey stood, and said, "Your Honor, we knew nothing about this witness. We weren't informed there was a witness by this name. We made every effort we could to contact all potential witnesses, but not this one because we didn't know about him."

Susan stood and said, "Your Honor, as you might note in the pleadings of this case, his name was listed as a potential witness along with everyone else that was there that night. We believe most of the people that were there were intimidated by the defendant after he was charged, and that's why the state had trouble getting people to admit they were there. But there was one he couldn't get too, and he's here today, ready to testify."

Corey turned and whispered to his client, who in return whispered back.

"Your Honor, we tried to find this witness and we were always unable to locate him."

"Not our problem. We found him and he's here. May we continue?"

"You may."

"Now sir, tell us what you saw."

"Well, I went in the bathroom. I had to…you know…go. The urinals were all busy, so I went in a stall. I was just ready to walk out—I had just opened the stall door when the defendant, that guy over there, hit John Ward and knocked him down. Everyone else got out of the bathroom. I just shut the door and kept still until the defendant left and there were people around the victim taking care of him. Then I walked out of the bathroom."

"Did you actually see the defendant strike Mr. Ward?"

"I did, yes. He didn't just tap him either—he hit him hard."

"Nothing further, Your Honor."

"Mr. Abbott, any cross?"

Corey stood. "Yes, Your Honor. Where do you live, Mr. Whitacre?"

"Nowhere in particular. I live around town, from place to place. Right now, I'm living with a friend here in Nashville."

"Did the state tell you to do all you could to avoid Mr. Wagner and his attorney?"

The witness smiled, and said, "No. I move around a lot because it's just the way I live."

Corey sat down, as he said, "How much did you have to drink that night before the incident?"

"It was still pretty early for me. I'm thinking maybe a beer or two."

He thought for a moment, then said, "How dark was it in that bathroom?"

"It wasn't dark at all. It was easy to see what was going on if that's what you're getting at."

He whispered to his client, who had lost the smile he had maintained throughout the hearing, clearly believing, at least until now, he had the hearing completely under control.

"We have nothing further, Your Honor."

"Please step down, Mr. Whitacre. Any additional testimony from either of you?"

Both attorneys indicated they had nothing further to submit.

"Okay ladies and gentlemen of the jury, I'm going to dismiss you for the evening. Be here at nine tomorrow morning to begin deliberations. Remember the admonition I gave you at the beginning of this trial, and I'll see all of you here, tomorrow morning."

As Susan was walking away from the table, Corey walked up to her, and whispered, "You hid that son-of-a-bitch, didn't you?"

Susan smiled and said, "Why Corey, I wouldn't do that to you, you know that. He was in plain view all the time. You just looked in the wrong places. Besides that, if justice *is* served, which it should be, that's the way these types of cases are supposed to end anyway, right?"

"Go to hell."

He turned and walked away.

"See you tomorrow morning…*Corey*."

He never turned around.

Knowing him as she did, she thanked God she wasn't living with him anymore. She just figured if some woman *was* living with him, she could find herself where she didn't want to be, once he arrived home from work tonight.

Chapter 22

Closing statements were completed before they left the courthouse for the day. The judge also read his instructions to the jury and informed them to be seated in the jury box by nine tomorrow morning. He told the attorneys to be there about thirty minutes earlier and, at that time they would discuss the schedule for the rest of the trial.

Susan still had almost an hour and a half before she needed to be in the courtroom. She had arrived at the office earlier than usual, thinking she would catch up and review files with pending issues before Amy arrived. But she was so tired, it took all the energy she could muster just to pick up another file to review before she left for the courthouse.

Trials always drained her both physically and emotionally. It never mattered how simple they were, or how significant they were, it was always a tiring experience and this trial was no exception.

She had just reviewed her fourth file, when she heard Amy walk through the outer office door.

"Morning, boss. How long have you been here?"

Susan leaned back in her chair, rubbed her tired eyes, and said, "To long. I think if I can get this trial over with today, I may take a day or two off. I feel like I'm burning the candle at both ends. On top of all these trials, I'm continuously thinking about the election."

"What's the schedule concerning the trial today?"

"I'll leave about eight-thirty and wait until I'm certain there's not going to be an immediate verdict. Then I'll come back here until they call me."

"Okay. I'll just start working on what you've already given me to do, and if you need me for anything special, just let me know."

Susan left for the courthouse a few minutes before nine. Once she arrived, she informed the judge she was available. She waited in the clerk's office until the court attendant told her he was ready to begin.

The judge once again admonished the jury about following all the jury instructions, then sent them to the jury room to deliberate. Corey never acknowledged her. It was apparent he was upset. He made certain she knew.

Once she returned to her office to await the jury's decision, Amy told her John Ward was on line one.

"Morning, John. How are you?"

"I'm good. Did the jury decide?"

"No. The judge just sent them out to deliberate. I wanted to tell you how well you did after you had finished testifying, but I couldn't locate you. I thought you really did a good job."

"Thanks. What happens now?"

"Well, they either find him guilty, not guilty or are unable to come to a verdict."

"What happens to him under each of those scenarios?"

"He's out on bail now. Most likely, that will continue until he's sentenced, if he's found guilty. If he's found not guilty, he'll be released. If it's a hung jury, he'll be out on bail pending a retrial."

"So, under all three of those things, he'll still be out of jail after the jury is finished figuring it out?"

"Most likely, yes."

"Okay. I'm not sure what I'm going to do. I'll let you know. Call me at this number when there's a verdict, okay?"

"Certainly. If he's found guilty, I'll ask the court to incarcerate him pending sentencing, but I imagine the judge will do the same thing he did when they first arrested him—just leave him out pending further proceedings. I'll contact you no matter what they do."

As Susan prepared for her next trial, set to begin in a week, Amy walked in and said, "Jim Arnold is on line two."

"Okay, good. I was going to call him anyway. He represents that Wilson guy I have to prosecute next week."

A few minutes later, Susan said, "Amy, can you come in here?"

"As she walked in Susan's door, she said, "What do you need?"

"Have a seat."

As she sat, she looked at Susan and said, "This must be serious. What's going on?"

"Do you know Jim's secretary, Judy something or other?"

She smiled, and said, "Judy Williams? Sure, I know her. We have been friends a long time."

"Hmm. You talk to her often? I mean, is your knowledge of her just through the office, or did you know her before you came to work here?"

"I met here through this office. Why? What's going on?"

Susan leaned back, folded her arms and said, "Do you two talk about the cases this office and their office have with each other?"

"No, not at all. Why?"

"Because he just told me his secretary, this Judy that you know, told him we had found a good witness in that Roberts case that would blow the case wide open. Did you tell her that?"

Amy said, "Hell no I…no I…"

Susan leaned forward and said, "Before you go any further, I know you told her that. Jim *told* me you told her and there would be no other way anyone in that office would know. I did not want them knowing about that witness until it was time…and, you know…*now wasn't the time.*"

Amy hesitated, then said, "You know, she was so smug and she was telling me all about their case and how good it was. I never talk about business outside the office but I just couldn't take that bullshit from her any longer and… I might have…"

"No 'might have' about it, Amy, you leaked information about a case to the opposing party. You know how I feel about that!"

"I know, I know, and I'm sorry. But, the situation…I'm going to kill her. I know what happened wasn't right but…"

"You're not going to say one word to her about it. This is all on you. You wanted to feel important…to know more than she did. The situation was completely your fault. She did what she should have done—she went to her boss and told him what you did. She understands the significance of breaching a confidence. I can't believe you did this…*again*. I told you the last time if it happened again, you would no longer work here. Now, Amy…"

"Wait, wait. Don't fire me…please. I really, really need this job. I'll never ever say anything again. I am so sorry. I will never…"

Susan put her hand up to stop her. "Go back to work. I'll figure out what I'm going to do once I get this trial off my mind. Go back to work. I don't want to talk about it now. I'll let you know what I decide."

She stood. "Okay, I understand." As she backed away from Susan's desk, she said, "Susan, I really need this..."

Susan stood and yelled, "Enough! I don't want to hear it. Go back to work."

A few minutes later, Amy told her Larry Whitacre was on line 1 and wanted to visit with her.

"Larry, how are you?"

"Fine, so far. Any verdict yet?"

"No, not yet. Where are you?"

"Staying with friends."

"Do you want me to call this number when we get a verdict?"

"Yes. Is he going to be out of jail if he's found guilty?"

"I'm afraid, based on one of the conversations I had with the judge, he probably will be pending sentencing. But let's just see what happens."

"I'm thinking of leaving town. I don't have any ties to Nashville, and I really don't want to be around if he's out of jail."

She hesitated. "I don't think you really need to do..."

"You don't know him. I found out all about him before the trial started. He's an animal. I think I'll get lost. Just call this number when and if you have a verdict."

"Okay. And Larry, thanks for..."

He terminated the call before she could finish her sentence.

Susan had her feet up and a drink nearby when Tom arrived home late that afternoon.

"You know, I tried to get in to see you all day. You must have really been busy."

She held up her glass. "Second one...already. Long day for fucking sure."

Tom smiled and said, "I can tell you've had enough. How long you been home?"

"Like I said—drink number two."

"No verdict?"

"Nope."

"Worried?"

"Yup. I thought it would be easy for them. There shouldn't be anything to even discuss. The little shit's guilty...end of story."

"There must be something bothering them that..."

She shook her head. "Just don't go there. I've thought it all through. There shouldn't be an issue of any kind…period!"

"Okay then. You want me to fix us something for supper?"

"I'll eat if you do. If you want something, fix enough for me. If you don't, get a drink, and we'll just drink our supper tonight."

Tom sat down on the autobahn she had her feet resting on. "What happened today? What went wrong?"

"Just a long day, Tom, a long day."

"Well, you didn't get a verdict, but were there other issues? I know you sometimes just get depressed just like I do, but something's obviously bothering you."

She hesitated, took a drink, and said, "You know, I told you my secretary, *my friend*, leaked information about a case maybe six months ago. You remember I told you how mad that made me, and I told her *never to do it again*? You remember that conversation?"

The smile left Tom's face. "Oh no. She didn't…*she didn't do that again did…*"

"Listen to this…"

Chapter 23

John, Larry and Susan waited quietly in the conference room, for the court attendant to let them know the jury was in place: ready to proceed.

John said, "I thought they were ready when they called you to come to the courthouse. You called us nearly two hours ago, and we've been in here almost an hour now. What's taking so long?"

"Sometimes it just takes the judge a little time to prepare what he's going to say, or he gets a phone call that takes a while to finish. His schedule always dictates the movement of a trial. He always has the last say in all steps of the process."

She thought for a moment, before she said, "Look, I know you two want nothing more than to get this over with. I'm just glad you were as easy to work with as you were and that you both decided to be here with me today to follow this through to its conclusion. There are times when…"

The knock on the door stopped her in mid-sentence. She stood and said, "It's time, guys. You two sit in the back of the courtroom and when the hearing is over, one way or the other, we'll come back here and discuss what happens next."

They walked across the hall and into the courtroom which was empty, with the exception of the defendant and his attorney seated at the council table.

Both John Ward, and Larry Whitacre sauntered to the back of the courtroom and sat down. She walked to the council table, and nodded at Corey as she took her seat.

He looked at her and said, "We need to talk before you leave."

"We'll just have to see how that works out. I have a lot to do today, so we'll see how long this takes."

"Whatever. Surely you can spend two minutes with me."

She smiled and said, "Maybe."

A few minutes later the jury filed into the courtroom. The judge walked in the courtroom from his chambers as everyone stood, and as he took his seat, he said, "Sit, sit. Now folks, it is my understanding you have arrived at a verdict, is that correct?"

One woman, seated at the far end of the jury box, stood and said, "Yes, Your Honor, we have."

"Is it unanimous?"

"Yes."

"Would the bailiff take the verdict from the foreperson and bring it to me so I can review it before it's read?"

The bailiff took the verdict from the juror and gave it to the judge for his review. He read it, nodded to the bailiff who took it from him, and handed it back to the foreperson, as he said, "Please read the verdict you have arrived at."

She unfolded the paper in her hands. It shook as she started to read.

"We, the jury, in the above-entitled matter, find the defendant…guilty of the charge of aggravated assault."

Susan smiled as she looked away.

The judge said, "Thank you. The jury is hereby dismissed. Check with the clerk's office before you leave to see when you'll be needed again in the near future."

The jurors all stood and walked by her as they left the courtroom. A few of them smiled at Susan as they passed by.

Once they had left the courtroom, the judge said, "Sir. please stand."

The defendant stood, along with Corey.

"You have now been found guilty of aggravated assault, which is a felony. Before I sentence you, I do want a presentence investigation prepared and presented to this court. You have been out on bond up until now, and I am going to allow that to continue until sentencing. I'll find out how long the report is going to take to prepare, and then set the date for sentencing based on that. Your conditions on release will be the same as they were before trial. Any questions from the defendant or either attorney?"

Susan stood, and said, Your Honor, the state would request he be incarcerated pending sentencing. He's been convicted of a serious offense involving injury and it's the state's positions he shouldn't be allowed back out on the streets."

Corey stood, and said, "Your Honor, we believe…"

"Hold it, Mr. Abbott. The defendant got along fine while out prior to trial, and I expect him to do equally as well now. If there are problems, all you need do is let me know and I'll set an immediate hearing. Anything further?"

Both attorneys remained silent.

The judge stood, and said, "Fine. We are adjourned."

Susan put her paperwork in her briefcase, and as she did, she could hear the defendant and his attorney whispering back and forth. What exactly the defendant was saying was unclear, but he wasn't happy and that was obvious. Not wanting to walk by the heated discussion going on between Corey and his client, she stood by her table for a few moments, and when it appeared the discussion was at an end, she picked up her files and started to leave. But she had taken only a few stops before Corey blocked her path.

He smiled as he said, "Pretty good move—calling that witness after my man testified. I would have never thought of that. Thanks."

"Really it wasn't that big a deal. I could have called him before you put on your case, but I wanted your client to lie under oath, then follow him up with a witness that was extremely believable. I wanted him to be the last witness the jury heard and to offset everything your client lied about. So, yes, it worked out well, but it certainly didn't take a genius to call him when I did, rather than earlier in the proceedings. By the way, it didn't sound like your client was very happy with the verdict—or to be honest, with you either."

"He wasn't. But he was upset with the whole process, not just the verdict."

"That's understandable."

"He was pretty impressed with you though."

"Oh, I don't think so. From what little I could actually understand, he was mad as hell at me."

"I must admit he was pretty angry with you for making him look like such a fool and such a liar."

"What the hell did he expect? He is both of those things. Is he dangerous? I mean, I know he didn't hesitate to beat the living hell out of a guy that got ahead of him in line. What's he going to do about someone that might have just sent him to prison?"

"No, he's not dangerous. He'll be fine. He's just blowing off a little steam."

"You don't think he might try to contact me, or harm me in some way?"

"Nope. Believe me, there's no problem. I took care of that issue while we were talking."

She started to walk away as he continued. "Did you think I handled my portion of the trial okay?"

She stopped, considered his question for a moment, then said, "What difference does it make what I thought of your presentation?"

"Just answer the question."

"Yeah, I guess so. You presented what you had. You just didn't have much to work with."

"Okay, so do me just one favor. If you win that election, just keep me in mind for a job. I hate the one I have and I think I could be a good prosecutor."

Susan laughed, and said, "You really think you and I could work together?"

"I do, yes I really do. Just keep me in mind."

She turned to leave, as she said, "Sure, I'll do that. I'll keep you in mind if I win."

She heard him say, 'Thanks.'

As Susan approached her victim and his witness, John said, "Okay, so I know they found him guilty, and that's good. But what else just happened?"

"Yes, the verdict was a good one, and I want to thank both of you for testifying, for hanging in there with me, before and during the trial. I know it took a lot for the two of you to sit up there and point your finger at this guy and say he was the one. But now that the trial is over, the judge has released him as he did prior to trial. He most likely will remain out on bond until the judge has a presentence investigation report recommending a sentence."

"So, we both need to continue watching out for him until he's sentenced?"

"Yes. I'm sorry but that's just the way it is."

John said, "I'm leaving town. I don't need to stay here and I'm not taking any more chances with that guy."

"Neither am I. I'm out of here,"

"I understand completely and I'm sorry. Make sure the office has your phone numbers before you leave so we can remain in touch. I'll let you know as soon as he's sentenced, and you can decide then whether you want to return or not."

Tom had long ago left the office, when Susan finally felt comfortable leaving for the day.

He was preparing supper when she arrived. She took her coat off, walked into the kitchen and kissed him.

As she walked in the living room, and kicked off her shoes, he said, "I understand you had a good day today. I tried to congratulate you but you were either at the courthouse or had someone with you all day. I finally quit trying a little after four and just came home. Obviously, my day wasn't near as busy as yours. You want something to drink. It'll be an hour before we eat."

"Yeah, pour me something…whatever you're drinking."

As he handed her a glass of wine and sat down, he said, "I hear you won your case."

"Yes, that went well. But, the judge unfortunately, released the defendant until he receives the presentence investigation and report. Leaving the defendant out on the streets scared the hell out of both the victim and the witness. In fact, they left town. I don't know if they'll ever come back or not, but they simply weren't staying in Nashville if the defendant wasn't incarcerated."

"Is he *that* dangerous? The charge wasn't murder, or something as serious as that—he just hit a guy."

"He didn't just 'hit a guy'—he damn near killed him. He really hurt him. And to hear tell, the guy's been doing that for a long time. This time, the victim just didn't let him get away with it. One thing though, really concerns me—I could vaguely hear him talking to Corey, and I know he wasn't upset with just the complaining witness. He was ripping me up one side and down the other. I asked Corey if he felt he was dangerous—if *I* might have a problem with him, and he told me unequivocally that would not be an issue. But it does concerns me a little."

Tom leaned forward and said, "Should we say something to law enforcement? What should we do? I sure as hell don't want him harming you, or even being a potential threat so that we have to keep looking over our shoulder all the time."

"No, I think we're okay. I don't put much faith in anything Corey tells me, but I also have virtually nothing to go on—to tell law enforcement, because I really overheard nothing that specific. No, I'm sure it will be fine. By the way, Corey wants to come work in the office if I win the election."

"He told you that?"

Susan smiled, took a drink and said, "He did, yes sir, he certainly did."

"You're not going to hire…"

"I would rather throw the election than have him work with us in that office. No, he won't be coming to work with us any time soon—in fact, never."

Tom thought for a moment, then said, "Whoa, you did have an interesting day. Why don't you just come over her on the couch, lay your head in my lap and let's watch the news until supper' s ready?"

Susan smiled, slowly stood and said, "My friend, other than 'guilty,' those are the best words I've heard all day."

Chapter 24

"Morning, Amy."

"Morning, boss. You should be feeling good after yesterday. Yesterday should have been a good day for you, right?"

Susan smiled and said, "It was, yes, it was."

"I tried to congratulate you yesterday and find out how everything went. But you had people waiting for you when you arrived here from the courthouse, and then you went home—without saying a word to me I might add."

"Long day. I was beat. I went to bed early and didn't come to work quite so early this morning."

"So, did they sentence the guy?"

"No. The judge is going to have a presentence investigation and report prepared. He'll probably follow the department's recommendation. I don't have any idea when the report will be ready, but as many as they do, it'll probably be a while."

"What about the victim? He should have been happy about the result."

"Yeah, he was, but both those guys, the victim and his witness, feel Wagner could retaliate. They are both talking about leaving Nashville. They just don't want to be around here with Wagner still out of jail. I can understand, but it's a shame they feel they need to leave town. Just let me know immediately if one or the other calls."

"I will. You got a number of appointments today. Did you look at the calendar?"

"I did. Is that some kind of bandage on your leg? Is that like an Ace bandage on your leg? What happened?"

"Oh, that. Yeah, that's one of those wraparound things. I really pulled a muscle or something last night—or bruised one maybe."

"What happened?'

"Oh, nothing really. My husband and I were lying together on the couch watching TV, and one thing led to another. He put his hand…

Susan put up her hand and said, "Stop."

Amy said, "What's wrong? You said you wanted to hear what happened. You don't now?"

"I don't want to know… where he put his hand. Just finish your story, without those kinds of details. You know what details I'm referring to."

"Okay, okay, sorry. So, anyway, he started to kind of get rough with me. I mean, obviously he's done that before, but not like this. So, I grabbed him and squeezed."

"Oh god, Amy why did you do that? Why the hell didn't you just get up and move away. Like, sit in a chair or something."

"Eye for an eye, Susan. You know that's how I roll."

"Whatever. What happened then?"

"Well…he got a little testy about that, and he pushed me off the couch. When I fell, I hit my leg on the edge of our coffee table sitting in front of the couch. Hurt like hell."

"What'd you do?"

"I watched him laugh for a minute, slapped him as hard as I could and went to find one of these bandages. I wrapped it, and it felt much better. But this morning, it's really bothering me. No big deal. I'll get through the day."

"Look, why don't you get your ass out of that house? Leave him?"

She smiled. "We're both good this morning. No problem. It just got a little hot there for a few minutes last night, but we're both over it now. In fact, he rewrapped the bandage for me before I came to work."

"A relationship like none I've ever seen. Whatever. Go to work."

"Before I go get started, I didn't leave you a message from one of the calls I got yesterday."

"Oh. Why's that?"

"I guess I figured the call was probably personal, and I should just verbally tell you about it."

"Why? Who was it from?"

"That Greg guy. The one you've had coffee with a couple of times. I told him you weren't in, and he called a second time later in the day."

"Did he ever say what he wanted?"

"No. He just said he needed to visit with you."

"Okay. Did he leave his number?"

"No. He said he'd call back."

"Thanks."

She hesitated.

"What's wrong? Go…go on…go to work."

She smiled. "You want to tell me what's really going on there? I mean, you know, just girl to girl."

"Amy, we've had this conversation before. *Nothing* is going on and that's the truth. We are just friends having a cup of coffee and talking over current events and our lives. There's really nothing going on."

"Okay, whatever. If he calls, should I put him through?"

Susan thought for a moment. "No. Just take a message. Tell him I'm busy, but I'll give him a call back when I can. He's no different than anyone else that calls in here, so just treat him the same."

"Well, if you want my opinion…"

"I don't."

Amy stood to leave. As she did, Susan said, "One more thing, Amy."

"Sure, boss."

"Last night, I gave a lot of thought to you discussing our office work with people outside the office. This is the last time I'm going to warn you. Don't let that *ever* happen again, as long as you work for me."

"Don't worry about that boss. It won't, I promise. I just…I just…"

"If it does that will be the last day you work here. That's not a threat that's a promise. Now, go on…go do your job."

Amy turned around to leave, as Susan said, "Oh, and by the way, I'll probably have you start making a few calls to people asking for their vote in the primary. It's coming up before long and there are a few business friends I want to remind to vote, *and t*o vote for me. I'll have some signs we can hang on the walls in your outer office, and I might have you go place a few of them around town. You okay with that?"

"Absolutely. I'll let you know if it's a place I've been thrown out of. They probably wouldn't want me walking through their front door, or leaving a sign for them to put up. There's only a few of those though. By the way, how's that all going? The election, I mean."

"To be honest, I'm not really sure. I haven't talked to Sally for a week. I see she's called half a dozen times, but right now, I still have a job to do, and to do it as well as I possibly can. So, I really don't have time to go out begging for votes. We'll look at my schedule later today and see if we can't find time for me to go do a little campaigning during the days before the election. I'll talk to Sally about that too. Put her through if she calls."

The rest of the morning was as hectic as her conversation with Amy. She had appointments every half-hour, and phone calls to return between appointments. As noon approached, after her last appointment of the morning, just as she was ready to walk out the door, Amy came into her office and said, "There's a Janet Hepner on the phone. She says she needs to talk to you. I tried to take a message, but she was having none of that. She wants to talk to you. I think she's the wife of that guy you're prosecuting for that robbery. I think his name is Sam…Sam Hepner. What do you want to do?"

She thought for a moment, then said, "Let's get it out of the way. I'll take it now. You go ahead and leave. Lock the door as you go out. I'm going to work through the noon-hour."

"Okay. I'll see you when I get back. Good luck with her. She's pretty demanding."

"Ms. Hepner, this is Susan Jackson. How can I help you?"

She hesitated for a moment, then said, "You're the woman that's prosecuting my husband, right?"

"I am, yes. Again, how can I help you?"

"Dismiss the case."

Susan hesitated. "I'm sorry, but I can't do that."

"Why not? He's not guilty. Why would you continue on, when you know he's not guilty?"

She leaned back in her chair, and said, "The evidence we have indicates he *is* guilty. To be honest, the officer involved in the case, based on his investigation, has no doubt he did it. Why would we dismiss under those circumstances?"

"Look, you need to understand. He's the only one bringing in any money to this household. We got nothing. I can't work. I have four young kids to take care of. I need his income to survive. Besides that, like I told our attorney, he was home all night that night. Now, based on that, can't you just dismiss and try to figure who really did this?"

"Based on all the facts *we* have available it appears to us your husband did what he is charged with. I have no choice. I have to move ahead with the case."

"Oh, you have a choice. At least, according to my attorney you have a choice. She says it's all up to you whether or not this case proceeds. Is that true?"

"Well, I have some say in whether we move forward, but no it's not all up to me. The officer has some say, my boss has some say in what we do, and we all have come to the same conclusion. That conclusion was to move forward."

"You know, I think you're just a power-hungry bitch. You made the decision to move ahead, you know now it's wrong, and you won't change your mind because you'll look weak. That's what I think."

"I'm sorry you feel that way, Ms. Hepner. But we decide whether to move forward in each and every case, based on the facts. The facts to us indicate your husband committed this crime. Now I'm going to hang up. Don't call back. If you need information, you call your attorney, but don't call back here. We'll not be talking again. Good day."

Chapter 25

"We don't have much more time, Amy. How many of those signs have you placed in the last week or so?"

"Oh, I don't know, maybe five or so."

"Maybe you should devote more than a half-hour a day to doing it—maybe take an hour. Would that work for you?"

"You're paying me, so if you're willing to pay me for a full hour, that's fine by me. It comes at a good time during my day. My work here, at the office, is over for the day. If I'm in a bar I can have a quick drink before I move on, and when I'm finished, I go home for the day. It's a schedule I enjoy, so if you want me to expand it by another half-hour, I'm more than willing."

"How much feedback are you getting?"

"Let's just say I'm not hearing anything negative. I have to tell you though, there's not much positive either. Not many people have heard of you, so I'm thinking it's really beneficial that you're doing this—getting your name out there in this manner."

"Sally is going to continue with ads in the paper. I'm speaking at about four or five events a week, so I'm thinking we're doing about all we can do."

"What about Chuck? Is he supporting you at all?"

Susan leaned back in her chair, thought for a moment, and said, "You know, I honestly don't know what he's doing. I've talked to him a couple of times during the past week, but he never says much. I assume he's supporting both Brian and myself. But I'm not going to push him. He knows what's at stake here, and I've always had confidence in his judgement."

"Did I give you your messages yet? I don't think I've given you all your messages yet from earlier this morning. You've been busy. Let me get them."

As Amy walked back in with a number of new phone messages, she said, "Just to highlight what's here, that attorney that represents that guy you're trying next week called, and so did that Corey you had a trial with last week."

She handed the messages to Susan, and said, "I'll increase my time campaigning for you starting today, so you know."

"Yeah, that's a good idea. Thanks."

A few minutes later, Amy told Susan that Teresa Wisner was on line one.

"Hi Teresa, I see you called before. Sorry I haven't had a chance to get back to you."

"I did call, yes, I did. I wanted to visit with you a few minutes about the Hepner case we're set to try next week. Do you have a minute?"

"Certainly. Do we have a problem or do you just want to generally discuss it?"

"Is there any way we can resolve this? By that, I mean plead the guy to a lesser charge and conclude this once and for all?"

"I assume you want me to reduce it to a simple misdemeanor? Is that what you're thinking?"

"Yes."

Susan hesitated. "Do I detect desperation in the tone of your voice? Are you having some issues with the case?"

"Have you had any contact with his wife—with the defendant's wife?"

Susan laughed. "As a matter of fact, I have. She called here and I hesitated to talk with her, but I did finally visit with her for a moment. Nothing to do with the facts, but only as to letting him plead to some lessor charge and letting him go. I told her in no uncertain terms that I wasn't going to do that. But, my conversation with her was *not* pleasant, I can tell you that."

"Oh God, Susan, she's awful. I get calls from her every hour of every day. She's continually on me about getting the charge reduced or they're going to get a different lawyer. I just keep telling her to go ahead and find one, but she won't—she just keeps calling me and wanting the same thing. I assume there's nothing else at this point you can do, is that correct? I mean, anything would work for me as long as he isn't incarcerated."

"I'm sorry, Teresa, but there just isn't. He does have a record, although nothing very serious. I can't reduce this charge to a lesser offense and I told his wife that. I'm really sorry you have to deal with her, but there is a light at the end of the tunnel—you only have a couple of weeks to continue putting up with her."

Susan could hear her sigh. "Okay, I understand. But, if you change your mind, call me right away. I've had about all of her and this case I can take."

She had no sooner hung up, than Amy walked in and said, "Corey is on line one. You want to take it or not?"

"Yeah, I'll talk to him. I have no idea what he wants, but I have no doubt whatever he wants isn't good."

"Hi, Corey. What do you need?"

"Morning. Need? Oh, I don't know. I just thought I'd call and see what you thought of the trial. Any second thoughts?"

She leaned back, and said, "Not really. It went as I expected it to. Evidence came in about like I anticipated. The outcome was as I thought it would be. So no, I have no second thoughts about it at all. In fact, I haven't thought about it at all since the verdict."

"You did a good job."

"Thanks. How's your relationship with that family now that the trial has concluded and he's been found guilty?"

"How do you think? But, you know, all is not lost. We're going to appeal. Maybe the whole outcome will be overturned."

"You know, you really have nothing to appeal. It's a waste of your time… and their money."

"Oh, come on Susan, the money's not why I'm appealing. You'll see. I've got a thing or two up my sleeve. You'll see before long. But that's not why I called."

"Okay, I'll bite. Why *did* you call, Corey?"

"How's the campaign going? Is it still looking good for you? I've heard some good comments."

"I have no idea how it's all going. Yes, I *think* from what I've heard, at least the primary looks pretty good. Why?"

"I just want you to know I'm doing all I can for you."

She sat up, cleared her throat, and said, "Why's that?"

"Because I want you to *win,* that's why."

"Oh, okay, well thanks. I appreciate that. Now, I've got a thousand things to do, and if that's it…"

"You know, we talked the other day about maybe a position in the office if you do win. You remember we discussed that, right?"

"No, *you* discussed it. I *listened.*"

"So, are you still thinking there might be a spot in the office for me if you do win? I want to know so if there might be, I can start campaigning like hell for you"

"Okay, let's settle this issue right now. No, there will not be a spot in this office for you, unless someone wins other than me. I would not even think about working with you in this office. If you were the last lawyer in Nashville and I needed someone to work here, I would rather find a way to do it all by myself than hire you."

He laughed. "You're kidding right?"

"Serious as hell, Corey. Now, are we done here?"

He hesitated.

"We done here?"

"I thought we had a better relationship than that. I really did."

"We have *no* relationship, Corey. From the day you hit me, that all ended. I know you. I know all about you. I'll never work in the same office with you, and to be honest, I don't give a shit if I ever see you again, let alone work with you."

He cleared his throat. "Sorry to hear that. And one of these days you'll be just as sorry you ever said it."

"You threating me!"

"See you around...*bitch.*"

He terminated the call.

Amy walked in shortly thereafter, and said, "I heard some of the end of that conversation. Everything okay?"

"Don't put him through again. Don't let him make an appointment with me. Let me know if he calls, but don't put him through...ever."

Later that night, as they finished supper, Susan said, "I got a call from Corey today."

"Your buddy, Corey Abbott?"

"Yes."

"What'd he want?" He smiled as he said, "Did he still want a job if you win?"

"Yes. He was an asshole. If I didn't know he was such a fucking coward, I might have been a little concerned about the rhetoric."

"What do you mean 'concerned.'"

"He got a little nasty. I told him never to contact me again."

"Is it something we need to report? How 'concerned' about him are you?"

"Let's just say my contact with him, other than if we meet in the courtroom, ended today once and for all."

"Okay, what the hell did he say to you?"

"Just forget it, Tom. I handled it. Believe me, if I thought he was a threat, I'd tell you. I learned long ago his bark was worse than his bite. He's a big talker. I took care of my relationship with him in every respect today."

She stood. "Now, I'm done discussing the negative. Let's leave the dishes, go in the other room, get comfortable, and discuss the positive. Let's figure out where we're going with this election from here on so I can say I'm proud to have been elected the first woman district attorney general in Davidson County. Believe me, discussing *that* subject, is one hell of a lot more important than discussing that stupid conversation I had with Corey."

Chapter 26

Susan had been in the office for a couple of hours this morning, when Amy informed her Officer George Black was waiting to visit with her. The early hours of this morning had quickly slipped away. She told Amy to send him in.

She stood as he walked in and said, "Morning, George. I just wanted to briefly touch base with you concerning the trial tomorrow. Are you ready to go? Do we need to review everything again?"

As he sat, he said, "No, I'm ready. We went over everything in detail the last time I was here. I thought maybe you might be able to resolve this case with the other attorney. She's a rookie and I just figured maybe she would want to settle it rather than try it."

Susan smiled and said, "Well, I'm not sure I would classify her as a rookie but I, like you, figured she would try harder than she has to resolve it. She's very inexperienced that's for sure. I know she's worried about trying it, but so far, we haven't been able to come to a meeting of the minds."

"What's the problem? Why is it so hard to resolve the case when what he did is so clear cut?"

"The problem, as I understand it, isn't him, it's her—his wife. She doesn't have any other source of income, and she wants him to continue working. His attorney wants to plead it down to a misdemeanor which I won't agree to do. So, we have a problem that is unresolvable, and I'm afraid that's the way it will remain. Do you have any other thoughts about that particular aspect of the case? Would you rather I settle it regardless of how much I'll need to compromise?"

"No, no, I don't want him to plead to something so insignificant that he'll just be back out there doing the same thing the following night. Certainly, I don't want that."

"Do you need to go through the facts or issues again while you're here today?"

"No. I'm ready to go."

Susan stood. "Good. I'll meet you at the courthouse around one. It'll take us all morning to select a jury and maybe longer. You don't need to be there for that. Once the jury is selected, both attorneys will have opening statements which won't take long. You'll be the first one I call to testify, so I'll contact you if it looks like you'll need to be there before one."

He stood. "That will work. I'll see you tomorrow afternoon."

As he walked out, Amy walked in. "Sally is on line one. You want to take it or call her back?"

She picked up the phone, and said, "Morning, Sally. We haven't talked in a while…what's it been, two hours now? How's everything going?"

"Fine. I made a couple of calls, and we're all set for tonight. I'll meet you there before the meeting starts, maybe about six. Is Tom coming?"

"No. He's working on a case. He's to meet with witnesses tonight all evening, so he won't be there."

"You still have next Thursday down for that meeting with all those police officers, don't you? They are really, really important supporters of yours and this meeting is really, really…"

"I know. It's important. All these speaking engagements are important, and I guarantee you I'll be at all of them you tell me about. Now calm down. You're worse than I am and you've been through this same process a hundred times. Relax. I'm all ready for tonight, and I'll meet you before the meeting, just inside the door, at about six, okay?"

"Yup, that'll work for me. Sorry. I do get a little wound up now and then."

"Not a problem. See you tonight."

A few minutes later, and as Susan was just finishing up preparing for her speaking engagement, Amy walked in her office and said, "There's a Dorothy Longmire down in the lobby wanting to see you. I'm not familiar with the name. Should I tell her to come on up?"

"Dorothy? What the hell is she doing here?"

"Who is she?"

Susan leaned back in her chair, put her pen down, and said, "She's an old classmate of mine that I hadn't seen in…"

"Oh, oh, that's right. You met up with her a while back for the first time in a long time."

"Did she say what she wanted?"

"No. Nothing other than she really needed to talk."

"Shit. I don't have time to…" She looked away as she remembered vividly the hell Dorothy had explained was her life. "Tell her to come on up."

"You sure?"

As she picked up her pin to conclude her notes for tomorrow, she said, "Yes, yes, just tell her to come on up."

A few minutes later, Dorothy walked through her office door. Once again, Susan couldn't help notice how old her clothes appeared to be. She also concluded they were most likely the best she had.

Susan walked around her desk, as she said, "Dorothy what a nice surprise. Come on in and have a chair."

Susan embraced her, and as Dorothy sat, she looked around and said, "Wow, what a beautiful office. This is way nicer than our home…and to be honest, probably about as big."

She continued to look around, as Susan said, "How have you been? How's everything going? The last time we talked, life was a little tough for you. Have things improved or is everything still about the same?"

"Oh, 'bout the same, I guess. Gosh, your office is really nice. I bet if you win that election, you'll have an even bigger one, am I right?"

Susan smiled and said, "I'm not really sure what office I'll have if I win. Did your husband ever find a better job? What's his employment status now?"

"He's working, which is good. But he leaves 'round noon, and doesn't get home until about eight. He's home this morning, which is why I was able to come see you today."

"How's the kids?"

"They're fine. Growing for sure. Doing good in school too. That's at least one positive in my life. How's the election looking?"

"You know, I have no idea. I think okay, but I'll never know until the last ballot is counted."

"Is there some way I can help you? Do you need someone to do odd jobs or little things for the election that you don't have time to do? I would love to help if you need me."

"No, no I'm fine. I have a campaign manager that takes care of most of those things. I just don't have time."

As Dorothy turned to look at the wall behind her, the lack of conversation between the two of them became somewhat uncomfortable, at least for Susan.

Finally, Susan said, "Dorothy, I've really got to get back to work. I have a trial tomorrow that I'm trying to get ready for. I'm sorry but this isn't the best time for us to catch up. Can we just plan on getting together another time and talk? Would that work for you?"

"Sure, oh sure. That's not a problem for me. But before I go, can I ask you a question?"

"Certainly. Anything."

"This is hard." She once again, looked around Susan's office for a moment, then looked at her and said, "Could you loan me some money? We are completely broke. I'm not sure we even got enough to pay for food the rest of this week."

Susan was stunned. She sat quietly, trying to figure out how to answer. Finally, she said, "Well, I…guess I could loan you some money. How much do you need?"

"Maybe a couple hundred. Is that alright? Is it too much? I'm sorry but I didn't know where else to turn."

Susan reached in her desk drawer and pulled out her check book. She wrote the check and handed it to Dorothy, as she said, "You know this is a short-term solution to a long-term problem, don't you?"

"I don't understand."

"I mean, that's all you're getting from me. You need to find a permanent solution to the problem—a solution that will last a while. Going around to your friends and asking for money, in the long-term, isn't going to work. Now, let me work with you, help you find a job or some other way to at least help the overall problem. I'll be glad to do that."

Dorothy stood, and said, "Thanks, but we'll figure it out. I don't really need any outside help."

"Apparently, you do. That check in your hand is from 'outside help.' Now, let me work with you and we'll figure this out together."

Dorothy looked around again. "You really got it good, that's for sure. You got everything you ever wanted, don't you? You got no idea what it's like to be in this situation. How could you possibly help me come up with a solution to a problem you've never experienced in your lifetime. You have no idea what it's like to come and ask you for money—to come crawling to you and asking for help." She stood quietly for a moment, then said. "I won't be back. Thanks for what you did for us, but I've had enough of you and your attitude."

Susan stood. "Attitude? Where did *that* come from? What the hell are you talking about? I helped you—I gave you what you wanted and offered to help you solve the problem. I don't understand."

"I assume, by your tone of voice, if I don't work with you on figuring this all out, you're not going to loan me any more money, is that right?"

Susan thought for a minute and said, "Just consider that a gift, rather than a loan. And you're correct. There's no more where that came from. Unless you can figure out something long-term, either with or without my help, that will benefit your family and you, don't come to me asking for any more money."

"You're just as big a piece of shit as the rest of my classmates are. Thanks for the help and you can go to hell. You won't be seeing me again, rest assured of that."

Susan watched as she walked out her office door. She slammed the outer door as she left.

Amy walked in shortly thereafter. "Wow, was she upset or mad about something? She made quite an exit."

Susan sat, and said, "She's not welcome here anymore. Let me know if you hear from her. If she just walks in and wants to see me, tell her I'm busy or gone—I don't care which. You understand what I'm saying."

"Without doubt."

Chapter 27

Susan sat quietly, as she continued to review all her notes and her questions concerning the trial that was scheduled to begin in about two hours. .

She put her pen down and leaned back in her chair. Thoughts concerning Dorothy Longmire had consumed her since Dorothy had left her office yesterday. She felt sorry for her—she felt guilty for doing as well as she had financially, while Dorothy was struggling. Susan was well aware she could do nothing for Dorothy in the long term. She was equally concerned that providing her with money yesterday might well have been the worst thing she could have done.

Dorothy needed to figure out a long-term solution, and quit using other people as a band-aid for her problem. Maybe she should call her and explain that she really needed to see a financial adviser. If she would go, Susan would pay the bill. She had a feeling however, that Dorothy would never expend any energy to solve the problem in that manner. She would, more than likely, prefer to accept donations from people and just tread water day-by-day. Maybe when she had a little more time, she would make an effort to discuss her thoughts with Dorothy and see how she responded.

Today, however, was not the day for figuring out Dorothy and what she did and didn't need. Today was the day for putting Mr. Hepner behind bars.

They had picked a jury and quickly concluded both parties opening comments. Because of Teresa Wisner's lack of experience, almost all jurors whose names were initially called, were allowed to serve. There were a number of potential jurors that Susan would have stricken because they clearly did not appear to favor the defendant. But Teresa was a rookie, and she made more than one mistake while selecting the jury. Susan figured it wouldn't hurt to discuss those mistakes with Teresa once the trial was over—just one attorney with a lot of experience, helping out another with no experience.

Someone with plenty of experience had helped her when she first began: she would pass along the favor.

During the noon break, she quickly consumed a sandwich from the small sandwich shop next door, then hurried back to the conference room where she was to meet George Black and briefly touch upon his testimony. They had been through it a couple of times prior to today, but they would quickly discuss any questions he might have concerning the procedure or his testimony, before she called him as her first witness of any substance.

Soon after they started the discussion, there was a knock on the door indicating it was time for them to be seated and start the day's proceedings.

The first couple of witnesses testified as to their ownership position with Carver Electronics, the store that was robbed. The witnesses explained the specifics of the operation of the business on a day-by-day basis, including opening hours, continuous video filming within the business and the overnight holding of cash within the store. None of the testimony was contested by the attorney for the defendant and it all took very little time to complete.

Officer Black was the next witness. After his basic background information was introduced into the record, Susan asked, "So how did you first become aware of the break-in at Carver Electronics"

"The station was called by a Tom Cavanaugh who told us he had just left a bar situated near Carver Electronics. He said it was obvious the business was closed, but he saw someone come out the door of the business, then take off running."

"What happened then?"

"I was patrolling nearby. I drove to Cavanaugh's location to visit with him."

"Based on that conversation, what did you do?"

"I checked the building and determined a window in the back had been broken out. I then called the owner who came down and confirmed the building had been broken into. Cash had been taken from a box he had sealed in the front portion of the business, but which had been broken into."

"Based on that, what did you do?"

"The witness got a pretty good look at the individual leaving the store. I had him come in and look through some mug shots of men that had been in trouble for this type of problem before. He picked out the defendant's picture immediately. I picked up the defendant and ran him through a lineup. The witness picked him out and told us he was, without doubt, the one he saw."

Susan heard someone whispering. It was loud enough to be heard throughout the front of the courtroom. She looked to her right, and the defendant's wife was clearly out of control. She was whispering, but loud enough for all to hear, as she also waved her arms to accentuate the point she was making.

The judge looked at the defendant's wife, and said, "Ma'am, please remain quiet, and stop all that arm waiving. We all need to concentrate on what the witness is saying, not on what *you* are saying *or* doing. Get yourself under control or I'll have you removed."

He turned toward Susan, and said, "Please continue."

"Officer, what did you do next?"

"I confronted the defendant with what I knew."

"What did he say to you, if anything?"

"Nothing. He never admitted nor denied. I just arrested him and took him to jail."

"Did you discover anything else that might have confirmed your arrest of Mr. Hepner?"

"I did. He had a roll of money in his pants pocket. I took it and asked him where he got all the money. He never did answer."

"Nothing further, Your Honor."

"Cross, Ms. Wisner?"

"Well, yes, did…did, the defendant ever admit he broke in?"

"No."

"Was there a camara in the business that might have identified the individual that broke in?"

"There was. But the picture, since it was so dark, wasn't very good. Certainly not good enough to identify the intruder."

"Did you talk to the defendant's wife about his whereabouts that night?"

"Yes. She said he was home all night."

"You apparently elected not to believe her?"

"Yes. There was just too much other evidence against him. I didn't believe what she told me."

Susan could hear continued whispering between the defendant's wife and Teresa. Mrs. Hepner was the one clearly steering this boat.

"Nothing further, Your Honor."

"Anything further, on behalf of the State?"

"Nothing, Your Honor."

"Sir, you may step down. Call your next witness, Ms. Jackson."

"The state would call Tom Cavanagh."

Once all the foundational questions concerning his competency to testify were asked and answered, Susan got right to the point.

"Mr. Cavanagh, do you remember the night Carver Electronics was robbed?"

"Yes."

The witness was clearly nervous. He continued to wring his hands, and his voice quivered when he spoke.

"Why do you remember it so well?"

"Just because I saw it happen."

"Tell us what you saw."

"Well, I had just left a bar which was located a couple of businesses away from Carver's business. I was waiting in the passenger's seat of my car, which was parked in the Carver's parking lot because the bar's lot was full. I was waiting for my girlfriend who had told me she would drive home. All of sudden, this guy came running out of Carver's front door. I thought that was strange because at that time of night the business was closed."

"Go on. What happened then?"

"Well, the guy never locked the door behind him, and he started running across the parking lot."

"Did he have anything covering his face?"

"No."

"Please continue."

"He ran right by me…right by my car. I watched him as he ran across the street and got in another car and took off."

"Is the individual that ran by you that night, here in the courtroom?"

"Yes." He pointed at the defendant. "That's him—the guy by the two women at the table."

"Let the record reflect he is identifying the defendant as the individual that left Carver Electronics and ran past his car the night the business was broken into. Your Honor, I have nothing more."

"Cross, Ms. Wisner?"

"Yes, Your Honor."

Susan could hear the whispers of Janet Hepner as she tried to guide the direction Teresa's cross-examination was to take.

"Okay, now sir, how much had you had to drink?"

"Oh, I don't know, a couple of beers I guess."

"When did you arrive at the bar that evening?"

"Actually, not until about nine. We were there a couple of hours overall."

"You only had a couple of beers during all that time. Who are you kidding?"

"Councilor, is that your question? Is your question really, 'Who are you kidding?'"

"No, no I'm sorry, Your Honor. Are you saying in two hours you only had two beers? Do you expect anyone to believe that?"

"Anyone can believe what they wish. But I had to get up and go to work at seven. It was already late, and I knew if I had much more to drink, I would have a hell of…excuse me…a heck of a time getting up and going to work. I've had this job a long time, and one of the reasons I still have it, is because I do not go to work with a hangover, or still feeling the buzz of the night before. I left at around eleven and I had two beers…period."

She thought for a moment, then said, "Okay, okay, now, it was dark right?"

"Yeah, normally it is that time of night."

"Might you have been mistaken concerning your identity of the man that ran by you?"

"No."

"That's it. Just 'no.'"

"Yes."

Clearly Teresa was in over her head. Susan couldn't help her, and this experience would assist her in the future, but for today, she was in over her head. She could hear the loud whispers as her client's wife continued to try to dictate the flow of her questioning.

But in spite of those whispers, Teresa simply said, "Nothing further, Your Honor."

"Any other witnesses for the state, Ms. Jackson?"

"None, Your Honor. The state rests."

"Okay, let's break for the day, and tomorrow morning, we'll start off with the defendant's case. The jury is hereby dismissed for the day, but be here by nine in the morning and seated. Why don't the attorneys meet me in chambers and we'll finish up reviewing the courts instructions to the jury. Now, you jurors need to remember the admonition I gave you about not discussing this case with others. We are in recess for the day until tomorrow morning at nine."

Chapter 28

"Was *anything* he testified to the truth? I mean, really, if you hadn't double checked it at the time, I would question whether he even gave us his real name."

Susan and Officer Black were reviewing the defendant's testimony, after he had just finished testifying in his own behalf. They had opened court at nine, and it was now noon. The court then recessed for the noon break before Susan had a chance to cross-examine him.

"You know," Susan said, "I'm not sure there's much to cross-examine him on. I mean, he basically said you were wrong, he was home all night, and he didn't do it. All I can really do is ask him about the incident and how our witness could be so mistaken…maybe ask him about the money in his pocket, which wasn't brought up on direct, and go from there."

She thought for a moment, then continued. "We already know what his wife's going to say. It's just all going to come down to which side of the case is more believable—which side has the most to lose by lying. Of course, that's pretty obvious. I don't think we have anything to worry about as concerns a verdict and I really don't want to screw that up by badgering him and going over and over the same thing time after time. So, I'm going easy on this guy and we're going to hope that was the right thing to do."

"No argument from me. I have no problem with that at all."

Court reconvened after the noon-break and the defendant, once again, took the stand. After Teresa had asked him a few additional meaningless already asked and answered questions, the court looked at Susan and said, "Cross-examine, councilor?"

"Yes, Your Honor, just a few questions."

Susan stood, and approached the witness. "As I understand your defense Mr. Hepner, you say you were home all evening and it was a case of mistaken identity is that correct?"

"Yes, Ma'am."

She stopped walking, as she said, "You really think it was too dark to identify you when you ran right by the witness and you had no mask on nor a cover over your face of any kind?"

"Wasn't me."

"You were home all evening?"

"Yes."

"Where'd all that money come from? You know, all that money that you had in your pocket, and which was dollar for dollar, the exact amount missing from the store. Where'd that all come from?"

"Like I told my attorney, I was holding it for a friend."

"Why?"

"Why what?"

"Why were you holding it for a friend?"

"Because he asked me too."

"What was his name?"

He hesitated. "I don't really think I should tell you. He gave it to me to hold, like, confidentially, and I'm doing that, so I don't think I better tell everyone here who it was."

"That's because he doesn't exist, isn't it? It's not because you're breaking a confidence, but because he doesn't exist."

"Not true."

"Where'd you get the money, Mr. Hepner?"

"I told you."

"Over a thousand dollars there, Mr. Hepner, where'd it come from?"

Teresa stood and said, "Your Honor, she's kind of badgering my client. She asked the question, he answered it. Isn't that supposed to be enough?"

"I'll move on, Your Honor."

"Where's the man whose money it was? Why isn't he here to testify on your behalf?"

He hesitated, looked down for a moment, then at her as he said, "Now, I can't find him."

"My, how convenient. When did he give you this money?"

"Two days before the break-in."

"Why?"

"I didn't ask him. He just told me to hold onto it. I said 'okay.'"

"He gave you over a grand and you asked no questions?"

"Nope."

"You worked for Carvers. You knew right where the money was kept didn't you?"

"Well, I...I didn't do this. I'm holding the money for someone else."

"You worked for him, didn't you? The question just calls for a yes or no."

"Yes, but I didn't..."

"Let's just let the jury decide that issue. So, to sum up your story, your wife will say you were home all night, the store was broken into and money was taken which was hidden in a place no one but someone that was working there would know about. You can give us no other details about all that cash that was found on you other than a friend asked you to hold it. Oh, and the eyewitness who said it was without doubt you, and said he saw you running through the parking lot, was all wrong about what he saw. Is that correct?"

The witness smiled. "Absolutely. That's just what happened."

"That's all a bunch of crap and you know it. I have..."

Teresa stood and said, "I object, Your Honor. I...

"I'll withdraw the word 'crap,' Your Honor. Sorry, if it bothered the court and opposing council." She looked at the witness for a moment, then said, "I have nothing further."

"Ms. Wisner, do you have any other witnesses?"

"Yes, Your Honor. I would like to call the defendant's wife."

"Please proceed. Call your next witness."

Teresa called Janet Hepner to the stand, and over the next hour, she said, "He was home all night," in as many different ways as the English language permitted.

Susan had not deposed the defendant's wife, already knowing exactly what she was going to say. When she testified, she let her repeat her testimony as many times as Teresa took her down that road. She simply did not want the jurors to think she was badgering the woman.

Once Teresa indicated she was finished with direct examination, the judge nodded toward Susan and said, "Cross-examination, Ms. Jackson?"

Susan stood and said, "Just a few questions, Your Honor."

"Is your husband's income the only source of income your household has, ma'am?"

"Yes. You already know that. I told you that myself."

"Ma'am, just answer the questions I ask you please. Where did he get all that money he had in his pocket that night?"

"He told you. He was holding it for a friend."

"How long had he been holding it?"

"Oh…" She hesitated. "Oh, I think a few days."

"That was quite a bit of cash for your household, wasn't it?"

"Yes."

"You knew he was holding it?"

"Yes."

"Why was he carrying it around in his pocket? I mean," she moved toward the witness chair, "here he was, with over a thousand dollars in his hands which belonged to a friend, and he was carrying it around in his pocket? Does that make sense to you?"

"Well, maybe I was mistaken, maybe he…maybe he only just got it that day."

"What other income do you have coming into your home?

"None, other than what he gets from his job."

"So, if he goes to jail for this, you have no other source of income do you, ma'am?"

She looked down, as she whispered, "No, we don't."

Susan considered asking a few additional questions concerning the evening in question, but she just figured she had made the points she needed to make, and she didn't want to create any additional sympathy for either the defendant or his spouse.

"Nothing further, Your Honor."

Teresa called no further witnesses. The court dismissed the jury for the afternoon. He told them to be seated by nine tomorrow morning. At that time, they would hear any rebuttal testimony from the state, instructions from the court, and closing statements from the attorneys. The case would then be submitted to them for a verdict.

As she put her files in her briefcase, she happened to look up, and the defendant's wife was staring at her. Once she saw Susan looking her direction, she quickly looked away. But seconds later, she could feel her icy stare while continuing to pack her briefcase.

As everyone left the courtroom, Officer Black came forward, and said, "Well, what did you think of her testimony?"

"She's a desperate woman, that's for sure. I'm glad I don't have to be with her in the same room this evening. She doesn't like me, that's just pretty clear. Other than that, I felt it went well. We got everything into evidence we wanted and I felt their case was full of credibility issues."

She smiled and said, "You did good today. You don't have to be here tomorrow. I'm not calling any rebuttal witnesses. We got in what we wanted to get in without any problem. Now, it just comes down to instructions, closings statements and waiting for a verdict."

He glanced in the direction of the council table, then said, "It looks to me like you're still getting some pretty intimidating stares from the defendant's wife. I was just watching her. Does that bother you?"

"No, no, not at all. She's upset and I understand that, but she doesn't bother me in the least."

"Okay, just let me know if she becomes a problem. Tomorrow is my day off. I won't be here, but would you call me if we get a verdict?"

"Certainly. You'll be the first one I call once it's all over."

Chapter 29

Susan finished reviewing all her phone messages just as Amy walked in the front office door to start her day. Once Amy checked her desk for notes from Susan, she walked into her office, and said, "Morning. So, how did you get along yesterday? Everything proceed as you thought it would?"

"It did, yes. All of our evidence has been introduced. Nothing, either as concerns our exhibits, or as concerned our testimony was excluded."

"What about their case? How did Teresa get along? I know she's a rookie. Did she do well?"

"She made a few rooky mistakes, but all in all, she did fine. She just didn't have an awful lot to work with."

"I see we got a call late last night. I think it's Hepner's wife's number. I haven't had a chance to check it though."

"She's upset, as well she should be. Her husband is in some serious trouble, and he's the only one bringing home a paycheck. If she calls, tell her I'm busy, and do it each time she calls until she finally quits. I don't want to talk to her. She gave me the evil eye all through the proceedings. I think she's just frustrated, but I also think she's harmless. On second thought, just don't answer the phone if you see her number come up."

"You're not worried about her, right?"

"You mean worried that she might harm me?"

"Yes."

"Nope. She can't do anything stupid now—her husband already has. If she did something that puts *her* in legal jeopardy, those kids would have *no* one to care for them at all if she got caught. I don't think… I'm not sure, but I don't think she's *that* stupid."

A few minutes later Susan left for the courthouse. Once she arrived, after visiting with the judge and Teresa concerning the schedule for the morning, she walked in the courtroom and took her seat.

Once the judge took his place, he asked Susan if she had any rebuttal testimony, to which she answered in the negative.

The judge then read the instructions of the court to the jury. The instructions defined all the legal issues in detail, explaining what the jury was allowed to do, and what they couldn't do. In addition, he explained what evidence they could consider and what facts they were prohibited from considering while arriving at a verdict.

Once, he was finished, each attorney gave a closing statement. Susan gave hers and once finished, Teresa presented her closing comments.

Once Teresa completed what she had to say, Susan was given a chance to respond. She took the opportunity to touch just briefly upon a few issues, then, not wanting to appear overbearing and repetitive, closed her comments and took her seat.

Once she sat down, the judge turned everything over to the jury and they were taken to the jury room to deliberate the fate of Sam Hepner.

As Susan watched the jury leave the courtroom, she noticed Tom Cavanagh sitting in the back corner of the room.

As she watched, George Black walked in and sat down near him.

Susan stood and walked to the back of the courtroom.

She smiled as she said, "Don't you two have any more to do than sit in the back of a courtroom waiting for a jury verdict that could take at least all day?"

George smiled and said, "I have the day off. I really don't think this will take long. I've been wrong on how long a jury might be out quite a few times, but I'm not thinking this will take long."

"You know, Susan, the wife of the defendant keeps looking over here. I'm not sure who she's looking at, whether it's one of us, or all of us. But if she's got one of us singled out, I feel a little sorry for whichever it is that she's glaring at, because she's got a real bad look about her."

"It's me. Don't worry about her. She has a few issues with me. She tried to call the office after we adjourned yesterday. She thinks I am the one that's caused her family problems. I'm not worried about her. She has way too much to lose if she really does get crossways with me."

As they continued to discuss different aspects of the trial, the bailiff walked in the courtroom, said something to Teresa, then walked to where all three were sitting. As he approached, he said, "Susan, the jury has a verdict. The judge wants everyone to take their seats. The court attendant will bring them in shortly."

Susan turned toward George and said, "That's probably a pretty good sign." She smiled as she said, "If they have already come to a verdict, we may have just set a new record—quickest verdict ever."

Once the jurors had taken their seats, the judge said, "Ladies and gentlemen, who did you appoint as your foreperson?"

A younger gentleman in the front row stood and said, "I'm the one they appointed, Your Honor."

"Has the jury arrived at a unanimous result?"

"We have."

"Hand it to the court attendant."

"He handed it to the court attendant who handed it to the judge. He reviewed it, then handed it back to the court attendant, looked at the foreperson, and said, "The court attendant will now hand you the verdict. Go ahead and read it out loud."

"We, the jury in the above-entitled matter, do hereby find the defendant, Sam Hepner, guilty as charged."

"Is that the verdict of all twelve?"

"It is, Your Honor."

"Alright. You jurors are now dismissed and may leave, but please stop by the clerk's office before you leave the courthouse to determine when you need to appear again during your term, if at all."

The jurors filed out of the jury box, and once they had left the courtroom, the judge said, "Mr. Hepner, you have now been found guilty of burglary, which is a class D felony. I am going to order a presentence investigation and report. I'll set sentencing once I have the completed report in my hands. You posted bond, didn't you?"

"Yes, Your Honor, I did."

"Bond will continue in the same amount until sentencing. This hearing is adjourned."

Susan stood, and started to put her paperwork in her briefcase. As she was finishing, she noticed Teresa walking in her direction.

Once she reached Susan, she extended her hand, smiled and said, "Congratulations. Well done.

As Susan shook her hand, she quietly said, "Teresa, you didn't have much to work with. You did a great job with the hand you were dealt. You're going to do well in the courtroom."

"Let's just say I learned from a pro. Until next time."

Teresa walked back to her table. As Susan pushed the remaining papers into her briefcase, and prepared to walk away, she heard someone approaching her from the location of the opposing council table. As she turned to look, she saw Janet Hepner extending her hand as she approached.

"Well done, Ms. Jackson, well done."

Susan shook her hand and said, "I'm sorry, Janet. I know what you must be going through."

"You got your conviction—I'm sure it's just another feather in your cap."

Susan drew her hand away, and said, "That's not the way this works. All the evidence pointed to your husband as the one that committed the crime. In my opinion, the jury got it right. No one wins. I got the conviction, but I'm not happy your husband may go to jail for what he did—I was just doing what the public pays me to do. What a horrible impact this could have on you and your kids. For that I am truly sorry. I don't consider this a win for me at all. I was just doing my job."

"You can justify it any way you want—I could care less. See you soon."

"What do you mean by that?"

She smiled. "Oh, you know, here, in the courtroom, or who knows where else we might meet up—the grocery store, the movie theatre—just hard to tell."

"Is that a threat?"

"Absolutely not. Just a promise."

She turned and walked away, leaving Susan wondering whether she should tell George about her comment or forget it.

A few minutes later, she was back in her office, removing files from her briefcase.

Amy walked in and said, "That had to have been the shortest jury deliberation in the county's history. Teresa must not have presented evidence that created much doubt at all."

As Susan continued removing paperwork, she said, "She just didn't have much to work with. Funny thing. After it was over, the defendant's spouse, you know, Janet, made some comment about 'seeing me again.' That's worries me a little, but I never said anything about it to anyone. I'm sure she was just frustrated, but it does bother me."

"You don't think she would try to harm you in some way, do you?"

As Susan sat, she said, "You know, I don't think so. She's frustrated, worried about her family, and she blames me for their troubles. But I really think she'll calm down. Harming me isn't going to solve her problems, and I think she's smart enough to figure that out."

"Even so, I'll watch for her phone number. If I see her hanging around downstairs, I'll let you know."

"That's probably a good idea, at least for now. Who knows? He may just get probation and still be able to bring at least *some* money into the household. I'm sure she won't do anything to mess that up, so if we do have a problem, it most likely won't happen until after he's sentenced, if at all."

"Just in case though, I'll keep an eye out for her. Anything happens to you I may not have a job, so I too, have a vested interest in your welfare. I can guarantee you one thing—she'll never get by me if she does walk in our door, and that's a promise."

Chapter 30

Susan hadn't slept all night. As she sat alone drinking her third cup of coffee, she wondered what her two opponents were doing. Were they as apprehensive as she was? Was it more than just another day for them? Did it mean as much to them as it did to her?

Voting would begin in a matter of hours. Where had the time gone? It seemed like only yesterday she had decided to run.

Susan needed to get moving and get ready to go to work. As she stood, she figured there wouldn't be many projects started or completed in her office today. The election was all that mattered. She would finish tomorrow what she had planned on finishing today, but *this* day was *all about the election.*

"Morning. How long have you been up?"

"Morning. A long time."

"Well, okay, let me put that another way. Did you sleep at all last night?"

"Not one minute. And I mean that literally. Not one minute."

"Nervous?"

"I am, yes. I'm confident, but nervous."

He sat down beside her and smiled as he said, "Nervous you'll lose…or nervous you might win?"

"Let there be no doubt—I want to win in the worst way."

"Certainly, a win would fit nicely on your resume."

She frowned, and said, "You know the resume isn't the issue—don't you? I mean, you understand I don't give a shit about how it fits within the rest of my accomplishments during my life. You understand that, right?"

"Oh sure, sure, but…"

"I want this job more than I've ever wanted anything in my life…other than…you, of course. I think I can make a difference."

"You've never mentioned running for the office in quite that way. Are you going to make a lot of changes? You've never defined the 'changes' you want to make. Will I still have a job?"

She smiled and said, 'That's the plan today anyway."

She looked away and remained silent for a moment before she said, "You know, ever since Chuck decided he was going to retire a couple of years ago, the office has lost its way—we just don't seem to have a defined direction. Everything is handled on a case-by-case basis. I want to change that. I want to set some definite guidelines and go by them no matter what. You know…if *this* is the situation, then *this* is what we do."

She looked at Tom and said, "I want our office to make a difference, whether through prosecution or through public awareness as concerns what we *do* and what we *can do* for the public. I want to make a statement. I want to provide structure and leadership, both of which have been absent the last couple of years."

Tom continued to stare at her, taking it all on, and remaining quiet while she finished.

"I could give a shit about my resume. I want to make a difference…*period.*"

Tom jumped up, clapped his hands and said, "Well, you by god, sold me. I'd vote for you even if I wasn't sleeping with you. Now, let's eat breakfast and get to work."

As the noon hour came to an end, Amy walked in Susan's office and said, "So, what are you hearing? Has Sally called yet?"

"She called just to say there is a strong turnout. She's going from precinct to precinct and said there are a lot of people voting. That doesn't really help me come to a conclusion one way or the other, but that's what she's telling me."

Susan looked around for a second, and as she continued to move files around on her desk, she said, "Did you bring me the Davidson file? I thought I told you to bring it in. Where…"

"You did and I did. Look under your left arm on the desk. It's right…"

"Oh, oh yeah, there…Sorry. Right there all the time. Thanks. Do I have any more appointments today? Did I ask you that? I think I asked you that. Do I have any more…"?

"No. And yes you did, but again, no is the answer. Why don't you get out of here? Brian's already left. You have no more appointments, and you have no hearings during the next few days. Why don't you go to Sally's and let me handle the rest of the day."

"Yeah, maybe I'll just do that. Where are you going? Are you coming out to Sally's house? She's got that big place…well you know where it's at. Didn't she invite you to come out? She said she did."

"She did, and yes, we'll be there. Go on and go. Tom's left already…I assume he told you he was leaving. He's already out there. I'll handle the office."

"Yeah, that's what I'm…" She stood. "Yup, that's just where I'm going to…go…just right now. I'll see you tomorrow sometime. No, I'll see you tonight, right?"

Amy grabbed her arm, walked her to her office door, and said, "Go. I'll see you soon."

Susan mumbled something under her breath, then waved as she walked out the door.

She squinted as she walked into the kitchen. The sun was shining, it was apparently a beautiful day, but why was she in her house and not at the office. Most days it was still dark when she went to work.

Tom put the paper down, stood and walked to the counter where he fixed her a cup of coffee, then turned around and offered it to her, as he smiled and said, "Good Morning. Have a seat. What do you want for breakfast? Winners have their choice in my kitchen so just tell me what you want and it's yours."

She kept rubbing her head, as she said, "What time is it?"

"Ten."

"Holy shit, ten! I need to go to work? Why am I still here—why are *you* still here? I need to go."

She started to turn around as he grabbed her arm and pulled her close.

"No, you don't—not today. You told Amy not to expect you this morning. Now, sit and we'll talk about all you missed last night—after you had consumed your fifth drink."

She slowly lowered herself into a chair, as she said, "I don't have any bottoms on. I just noticed. Where did they go?"

"Well, you took everything off after we got home, when you said you wanted sex and you wanted it now—that was at about two this morning."

"You're kidding? I'm sorry I don't remember that at all."

"Rightfully so. You fell asleep when we started. Nothing happened. I just threw a blanket over you and you never woke up. Left me empty-handed so to speak, but at least you got a little sleep."

"Okay, I kind of remember I won. But can you fill in a few details? Is there anything else I should know before I go to work this morning? Would you get me some aspirin and a glass of water?"

When he returned, as she swallowed both pills, he said, "You didn't really drink all that much until after the final results were in. So, actually you weren't that way...drunk...until the party was basically over. A few people lingered, but when I saw how bad you were getting, I just walked you to the car and we came home."

"I can't remember the final results. Was it close? I just remember I won."

"No, it wasn't. You killed both the guys that were running. The margin was impressive to say the least. It looks like you could have a real shot at winning in the general election, regardless of your opponent."

"Do you know who that's going to be?"

"Oh yeah. He called to congratulate you, but it was after you had gone over the edge. I told him I would pass it on, and you would talk to him in the morning."

"Brian?"

"Yes."

"Did he win as easily as I did?"

"I don't know the actual numbers. I just know he won."

"So, we'll have our work cut out for us at the next election."

"We will, yes, but as easily as you won this one, I think you have a good shot at beating him. He's not very well-liked, at least in the office, and I assume the same demeanor that makes him not well-liked *in* our office, is the same demeanor he has *out* of the office."

He walked around the table, leaned down and kissed her. "But that's to worry about another day. We can worry about the next election tomorrow or the day after that. Today let's celebrate a great victory for you and figure out how we're going to defeat Brain tomorrow."

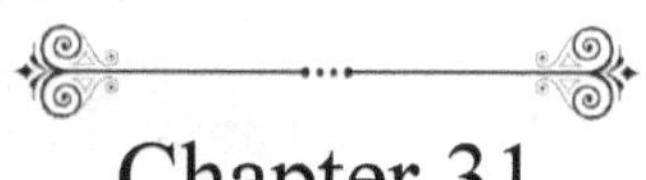

Chapter 31

It was mid-afternoon when Susan finally walked in her office door. As she did, Amy stood, and embraced her. "I'm so happy for you. You worked really hard to win, and your efforts paid off." As she returned to her desk, she said, "You really smashed those two you ran against. Now, next is Brian, right?"

Susan walked back to her desk with Amy close behind.

"Yes, he's next."

She took her sunglasses off and Amy said, "Whoa, I'm sorry, but you look awful. I'll try to keep people away from you today, so you don't scare them away."

"Oh, come on, I don't look that bad, do I?"

She pulled a small compact out of her purse and flipped it open. As she looked at herself in the mirror, she said, "Holly shit, this is worse than I thought. Yeah, you better just make appointments for me some time other than today."

"Good Idea. By the way, Chuck wants to see you."

An hour later, while Susan was still sorting through her desk for messages and files she needed, Chuck walked in.

He had a broad smile across his face. He extended his hand as he said, "Susan, Susan, I am so proud of you. You did it! You beat the hell out of both of them. Well done, well done."

After he shook her hand, he sat down as he said, "You didn't just win. You had a huge win. You could combine the votes of those two guys you beat and they still wouldn't have as many votes as you got. You apparently had a good plan, and whatever it was worked well. I can't tell you how proud I am of you."

Susan did the best she could to smile through her splitting headache, as she said, "Thanks, Chuck. It was certainly self-satisfying to have the results end up the way they did. It's nice to know you can still work your ass off and be rewarded for it."

"So, what's next? You got a plan in mind for this August?" He lowered his voice as he said, "It won't be so easy beating Brian, you know. He'll be a tough nut to crack. I hope you got a good crew working with you and a good plan to beat him, because he will be tough."

"Yeah, I suppose he will. To be honest, I haven't even thought of that election yet. I'm just going to appreciate what happened last night for a few days before I even consider the next step in this process."

"Sally's staying with you, isn't she? I mean, she's really good at what she does. I hope you've held on to her, because she knows what she's doing. Not that you don't of course, but she's a truly a pro."

"She's been a lifesaver for me. Having to work full-time *and* run for the job wasn't easy. That will also be the case this time around, so yes, I'm glad she's in my corner."

He stood. "I need to move on. Again, congratulations and all the best in the next election."

He shook her hand and walked out.

Amy walked in and said, "Brian wants to see you. He wanted me to call him when you were free. Shall I give him a call or are you ready to go home?"

"Yeah, I'm ready to go home, but call him and have him come down. Should be an interesting conversation. After he leaves though, I'm going home so don't schedule anything else for me today."

"Got it." She turned as the outer office door opened, and Brian walked in.

"He's here."

"Go ahead and send him in."

Brian walked in her office with a smile plastered across his face and his hand extended.

She had seen that smile before—a number of times. Never did it appear more disingenuous than it did at this moment.

"Susan, Susan congratulations. What a great win. You not only beat those two nothings, you slaughtered them. Nice job. But I knew with Sally on your side, you would have an easy time of it. She gets the job done with most of those whose campaigns she handles."

"Thanks, Brian. Same to you."

"It's interesting both candidates are from this office. I figure that might well be a first."

"Probably right." This was going to be a one-sided conversation. For one thing, she just didn't like him, and for another, she was too hungover to carry on any type of intellectual conversation this afternoon. She just needed to get through the conversation and go home.

"You starting your campaign right now—by that I mean yet this week?"

"Oh, I don't know. I need to talk to Sally and see what her thoughts are. I haven't had a chance to even visit with her about yesterday yet."

"I think you and I should talk before we get to far into this—maybe discuss what happens when the election's over and one of us gets beat—like where do we go from there."

"Yeah, you're probably right."

"You don't seem to enthused. Not that I intend to lose. I'm sure you don't either. But on the other hand, one of us isn't going to make it, and I'm just thinking we should talk about that *before* the election, rather than after."

"Yeah, sure, I agree. But not today. I really need to move along." She stood and extended her hand. "Let's continue our discussion about that another day. I'm ready to go home."

He smiled and stood. "You look…well, let's just say you look like it was a short night at your house."

"Yeah, let's just leave it at that. We'll talk another day concerning all of these…issues, when I'm a little more in the talking mood, okay?"

"Absolutely."

Later that evening, as she sat on the couch, half in and half out of sleep, Tom said, "Did you talk to Sally?"

"You mean, today?"

"Yes."

"No, not yet. She called the office, but I didn't return any calls. I'll talk to her tomorrow and we can talk about what's next then, but I couldn't go down that road with her today—not today."

A few minutes later, she said, "Did I tell you Brian was in and congratulated me?"

"No. What'd he have to say?"

"Just congratulated me. That's about it."

A few minutes later, she said, "Oh, he did mention something about what might happen to the loser of our race. I think he was wanting me to tell him if I won, he would continue to maintain his position and vice versa. I wasn't about to discuss that with him today."

"So, what *are* your thoughts about that? I assume he would keep you if he won, but what about you—what are your thoughts about keeping him around?"

"You know, I told you changes were needed in that office. He's part of what needs to change. He's a poor prosecutor, he makes bad decisions, and he's a poor representative of our office even when he isn't prosecuting. I'm thinking right now I wouldn't want him around. But then, today's been a long day. Maybe I'm just a little negative about everything."

"Sounds like to me you've already thought it through. If you tell him that, I suppose if you lose, he probably would feel the same about you."

"He'd be a fool if he terminated me, but I think you're right. I would have to find a job somewhere else. The difference between the two scenarios though, is that I am highly employable—I know that from other offices that have contacted me and tried to hire me away from the district attorney's office. He's not. Unfortunately for him, everyone knows him. But I'll wait and see what happens. If I beat him today, he would be out of there tomorrow. At least that's the way I feel at this moment." She stood. "I'm going to bed. I'll see you in the morning."

Chapter 32

The beauty of a late spring day consumed her. She sat in her office looking out the window and wondering if she would have the luxury of this moment if she went on to win the general election. She had been in her office since seven. But before Amy arrived, and the office moved to a new level of activity, she wanted to just stop and take a deep breath. While she was doing that, thoughts of whether or not this was really all worth it filled her head.

If she *did* get what she wanted, if she *did* win the election, was that really the way she wanted to spend the next few years—having complete authority over the whole office. The responsibility, the pressure, the time it would take to do it and do it right, would take double the energy and time her job was taking now.

Maybe if she…

"Morning. You got a lot going on today."

She never turned around as she said, "Yeah, I know. More than I want. Don't schedule anyone for late in the day. I'm taking off early."

"Something special or…"

"Nope, I'm just tired, mentally tired. I need a few hours extra this weekend to just do nothing. I think we're going out for supper tonight. Tomorrow afternoon we're heading to Percy Warner Park to walk the trails if this weather stays as beautiful as it is now."

"Sounds like a great way to spend at least part of the weekend."

The phone rang, and Amy walked out of Susan's office to her own desk to answer it. A moment later she walked back in and said, "Sally's on line two."

She picked up and said, "Morning, Sally. Everything alright?"

"Certainly. Couldn't be better. You already for Sunday night? I mean, that's a really big event for us. There are a lot of people signed up for this, and there's lots of old money involved. This could really take care of all your expenses for the whole campaign if it goes right. Are you ready for it? I mean, not that you're not normally ready for all speaking engagements, but this one…"

"Sally, I get it. Yes, I'm ready. How's everything else look? What about other speaking engagements? Are we getting a few lined up between now and election day? Are you happy with the way it's all coming together?"

"Absolutely. Yes, everything is moving along exactly as planned. From what I hear, you two are neck and neck. We need to just keep pushing and we'll get there. I expect you to win—you should expect the same thing."

"I agree. But you and I don't have quite the same outlook on life, or on this election. You are the eternal optimist and I'm a little laid back. Nothing wrong with either approach, but I'm never going to be quite as optimistic as you are—about anything."

"Gotta go. I'll see you Sunday. Tom's coming, right?"

"Yes, yes he'll be there."

Sally terminated the call without saying another word.

Midmorning, as Susan finished reviewing one file, and picked up another, Amy said, "Chuck's out here. He needs a moment. You want me to let him come in?"

"He runs this place—probably a good idea."

"Morning, morning, Susan. How are we doing today?"

"Fine, Chuck. Doing fine."

"Do you have a moment?"

"For you, certainly. Have a chair."

As he sat, he said, "How's the campaign coming?"

"Good. Really good. I have a rather important event Sunday evening. We're expecting a lot of people and hopefully a lot of donations. This is not a cheap process, as I'm sure you already know."

"Oh, I do, I certainly do. Are you running into any particular issue that's creating a problem? I mean, is the fact you're a woman, an issue, or your record of convictions, is it an issue? Any particular problem at all?"

"No, no, no problems of that nature at all. Why?"

"I just wondered." He sat back in his chair, and said, "You know, I been thinking about the two of you running for the job and whether I should make a recommendation concerning either of you. Initially, I wasn't going to. But I've changed my mind. I really believe the public has a right to know which of you I feel is the best for the job. I believe they should hear from someone that's worked with both of you for a substantial period of time and knows the two of you very well."

Susan's heart skipped a beat. Where the hell was he going with this? Surely, he wasn't going to support one and not the other. If he was, who the hell would it be? Did she really want to know? Maybe it would be better if he supported both.

"So, I've decided to back you in this race. I really feel you're best suited for the job, and I feel the public has the right to know that."

Susan cleared her throat, and took a couple of deep breaths before she said, "Thank you, Chuck. Thank you so much. I don't know what else to say. Thank you for putting your faith in me. If I do win, I will not let you down, I promise you that."

He smiled as he stood. "I know you won't. I need to go see Brian. He's not going to be happy. But I have to do what I think's right for the office. I've spent way too many years here working my ass off, and I want to see the office maintaining the level of competency I feel we have maintained while I've been in charge. Now, get out there and work *your* ass off so they elect you."

"Thank you, sir, I will."

As he walked out, Amy walked in. What was that all about?"

She smiled. "He's supporting me for the job. Shocked the hell out of me. Brian is going to be pissed off. Cliff's support in Nashville is a big deal. It most likely will really effect Brian's campaign."

"Congratulations, boss. That's great. I am so happy for you. I assume I'm going with you when you win. I mean, I get to be your secretary when you win, right? I don't want to be Brian's secretary. I mean…"

"Yes, yes, yes, if I win, you're going with me. Now get Sally on the phone for me. Close my door as you leave, and don't let anyone in or out until I tell you."

An hour later, Amy walked in, and said, "Brain was just here. He wanted to see you. I told him you were tied up. He wasn't happy but he said he was leaving for the day and would see you the first of next week."

"Hmm. Wonder what he wanted. I'm still going to need to work with him until this election's over. Monday when he calls, or stops by the office, either tell him to sit and wait if I'm busy or let him in if I'm not. Might as well get it over with."

Amy sat down. "There's something I need to tell you."

"What? What is it? I'm ready to get out of here for the day."

"That Dorothy whatshername called about an hour ago. She wanted to talk to you."

Susan leaned back in her chair. "What did you tell her?"

"I did what you told me to do. I told her you were busy. Then she wanted to set up an appointment."

"What'd you tell her then?"

"I told her you were booked up with appointments, hearings and trials for the next few weeks, just like you told me to."

"How'd she take that?"

"Not well."

"Did you tell her what I told you to tell her about seeing someone that might help her sort out her financial issues? Did you tell her I would help her find a financial advisor and a marriage counselor if she needed one? Did you tell her I would pay for it all?"

"When nothing else I said seemed to suit her, I did. Yup, that's exactly what I told her."

Neither said anything, until Susan said, "Well, go on. What did she say to all that?"

"Let me put it this way. The nicest thing she said after I told her all those things, was to tell you to go to hell."

"I figured that would be her response, but I wanted to at least give her the opportunity. I'm not giving her money every time she comes up to see me."

"She was crazy on the phone. She called you just about every name in the book and a few I've never even heard before. I'll have to look those up when I go home tonight. She was extremely distraught to the point where I now honestly feel there's something mentally off with her. She said you wouldn't have to worry about seeing her or hearing form her again. To be honest, I got a feeling you are really lucky in that respect. She is trouble."

Susan thought for a moment. "If you notice she calls again, just don't answer. If she comes in, tell her I'm out or busy. We are done. I tried to help her the only way I know how. That didn't work. She's on her own. I doubt she calls again, but if she does just let me know.

Chapter 33

As she waited for Amy to arrive, she thought perhaps if she were elected boss over this office, she just might not come in on Monday mornings. She would tell everyone else to be here early Monday morning, and she would be in around one that afternoon. Or, on second thought, maybe she would come in around ten. That would be better.

As she considered all the ramifications of that scenario, upon reconsideration, most likely the *truth* of the matter was that if she were elected, she would be here from about four in the morning, *every morning,* and work until about ten *every night*—definitely a possibility she and Tom would need to discuss. That would not set well with…

"Morning. How did that event work out last night?"

"Oh, hi, I didn't hear you walk in. There were a good number of people there and they stayed well into the evening. We didn't get home until around midnight. It was a short night."

"Any contributions to the campaign?"

"Yes, there were many. When is my first appointment? I have some issues I want to review before they get here. How much time do I have?"

"Well, your first appointment is with a co-worker. Brian is on the schedule for nine. You don't have anyone else until about eleven, and it's that cop that was the arresting office in the case involving that drunk that drove over that guy and killed him."

"Is he the man Bob Rivers represents?"

"Yes."

"I hate to say this, but Bob is a horrible attorney. I honestly don't know why anyone goes to him."

"Not very many do. I know his secretary and she says their business is way down."

"Let me know whenever Brian gets here. I'll get him out of the way as soon as he comes in."

A few minutes later, Amy let her know Brian just arrived. Susan told her to send him in.

As he walked through the door, the first thing she noticed was that his broad, disingenuous smile that was there the last time he paid a visit, was now gone.

She stood and said, "Morning, Brian. Have a seat."

Susan was somewhat hesitant. She had no idea how Chuck's decision might affect Brian's demeaner or his attitude toward her.

Brain sat as he said, "I understand you had a good night last night."

She smiled and said, "I did. Who told you that?"

"Oh, I have my sources. Doesn't matter anyway. I'm glad it went well for you. The election, as you might imagine, is what I want to discuss. I was really surprised when Chuck altered his position concerning his recommendation."

"You mean switching from neutral to actually recommending someone?"

"Yes. I really thought he would remain neutral—not really take a position, and just let the voters do their own homework. But apparently that's all changed."

"Apparently so. Without commenting on how I feel personally, I can understand why he decided to pick one or the other. I mean, his reasoning made sense to me, no matter which of us he felt was most appropriate for the job. I think the voters have a right to know which of us he prefers to win, whether that was you or me."

"I guess. Of course, that's a lot easier for you to say, since he's supporting you."

"Really Brian, I don't think so. I really think if it had been you, the reasoning behind him making a selection would remain valid. I wouldn't have liked him selecting you, but his reasoning to me was appropriate no matter whom he supported."

He looked away, as he said, "Yeah, I suppose."

He said nothing for a moment, appearing to Susan as if he were organizing his thoughts before he spoke.

He finally turned toward her and said, "Susan I'm not really here to discuss who he did and didn't support. That's something that's beyond our control. But I do want to talk about what happens *after* the election, no matter which of us wins."

Susan had been concerned this conversation was going to happen. She was hoping it would happen later not sooner.

"How so?"

"After the election, what are your thoughts about the loser remaining in the office? I mean, you win, I stay, I win, you stay—just giving each of us a bit of job security, no matter what happens."

She leaned back in her chair, considering whether to ease out of the conversation and tell him she would have to think about it, or just jump in with both feet. She quickly concluded she might as well get it over with.

"I'm not sure about that, Brian. If I win, I'll have to assess the performance of everyone in the office, including you, and make some tough decisions, as will you if you win."

"So, you're saying if I get beat, I should look for another place to work?"

"No, not at all. I'm just saying if I win, your job here is not guaranteed. I assume it will be the same situation if you win."

"No, it won't. Not at all. If I win, I will guarantee you a job right here, doing what you've always done. Now, can you do the same?"

"No." She waited for him to respond. He said nothing.

Finally, Susan said, "I can say you would have a *good chance* at working here, but…"

He stood. "You don't need to say anything else. You've made it pretty clear that I should plan on looking for a new job if I lose. I have no doubt if you thought I was an irreplaceable, integral part of the process here, you'd tell me—you wouldn't let me leave here for any reason."

She stood. "Like I said, I would want to …"

He raised his voice as he said, "What you said was I would need to find another place to work." He moved forward and leaned against her desk. "Guess the best thing to do is beat your ass so I don't have to worry about it." He walked toward the closed office door, opened it, smiled and said, "Glad we had this little talk. At least I 'm sure where I stand…and I know now, where *you* stand."

He walked out, slamming her office door as he left.

Amy opened the door and slowly walked in Susan's office as she said, "Whoa, what the hell was wrong with him?"

"He's having a bad day."

"I guess he is. He said nothing to me as he left, and he slammed the outer door as hard as he did yours."

"He'll get over it. I wasn't sure whether to go ahead and tell him today that if I won, he might not have a position here or just let it lie until the election was over."

"You apparently told him now."

"I did. What happened while he was in here? Anything I should know about?"

"Yes." She smiled as she handed her a small piece of paper. "Your friend Greg called. He wants to talk to you. He wanted to know if you had any free time today."

"What did you tell him?"

"I said I wasn't sure. He would have to ask you."

"Thanks. Shut the door on your way out."

"Are you going to meet with him? I didn't think you were going to…"

"Shut the door on your way out."

"Okay, okay sorry." She turned and quickly left Susan's office, softly closing the door as she did.

She looked at the message for a few seconds, trying to conclude whether to call now or wait until later in the day. She finally decided to get it over with. This would be as unpleasant a conversation as the one she just had—and the end result most likely the same. She was certain what she was about to tell him was not what he wanted to hear.

"Greg, Susan. How are you?"

"Hi Susan, I am well. Great to hear your voice."

Both remained quiet, until he finally said, "How's your schedule look today?"

"Crazy. I have appointments off and on all day."

"Can you squeeze me in somewhere?"

"As in 'squeeze you in' how?"

"Do you have time to grab a cup of coffee at that little shop down the street?"

"Not really. Sorry, I am really busy. The campaign has unfortunately interfered with office work. Maybe another time?"

"What about tomorrow?"

"Busy. I am busy all week, Greg."

He remained quiet.

She had decided it was time to put an end to this. He apparently wasn't going to give up.

"Greg, maybe we shouldn't see each other for a while. I have so much going on and I know you have to be busy with your practice."

"No, no I don't want to do that. Let's set up a time next week. I really need to see you—even if it's for only a few moments."

"Why, what's the problem? I don't understand."

He hesitated. "Susan, as I told you the last time we were together, I love you. I meant it. I don't want to let you go. You were the best thing that ever happened to me. I know that now. Can't we just get together and…"

"No, no, no Greg. I had no idea your feelings were that strong. I love Tom and there's no room for anyone else in our relationship. We had our chance and it didn't work out. I don't think we should see each other again. I'm sorry, but I really think that's best for both of us."

"But what about just a time or two a week? What about that? Does maybe just once or twice a week work for you?"

"No. *No* time a week works for me. Now, Brain I have to go. Don't call here again. Good luck and goodbye."

"Susan, don't hang up. Don't hang…"

She terminated the call and sat there, reconsidering what she had just done. She concluded it was absolutely the right thing to do, and picked up another file to review the paperwork before her hearing at nine tomorrow morning.

As she did, Amy walked in her office and said, "I thought that was Greg you just talked to."

"It was. Why?"

"He's on line one…again. He said you needs to talk to you."

"Okay, now here's the deal. I'm busy and I'll be busy every time he calls from now on. Do you understand."

Amy smiled, and said, "I do. I'll take care of it."

Late that afternoon, Susan walked in the front door of their home, where Tom was on the deck, reading, and enjoying an incredibly beautiful day. She grabbed a glass of wine and walked outside.

Tom turned and said, "Hey, how'd the day go? I tried to get in to see you a couple of times, but you were always busy. Do you have a lot of hearings coming up?"

She dropped down into one of the chairs, leaned back and said, "You won't believe how my day went."

Tom set his book down, and said, "So, tell me about it. What happened?"

"It all started with Brian and it quickly went downhill from there."

Chapter 34

Susan was just returning to her office from the courthouse. As she walked by Amy, she said, "Anything go on while I was gone?"

"That didn't take long."

"I told you it wouldn't." She continued walking to her desk as she said, "I also told you Bob Rivers wasn't much of an attorney. He filed a motion today that was a loser before he ever had it typed up. I really, really like the guy. I mean, he's very personable, but he is such a poor attorney. I cringe whenever he's representing someone I am prosecuting because I'm afraid he'll make a mistake that might be appealable. He's a great guy, but a piss poor attorney."

Amy followed Susan to her desk. "Sally called. She wanted you to call her when you had a chance."

"Anything else happen?'

"Not really. Bob River's secretary, Traci is her name, called and wanted to visit about another case you are handling. I don't much like her. She's pretty snipy."

"Is she new?"

"No, she's been there awhile, but she just really thinks she's above everyone. I don't like dealing with her. I tolerate her, but I don't like her at all."

"Get Sally on the phone for me, will you?"

A few minutes later, Amy told her Sally was on line one.

"Hey, Sally, Amy said you called. I just got back from a hearing. What's going on?"

"I'm just trying to schedule a few new speaking engagements near the date of the election. You're pretty well booked up in the near term, but you don't have much going on immediately before the election. But another reason I called concerns your opponent, Brian. Did you two have a falling out? I've noticed a few negative ads about you from their side that just surfaced today."

"Yes, we've had a slight falling out."

"What about? Is it a problem? Is it something that might cause Chuck to alter his support?"

"No, no nothing like that. We had a meeting and he just wanted to make sure his job wasn't in jeopardy if he lost and I told him… it was. He took issue with that."

Sally hesitated. "Well, I can see why the tone of the ads have changed. You think that was the thing to do? You want to rethink that?"

"Nope. That's the way it is, and that's the way it's going to stay. If I win, we'll address his issues and his problems at that time."

Sally hesitated, then said, "Okay, you're the boss. I just hope he doesn't have anything on you that could embarrass you, because from what I hear, his back is against the wall, and he's ready to try anything."

"Not concerned in the least."

"Okay. If I don't talk to you sooner, I'll see you tomorrow night."

"We'll be there."

The day remained unremarkable, until a late afternoon call, lasting almost a half-hour, resulted in Susan messaging Amy that she needed to see her.

As Amy sat, she smiled and said, "What's up? I about got all those subpoenas ready to hand over to the officers for service."

The outer office door opened and two officers walked in.

Amy stood, and said, "Let me take care of them. I'll be right back."

As she started out the door, Susan said, "Stay here. Sit down."

"But, I'll only…"

"That wasn't a request. Now, *sit down*."

"Well, okay. What's going on?"

"You remember what I told you not long ago, when I said nothing discussed here could ever leave this office? You remember that conversation, because it wasn't but a few weeks ago we had it."

"Yes, of course, I remember. And I've done just as you asked. I haven't talked to anyone about anything that's gone on in this office."

"Did you talk to Bob Rivers secretary this morning?"

"Yes, but…"

"Did you tell her what I said to you about how incompetent her boss was?"

"No…I…I don't think I did."

"Then how would she know, word for word, what I said about him? You're the only one I said it to. And *I* sure as hell wouldn't have told him…or her. How did she know, word for word, what I said?"

"I might have said something…that…"

"No, you told her, word for word, because that's what he did with me…he repeated what I said about him to you, word for word. And that all came from his secretary--and that all came directly from you."

"Well, what she said about this office and about you…I just wasn't going to…"

"Now, because of what you've said, you have created an impossible working relationship between us—one in which he'll file every motion he can think of, call witnesses that are questionable at best and just take up everyone's time. He'll fail to return my calls…well, you get the idea."

"I'm sorry. I didn't think about…I won't let it happen again. I promise."

"Too late." She stood. "I've asked these officers to come up and escort you out of the building. I want you to pack up what belongs to you, while they watch, and then get out. Draw unemployment if you can, get another job if you can, but first and foremost get out of here. Officers, come get her."

She stood as she said, "Please, Susan. Give me one more chance. I need this job. Don't do this to me, to our family."

"You had your chance…no more chances in this office. Get out."

As she started to move forward toward Susan, an officer on each side grabbed an arm and moved her toward the door, out of her office.

"Susan, I swear to god you'll be sorry for this. If it's the last thing…"

Susan shut the door between both offices. She started to cry. Once she heard nothing else, she opened the door, and watched as the officers walked her down the hallway to the elevator.

She walked back in her office, wiped her tears away, picked up the phone, punched in an interoffice number, and said, "Chuck, I'm going to need a new secretary."

A few hours later, she looked at Tom, and said, "Fill it up again."

He smiled. "You sure? You've already had two glasses now. Three is normally your limit. That's normally the number it takes to put you into another intellectual zone which doesn't become you."

"Pour."

"Okay, this is your party." As he poured, he said, "I'm surprised you didn't hear from her again. In fact, I'm surprised you haven't heard from her *tonight*."

"Oh, I've heard from her. I just hadn't mentioned it."

"When?"

"Once, just as I was getting out of the car here at home."

"Really? What type of contact?"

"She sent me a text that said, 'You made a big mistake. You shouldn't have done what you did.'"

"Did you respond?"

"I just said don't contact me again or I'll charge you with harassment."

"Have you heard anything since?"

"No."

"Do you think she's dangerous?"

"I think she could be, yes. I'm not worried about her, but I do think, based on how well I know her, she could be dangerous. That's why I had those officers present—to make sure there were no problems while I got her out of the office."

"You worried about her confronting you somewhere?"

"Not really. She is going to need a job to support her worthless husband and those children. Harassing her former employer probably would not be something a prospective employer would want to hear about."

"Who's your new secretary? Someone told me, but I didn't recognize the name."

"Joan Mathis."

"Is she going to work out?"

"She's a little slow, but she'll be fine until the election. If I win, I'll have Chuck's secretary and she's a real pro."

"You've had an interesting week, to say the least."

"I have had a week from hell. Luckily, it's been nothing I couldn't handle *and* it's nothing the public would have any interest in, *or* anything which might affect the election. But I sure as hell don't want to go through another week like it, I can tell you that."

Chapter 35

They both remained quiet, each content to simply live in the moment, enjoying each other before they jumped out of bed and began the day.

"You know how much I love you? Have I told you lately, just how much I love you?"

She whispered, "I think you did a minute ago, but to be honest I was so busy, I'm not sure exactly what you said…or even what I said in response."

"Well, then I'm glad I said it *now*, while you're lucid and cognizant of what's actually going on around you" He pulled her close and said, "Can we just lie here all day? Are you really that busy? Maybe in a couple of hours we could do it again…and then in a couple of hours, again…then…"

She sat up, looked down at him and said, "You're a big talker, that's all you are. You know as well as I, after about the second time, you will say you've had enough and just leave me behind. Nope, I've been down that road before hot shot. Besides that, I have way too much to do than to stay here the rest of the day with you. So, get up, get dressed, let's roll."

He reached out, put his arm around her, and said, "Just once more. Let's compromise. Just once more for the road."

She smiled, pulled the sheet back, and said, "Okay, but this is it. Then we need to get to work. I don't know about you, but I got…"

"Come here."

"Morning, Joan."

"Morning, Mrs. Jackson. You're a little later than usual this morning."

"I am, yes I am. But this is the exception rather than the rule. Normally, as I'm sure you've already noticed, I'll be here most mornings before you are. Any calls I should be aware of, or just the usual cast of characters?"

"The only one that you haven't talked to or met with since I started here, is a Brian. He said he wanted to see you for a moment, and he would stop by about nine. I told him I would tell you and that I'd call him back if that was unacceptable."

"Humm, wonder what he wants. He works in our office and is the one I'm running against for the district attorney's job. That's fine, I'll see him when he gets here."

Susan walked away, but just as she reached her office door, she stopped, turned around and said, "How are you getting along here, Joan? Anything else you need from me for your desk, or is there anything else you need to know that might have come up and we haven't discussed yet? By the way, you're doing a good job. I am really pleased with your work."

"Thank you. I'm fine for now. By the way, after what you told me about your prior secretary and why she left here, I've tried to be really careful about what I say. Just so you know."

Susan smiled and said, "Not a problem. I hear nothing but good things about you so just keep up the good work."

She sat down at her desk and started to prepare for a trial scheduled in a few days. Just as she opened the file, Joan indicated Brian had just walked in and wondered whether she could send him in.

Susan told her to send him in and she stood as he walked through her doorway.

"Hi Brian, good to see you. Have a seat."

As he sat down, he said, "Thanks. I see you have a new secretary. I heard about that one you had. You did the right thing. At least in my opinion."

"Yeah, it was tough, because she was really good at what she did. But I couldn't handle what she was saying outside the four walls of our office, so one of us had to go."

"I'll get right to the point. There are a couple of reasons I'm here. First of all, she, your former secretary, wanted to see me. She told me she had some things she wanted to tell me about your campaign. I told her to go to hell. That's the first thing. Second, I want you to know I got off track a little when you told me you'd have to consider whether to keep me here at the office if I lost the election. That was wrong. I shouldn't have responded the way I did and I'm sorry. My campaign went a different direction when you said that, and the ads reflected that. But no more. If I can't win without slinging mud, I don't want to win it at all. I just wanted you to know that."

Susan smiled and said, "I can tell you now, that I really thought you were getting a little out of line with some of your ads, but I have noticed lately that's changed. Thank you."

They discussed insignificant issues about the job, about the campaign and about their personal lives until he left, and she was able to continue preparing for trial.

A little after five, Joan walked in her office and said, "You okay with me leaving now, Susan?"

"Absolutely. Nice job today. I'll see you in the morning. Lock the front door when you leave."

An hour after she left, Susan picked up her phone and called Tom.

"Hey, what's going on? How long have you been home?"

"Unlike you, I left the office two hours ago. I shouldn't have left early, but I had had enough. When are you coming home?"

"Oh, I got distracted a couple of times today and I'm not entirely prepared for that suppression hearing tomorrow morning. So, I'll leave here in maybe an hour…maybe around seven. I should be home about seven-thirty."

"I'll plan on that. I'm fixing us a good meal. I got a pork roast cooking, which we'll have along with mashed potatoes and gravy, and asparagus with a hollandaise sauce. I also picked us up a desert from that little shop down the street before I came home. So, I'm going to plan on seven-thirty. Do *not* be late…please."

"I won't. I had a nice visit with Brian today. I'll tell you all about it when I get home."

"That smacks a little of an oxymoron. Nice visit…with Brian…in the same sentence seems somewhat inconsistent."

"It was until today. I'll see you in about an hour."

At six-thirty, she put her pen down and closed the file. She rubbed her eyes, quickly organized the files on her desk and walked to her car.

Traffic downtown was heavy as usual, but as she approached home it disappeared as it always did.

She stopped at the last stoplight before she reached the house. As usual, since the road she would continue to drive ended in their subdivision and wasn't a through roadway, the traffic was light.

While sitting there, she noticed a car drive up alone side, and stop for the stoplight. Whoever it was, honked their horn. She paid no attention. They honked again, and it was then she noticed the passenger window was down.

Concerned there might be a problem, either with them or with her vehicle, she lowered her window. As she strained to see in the darkened car, she observed a reflection from what appeared to be a piece of metal.

She quietly whispered, "What the hell…is that a gun?"

Tom waited until seven-thirty to call her. The food would have to be microwaved—it was all just sitting on the counter. She never answered his call.

He tried again and again it went to voicemail. By now it was near eight and still, he heard nothing. This wasn't like her at all. She was always on time, or she always let him know she would be late.

As he waited in the kitchen, trying to keep everything warm, the doorbell rang. He walked to the door, looked through the glass adjacent thereto, and noticed a couple of law enforcement officers.

He opened the door, smiled and said "If you're looking for the assistant DA, she's not home yet. I expect her any minute. You guys can come in and wait for her here with me, if you wish."

"Sir, we've got some bad news. Can we come in?"

Tom hesitated. The smile left his face. "Sure, come on in. What's going on?"

"Susan's not coming home."

Chapter 36

Three years later

As Andy Price drove to work the following morning, he called Jessica. She didn't answer, which was not unusual. A few minutes later, he tried again.

"Okay, what do you want."

"Morning to you too, sweetheart."

"Andy don't give me that 'sweetheart' crap. What do you want? I'm getting ready to go to work. Now, *what do you want?*"

"How did Kim get along last night? Everything go okay? Was she late getting home?"

"She got along fine. She really likes this kid. Not that that means much at this age, but she really does like him. Now, is that it? I got a few things to do around here before I leave for work."

"How's everything going at work? Do you like those guys you work with? Are they all as good at selling real estate as you are?"

"What are we into now—just small talk before the day begins? I don't have time for that. Now is there anything else you need, or are we done here?"

"Yes, there is. I need my family back, that's what I need."

"Bullshit. You will *be* with your family in a few minutes—when you get out of your car and walk into the station. *That's* your family—you know it, so do I. Now, if you have nothing else important to ask or tell me, I need to go."

"Now, come on. Can we discuss this later?"

"Good bye, Andy."

She terminated the call before he could get another word out of his mouth.

Basically. It was the same conversation every time they talked. He often wondered why he even tried. Their conversations could just be a recording—the issues were always the same. Nothing he said changed her mind. Of course, he knew there were a couple of things he could do to make things right, both involving his occupation. But he didn't want to make those changes, nor did he feel he was in a position with the department to change *anything* right now, even if he wanted to.

"Morning, Garth."

Andy sat down, and started to look through a few phone messages that he had received after he left work last night.

"Hey, do you work today?"

Andy looked up from one of the messages, and said, "What the hell you think I'm doing here? Of course, I work today."

"I thought you were off today. Besides that, we both know just you being here don't mean you're going to work anyway. You can *look* like you're working but not be doing a damn thing better than anyone I ever knew. What do you have planned, if anything?"

"I think I'll contact Harlan Anderson and find out if he can see me today."

"You going to start looking into that Jackson murder?"

"Yeah. I'm just going to ease into it. If it looks like there's nothing to follow up on as I review everything in the first few days, I'll just let it go. But their story is compelling and really deserves an ending. At least that's the way I look at it."

"Yeah, well, good luck. Harlan always was damn good at his job, and *he* couldn't figure it out. Besides that, their story is already three years old. Everything's got to be pretty cold by now."

"I know, I know. You're not telling me anything I don't already know."

Later that morning he contacted Harlan and set up a time to meet with him. He then started to review the file, pulling out all the paperwork he could find concerning the case that appeared relevant. He specifically wanted to review all of the investigating officer's own notes.

At precisely one p.m., Andy knocked on Harlan's door.

Harlan showed him in, and for the next half hour, they discussed old times and how much everything had changed in the cop business since Harlan first because an officer.

Finally, Andy said, "Look, I'm really sorry to take up your time today, especially since you're retired. But that newspaper article concerning the Jackson murder really caught my attention. I assume you read about the suicide of Susan Jackson's husband in the paper last Sunday."

"I did. Actually, to be honest, it brought a tear to my eye. It was really upsetting that I couldn't come up with something before I left the department, but unfortunately I just wasn't able to."

"Why? Were there no viable suspects, or just no evidence of any kind?'

"No there were plenty of suspects, but I just couldn't put any of them at the scene. Whoever did this, did a hell of a job of covering his or her tracks, because I just couldn't come to a definitive conclusion."

"Now, this happened at the intersection of Pine and Cedar, right?"

"Yes. That intersection had no cameras installed. It was a new area. They just had no camaras anywhere. And since it was new, and was servicing a new area of construction, there just wasn't a lot of traffic. No one witnessed it."

"From what I read she was gone before another car arrived at the scene."

"Whoever shot her, used a .38 and struck her right in the middle of the forehead. She never knew what hit her."

"What was the husband like? Apparently, he was never considered a suspect."

"Well, you know how that goes. Everyone is considered in the beginning. But it didn't take long to rule him out. He was so distraught—he called every day, at first. Then as time went by, he started calling every other day, and finally it was once a week. But he never quit calling, even when it got down to once a week. He never remarried. Basically, when the killer ended her life, they ended his too."

"So, as I review your paperwork, there are a number of people that you came up with who might have had a motive. It appears you talked to all of them, but just couldn't tie anything down."

"I did. I talked to everyone that might have had a reason to be upset with her, or have a reason not to want her around anymore. She was running for office, and just recently she had been involved with a few people what might have had a reason to wish her harm."

"Apparently, none of them were strong enough suspects to charge them?"

"Nope. Either they had an alibi, or I couldn't put them at the scene, or there was some other reason I just couldn't charge them."

"I see you concluded that no one you interviewed owned a registered pistol."

"Yes. At the conclusion of my investigation, there were multiple reasons I didn't follow up and charge anyone. I just couldn't find anyone that I felt could be charged *and* that I felt could be convicted. Everyone I interviewed had a reason of some type or another to do her harm, but to *kill* her—to *shoot* her? I just couldn't find anyone with that much hatred that I could charge. You got a tough road ahead of you, Andy."

"What about the press? Did they create any issues for you?"

"They were unmerciful—unrelenting. They just never stopped. I had them at my door all the time and, of course, that created even more pressure on our department to do something. But even then, even with that extra layer of pressure, I couldn't find anyone I felt comfortable charging."

Andy smiled and said, "Wow. What a case. What pressure that must have been for you on so many levels. Well, you know, I'm not going to devote the rest of my time with the force to this one case. And I'm certainly not saying anything to the press about this new investigation. If I just can't come up with a viable perp, I'll let it go. But I wanted to at least give it a shot."

He stood. "I better get back to the station. I'll keep you updated. If I have questions, I assume you'll help me along the way?"

He stood, and extended his hand, as he said, "Certainly. Just let me know what you need. I'll be available anytime."

Upon returning to the station, as he continued to review the paperwork in Susan's file, Garth walked by his desk. As he did, he said, "How'd your meeting with Harlan go?"

"Good, it went good. He's a classy guy—always has been. I went through his notes with him and we just talked in general about the case. He was stumped. He could never place anyone at the scene, nor was he comfortable enough to ever charge anyone. That all worries me. I mean, if he couldn't come up with anything at the time, what are my chances three years later?"

As Garth sat down, he said, "You know, it's funny though. Sometimes people remember little things later that they never thought meant much at the time—selective memory or something like that."

"You want to work with me on this?"

"Nope, it's all yours. What's up next?"

"I need to go see her former boss. I called him on the way back to the station. He's still around and seemed willing to talk, so I'll start with him."

"You're really into this aren't you? I mean, you seem almost consumed by the case and you only just opened the file."

"I don't know if 'consumed' is the correct word, but yes, this case interests me. That note her husband left, pulled me in immediately."

He looked away for a moment, before he said, "The personal life the two of them enjoyed interests me too…they were so devoted, so much in love…so much…"

Andy hesitated, looked at Garth, smiled and said, "I'm going to do whatever I can, even at this late date, to figure out who ended such a beautiful relationship. Hopefully then, Susan and Tom can both finally rest in peace."

Chapter 37

ndy had known and been friends with Chuck Manson for many years. The first time Chuck ran for the district attorney general's position, he had asked Andy for his support. Andy never hesitated. Chuck won, and they had enjoyed a good working relationship along with a deep friendship ever since. Both respected the professionalism each displayed within their job and the mutual respect they had for one another was palpable.

"Andy, it's been a while since we've talked. When was it—shortly after my retirement party? Has it really been that long?"

The years had been good to Chuck. He looked like he had just begun his career, rather than having retired three years ago.

"I think it has, Chuck. Have you got a few minutes to talk?"

"Certainly, have a chair."

The next twenty minutes were spent reminiscing about the "good old days." For each story Chuck told, Andy had one to match.

As Chuck finished one of his stories, Andy said, "I don't want to bother you anymore than necessary, but could we talk a few minutes about the main reason I'm here? I think I mentioned it involved Susan Jackson. Can we talk about her and about her employment, for a few minutes?"

"Certainly. Breaks my heart every time I think about her. What is it you are doing that involves Susan? You didn't explain over the phone—you just said you wanted to talk to me about her."

"Did you happen to read that piece in the paper not long ago—the article about her husband Tom committing suicide."

"Yes, I saw that. You know, he worked for me too. At the time, I was on my way out and I didn't have a lot to do with the office. I was just letting the people who would remain in the office handle most everything."

"Tom must have been beside himself when she was murdered."

"He was. He was inconsolable. I told him to go home for a couple of weeks and just to come back when he was ready. He was only gone a couple of days and told me he needed to get back to work. As much as anything, I had no doubt he came back to try and forget, at least for the day. Let me ask you Andy, why are you working on this now? It's an old case and wasn't solved by the detective working on it at the time. Why are you involved now, at this late date?"

"The story in the paper about Tom committing suicide caught my attention. I wanted to take a fresh look at the crime as someone who had absolutely nothing to do with it from day one. My boss told me to go ahead. I've just started, but I wanted to talk to you early on in my investigation and discuss your thoughts since you were her boss and knew both of them."

Andy sat back in his chair, folded his arms and said, "What was their relationship really like, Chuck? Were they as close as Tom's suicide note said they were?"

"Closer."

"They really were as close as everyone says they were?"

"Yes. I was a little concerned about hiring Tom since Susan was already working with us. I told them if their marriage interfered with our work product, one of them would need to go. They agreed to those terms and there never was a problem."

"Were they together all day every day?"

"No, no, not at all. Some days they never saw each other. Some days they had coffee with each other a couple of times during the day, or went out for lunch together. It really depended on their work load and what was going on. They just loved to be with each other."

He looked away for a moment, clearly deep in thought. "But it was obvious that situation didn't come about without both of them working things out. It didn't come about without a lot of trial and error, while they were each figuring out what the other wanted to do and then working it into both of their schedules. That took effort on the part of both of them to get to the point where they were comfortable being together all day and all night too."

Once again. Andy hesitated before he said, "But why are you asking about how they got along? What difference does that make? Aren't you interested in the crime, not the relationship?"

Andy cleared his throat, and said, "Certainly, yes that's right. Let's just talk about her—about her relationship with her coworkers or any other issues that you think might be something that needs some looking into."

"Well, really as I told Harlan at the time, there was nothing I ever saw or heard that would have shed some light on her murder. Everyone in the office seemed to get along well. She did have some trouble with her secretary not long before she died, and I did discuss that with Harlan. She also had a few issues with the guy that ran against her, Brian. But I think those two worked all that out before the election. At least that was what I was told."

"I realize this would seem to be way out of character, but while they both worked with you, had you heard any whispers about any inner-office relationships which would have involved either of them?"

"No, never. There was never a word said about that involving either Tom or her."

He stood, as he said, "Okay, well Chuck I think that's about it. Is there anything else you can tell me about them that involved the murder that might have crossed your mind since Harlan initially interviewed you?"

Chuck stood as he said, "Not really. There were one or two people I thought at the time might have a problem with her, and they were part of my discussion with Harlan. Other than that, if I think of anything else, I'll certainly let you know. Are you going to visit with her secretary concerning their issues? She's still working for Susan's replacement."

"I'm going there right now. Thanks for all your help, Chuck."

"Afternoon, Ms. Mathis, I'm Andy Price and I'm with the Nashville police department. I'd like to visit with you a moment. Do you have time right now to answer a couple of questions for me?"

She hesitated. "Well, I guess. What's this about?"

"Susan Jackson."

"I wondered if that suicide note might renew an interest in her murder. Yes, I have a few moments before my boss gets back from court. It'll be crazy then, but for now, how can I help you?"

"Did you work that day?"

"Yes. I had only been here a few weeks though. I didn't know many of the people that were working here."

"Why were you so recently employed? Now, I know you've probably heard all these questions before, but I'm new to the case and I really just want to start over. So please forgive me if you feel like you're answering a number of these questions all over again."

"I understand. She had terminated her prior secretary and hired me just prior to her death."

"Were you made aware of anyone that might have held a grudge against her, or that might have had a reason to have done her harm?"

"No, not really. Except…maybe…"

"Please finish that thought. Who do you have in mind?"

"Her former secretary was really hot about getting terminated. She called me a couple of times and tried to tell me how much of a…bitch…Susan was, but I just hung up both times. She was Susan's secretary for quite a while, and I think they were pretty close. But it didn't end well."

"Do you know where she's working now?"

"I think she's with a real estate office…just a moment."

She reached into one of the desk drawers and pulled out a legal pad with a number of names and numbers.

She pointed to one of the names, and said, "That's her name and her phone number."

He wrote both down as he said, "Were Susan and Tom, in your opinion, really as close as everyone said they were?"

She thought for a moment, then started to say something but stopped. She reached across the desk and grabbed a tissue. She dabbed at her eyes, and said, "Yes. They were incredibly close. It was awful to watch Tom after she was murdered. He was never the same. But to answer your question, yes, they had this marriage thing figured out, and their solution was something all of us that are married, should strive for."

"Hi, Dad. What are you doing? You don't normally call during the day."

Andy said, "I'm driving back to the station after interviewing a couple of people. I'm just working on a case. What are you doing?'

"Getting ready to go to work."

"What are your hours? Why are you going to work so late in the day?"

"Dad. I told you I work at that ice cream shop down the street from us. I also told you, but obviously it wasn't important enough for you to remember, that I go to work around two and don't get off until eight."

"Sorry, sorry, you're right. I remember now. How about a burger at that little hamburger joint where we've met before when you get off work tomorrow night?"

"No, no, I…I have to…"

"No, you don't. Come on, have supper with me. It's been a long time. I'll pick you up at work. It's fast food. It won't take much of your time. Just humor me for about forty-five minutes."

She hesitated, took a deep breath, then said, "Okay, Dad, but only forty-five minutes. Pick me up at eight."

"Great. Looking forward to it. I'll see you then."

Chapter 38

Andy was on time and she was waiting. He drove to a small diner where they had met before. He spotted a small table for two situated in the far corner, where they could talk with little chance of being overheard by those not invited to their limited party for two.

After they had ordered, he said, "So, how was work today?"

"Fine."

"What do you normally do?"

"Just work." She continued to look around, failing to make eye contact with him. It was obvious she was wanting to be somewhere else, most likely anywhere other than here.

The waitress came and took their order. After they had ordered, as the waitress started to leave, Kim said, "I'm in kind of a hurry, could you put a rush on it?"

The waitress nodded and walked off.

Andy looked away for a moment, then turned toward her, and said, "Why are we in 'kind of a hurry?' Are we going somewhere I'm not aware of? What's going on?"

"I told Jack to pick me up here. He's always a little early, so he'll probably be here between eight-thirty and eight forty-five—just so you know."

"While we're on that subject, you know, the subject of *Jack,* why don't you tell me a little about him?"

"What do you want to know?"

"Oh, just the normal things dads want to know about guys dating their daughters. Standard stuff—does he beat you, is he honest and up front with you, is he all hands when he takes you out, what's his…"

"That's enough, Dad. Okay, he's good to me. He's not handsy. We've been dating off and on now for quite a while. He's a true gentleman all the time. We get along way better than you and mom, which isn't saying much I know, but we do. What else do you want to know?"

"I guess that's enough. Where are you going after you leave here?"

"I've gone all through that with mom. She knows I'm going out with him and where we're going. I've already been through all that with her."

"How old is he?"

"A year older than me."

"Does he have a car?"

"He uses his folks when we go out."

"What kind of grades does he get?"

"He's a good student. In fact, he gets better grades than I do, and you know I made the honor roll last year, in spite of not having a father at home to help me when I needed him."

"Now, that's not really fair. I try to be there when I can—whenever   you say you need me."

Both remained quiet. A few minutes later, the waitress brought their food. As they ate, Andy said, "How are your grades *this* year?"

"Good. Mom helps me if I need some help, and, because of that, they are good."

"You know, I'd help you too if you'd let me know you need help. I'm only a call away. I've told you that before."

She continued to eat her hamburger and fries as if the building were on fire and she needed to evacuate. Her eyes remained fixed on the front window, clearly anxious for her ride to arrive.

"Really Kim, I'll help you with schoolwork, or whatever else you need whenever..."

She pushed her plate away, as she said, "What's the problem with you and mom? I mean, I don't get it. You've told me repeatedly now much you love her, how much you care for her, but here we are. When I leave here, when my date is over, I'll go one way, and when you're done at work, you'll go another. I just don't get it. And to be honest, I really think it's all your fault. So how do you respond to that...*DAD*? What's your take on our family mess?"

He looked away for a moment, then faced her and said, "Well, first of all, I don't consider it a mess. We do have a few..."

"No, no, stop right there. It's a mess. And from my standpoint, I'm really sick of it. Most of all, I just don't understand. I want us to be a family again…the way it used to be. But all I get now is her telling me the things that so irritate her about you, and you saying, 'Well, it's not a mess, it's a…a…' It's a *what* dad? Why don't you two figure out what the hell *your* problem is and *fix* it. Or get a divorce. Just end the marriage, and you two can ship me back and forth like real divorced couples do…a little time with her, a little time with you."

She started to cry.

He leaned forward, and said, "Honey, you don't understand. It's…it's…"

She looked out the window at the car that had just pulled up to the curb.

She stood. "You're right. I don't understand, Dad. I talk to her, I talk to you, and I just don't understand what the problem is between you. Even with your job issue, and the time you devote to it, you should still be able to work things out like other cops do—some of them *surely* have normal families. Work it out, Dad. I'm really sick of this little arrangement you two have with me in the middle."

"Do you have to go? Let's sit and disuse it a little further. Maybe…"

"You need to work this out with mom, not me. I need to go. Thanks for the burger."

"Hold on Kim. Let's…"

She was out the door before he could say another word.

As he stood to go, he figured if nothing else, his daughter had certainly learned how to express herself. She left little doubt about her position concerning him as a father and the status of the marriage.

A couple of hours later, once he had left the station and gone home for the night, his phone rang.

He had just poured himself a short glass of bourbon over a few ice cubes, and dropped down into his chair wanting to relax for a few minutes before he fell asleep.

"Hi, Jess. Calling a little late, aren't you? I didn't know you still stayed up this late."

"Normally, I don't, but I did tonight. I've fought with myself for the last half-hour wondering whether to call you at all, but anger took over, and I finally just decided to call. I figured if I don't like the path the conversation takes, I'll just hang up. So, you've been forewarned."

"You're right, I have been. And certainly, we both know you've become the *queen* of ending discussions by hanging up in the middle of one. Now, go on. What's the topic of discussion tonight? Have you just reached a new level of disgust with me?"

"I want to know what you and Kim talked about tonight."

"No problem there." He hesitated. "Why? It certainly wasn't anything earth shattering that's for sure."

"Well, *she* seemed to think it was. I asked her how you two got along, and she said, 'Fine, he just frustrates me. He's my father and I absolutely can't talk to him anymore.' So, what did you frustrate her about? Did it involve us? I don't want you talking to her about us. You leave *us,* between *us,* Andy. I don't…"

"Jess, don't get all wound up here. I hardly said a word. It was all her. She wanted to understand what was going on between you and I. It was her doing all the talking. I did little but listen."

"Knowing you Andy, you got your two cents in wherever you could. She wouldn't tell me the specifics and she was upset—I didn't push her. You need to keep her out of the middle of this Andy, you really do."

"I'm telling you I didn't do a damn thing. She did all the talking. She just doesn't understand the problem. Maybe you should sit down and have a talk with her—tell her what our problems are so she knows."

"Are you nuts. I'm not getting her involved. This is up to the two of us to settle and if we can't resolve these issues, then we need to get the divorce and get it over with."

He sat up in his chair. "Jess, you know I've been telling you since before I moved out, I'm willing to talk to you anytime about our problems. I don't want a divorce. You know I still love you, and I would do most anything to resolve these issues. What do you say we…"

"You going to give up that job?"

He hesitated. "Is that the only way this can be resolved?"

"Yup."

"Can't we sit down and just review all the other options that might be available to the two of us…"

"Are you going to give up that job?"

"I can't really do that right now. Besides, that doesn't appear to me to be the real issue, because…"

"I needed a yes or no to my question. You just answered it the same way you always do. You be careful what you say around our daughter, Andy. Leave our problems to us. You understand?"

"But Jess, I…"

"We're done here. You remember what I said or in the very near future, you and I are going to have a lot more issues than we have now."

Chapter 39

Andy slept off and on the remainder of the night. Each time he woke up, his thoughts would return to the time he had with his daughter, and the resulting conversation he had with Jess.

Once he reached his office, he pulled out the suicide note Tom Jackson had written. He read it again, as he had so many times since first seeing it in the newspaper. He compared the writer's thoughts and emotions displayed in the note, with what had happened last night, both as concerned his daughter and his subsequent conversation with Jess.

What had happened during his marriage that resulted in the relationship he now had with his wife and child? Why was his marriage so different than the one described in the note he was just now reading? It didn't make sense. He felt he loved Jessica and his daughter as much as Tom loved Susan. Why did *their* marriage work and *his didn't?*

"Hey Andy, what are you reading so intently there? You pick up a little porn somewhere?"

As Garth laughed, Andy said nothing.

He sat down, then waited a couple of minutes before he said, "What's on your agenda today, Andy? Anything of interest?"

He looked up, and said, "Maybe. Right now, I'm reviewing that suicide note written by Tom Jackson. I plan on working that case most of the day."

"What did you do last night?"

"Went out for supper with my daughter."

"How do you two get along? I know you've mentioned you had a bit of a rocky road with both Jess *and* Kim once you left the house. How did the two of you get along last night?"

As he put the suicide note back in his file, he said, "Really, not very well. She met me for supper, but it was clear throughout most of the meal, her thoughts were somewhere else. When her mind *wasn't* on something else, she lectured me on fixing our marriage and working things out with Jess. All in all, it wasn't a very pleasant meal."

"You know, it doesn't sound to me you're doing much to resolve anything. You and I have talked about it enough times and it appears to me that you're really doing very little about trying to save it. Do you really want the marriage to end?"

"No, I don't. *I don't.* But it's always the job with her. Oh, there's other smaller issues we fight about too. But I love my job. I'm not going to give it up. To be honest, I can't. There's really nothing else I know how to do."

"Andy, I *know* your job is an issue, but it seems to me based on what you've mentioned through the years, there really is more to it than that. If you didn't have the job issue, how would your marriage be? Would everything *really* be okay? Have you ever tried to discuss other issues with her, or does the conversation just start and end with your job? All your discussions with me seem to revolve around your profession, but are there really other issues there you haven't told me about? Just saying."

"Well, you're right about one thing. We have trouble getting past the job issue. But you know, I really do love her—I really do. And that daughter of mine, she's…"

"I know what you're saying, but to be honest, you just don't sound like you do much to show it. Maybe you should at least find out how she really feels about those other issues and how things would be between the two of you if the job *wasn't* an issue. Maybe she really doesn't give a shit about you one way or the other. If that's the case, then all this discussion about your job can end and you can go straight to a divorce. See how easy it is to figure these things out? Now, I'm no expert, but…

"Hey Andy, you got a minute?"

Andy stood, and as he walked toward the office of his boss, he said, "I do, boss, yes."

As he walked in his office door, Arthur said, "I won't take much of your time, but how's this investigation concerning Susan Jackson going? I haven't heard from you since you started. Is it a waste of time or not?"

"I've talked to a couple of people so far, and I've got nothing, but I've only begun. I just heard from her former secretary. She wasn't very cooperative, and really didn't want to talk, but that'll change before the day's over. She'll talk to me. I'm anxious to see what she has to say. Why? Do you want me to work on something else while I'm working on this dead file?"

"I don't want you spending a lot of time on that case. I'm glad you're looking into everything one last time—she certainly deserves that. But you're on a short leash here Andy, and I just don't want much of your time devoted to what happened three years ago."

"I talked to Harlan as I told you I would. He didn't know much about who might have killed her, but he gave me a little information I might be able to use later on in the investigation.

Garth leaned against the doorframe and said, "Not to bother, but Andy, I know you were interested in someone by the name of Amy Smith. She's on line one."

Arthur said, "Go, go on, I said what I wanted to say. Just keep me updated. I'll give you another couple of weeks on this and if we don't have much, I'll want you to move on. So instead of me remembering what I just said, you stop in about two weeks from now and let me know where you're at."

"Will do boss. Thanks."

Andy walked to his desk and picked up. "Andrew Price. Who am I speaking with?'

"This is Amy Smith. You called me a day or so ago and wanted me to call you back. What's this all about?"

"Well, Amy, I'm working on a cold case, and I wanted to visit with you about it when you have time."

"A cold case? What the hell would I know about some 'cold case.' Who does it involve?"

"Your former boss, Susan Jackson."

She hesitated. "Why you looking into that case again? I thought that was all done with. I heard they quit investigating the case years ago because they couldn't come to any conclusions concerning what happened."

"That's correct, they did. But I'm looking into it again with a fresh set of eyes. Do you have time to visit with me?"

"When?"

"Maybe this afternoon?"

"No, no, not today at all. To be honest, they took my statement years ago and what's in it is all I know. I just don't have time to fuck with it anymore. It's old news and I'm busy. Is this all coming up again because of Tom's suicide note? Is this all being investigated again because of that note in the paper?"

"Yes."

"Well, I don't have any information about that other than what I told that other guy years ago. So, no, I don't have time today."

"What about tomorrow? I'll be brief."

"Nope, not tomorrow either—nor the next day, or the next. I can't afford to spend any more of my time on Susan Jackson—been there, done that. Go find someone else that knew her and may have a little information for you. She had a lot of friends. One of them might be able to help, but sorry, I can't. Good luck."

She terminated the call.

As he hung up his phone, he looked at Garth and said, "Well, that potential witness just flew out the window."

"What happened?"

"She didn't want to talk…at all. Something wrong there. I think I'll try to contact her next week, and…"

A voice through the intercom system said, "Andy, you have a call on line one. It's Amy Smith. She said you two were just talking. She needs to visit with you again."

"Thanks." He punched the button for line one, and said, "This is Andy."

"Amy Smith. Be here by one. I'll give you a few minutes then, but I won't have any more time than that. It's an inconvenience the way it is, but I'll give you a few minutes. Can you be here then?"

"Absolutely. See you at one."

Chapter 40

Andy walked in the real estate office where Amy Smith was employed, precisely at one. Seated at the front desk, was a middle-aged, well-dressed woman who stood as he walked in the door.

"You must be Andy Price."

He extended his hand, smiled and said, "You must be Amy."

"I am. Let's go in the conference room. Someone else in the office will answer the phone and handle the front during the few minutes I'm with you."

As they sat down across a large conference table from each other, she said, "What can I help you with? Please remember, I already told you guys what I knew three years ago. So, if you're expecting much from me, I'll be right up front with you from the start—you are wasting your time."

The same defensive attitude she displayed during her earlier conversations, was as obvious in person as it was on the phone.

"First, let's just, in generalities, discuss your relationship with Susan. Can you tell me about the two of you and how you got along?"

"I worked for her for almost as long as she worked for the district attorney's office. There was only one day during all that time we had a significant dispute and that was the day she fired me."

"You never had any problems before that day?"

"Oh, we had some differences of opinion, but to say it reached the point where there were issues between the two of us, no. That only happened once, and that was the day I left."

"Tell me, what was she like to work for?"

"Easy. She was never really demanding, although she wanted the work done in a timely manner and she was the one that determined what 'timely manner' meant in each situation. But as long as you got the work done, she was easy to please."

"What did you observe about her relationship with Tom, her husband?"

"To be honest, it was almost sickening. They were all over each other all the time. Their relationship was like none I have ever seen. One in a million—that's what their relationship was." She looked away for a moment, then reengaged as she said, "And I envied them every minute of every day."

"Did she fire you?"

"Yes."

"Why?"

"I made two or three comments outside the office about our business and she found out. She gave me minutes to get my belongings together and get out."

"How'd you feel about that?"

"I hated her. Still do."

"Did you not deserve what happened? I don't understand. You've made it clear you violated an important privacy requirement by talking outside the office. Why were you, and why *are* you still upset about her terminating you? It sounds to me like you were strictly to blame for your own termination."

"I was."

Again, she hesitated. She thought for a moment, then leaned forward in her chair, and said, "But, I *cared* for her. I worked hard for her. I just felt she should have given me another chance, that's all. She should have given me another chance, and because she didn't, I left there with a bitter taste in my mouth which I still have and always will."

"That bitter taste in your mouth strong enough to kill the reason it's there?"

She sat back, smiled and said, "Nope."

"Where were you the night it happened?"

"I don't remember. It's been too long ago."

"Your statement said you were 'just driving around,' or something like that. Is that what you were doing?"

"If that's what it says, then yeah, that's what I was doing."

"You don't remember though?"

"You know, the fact that she was murdered didn't and doesn't change the way I feel about her. I hated here then and I still do. I have no desire to help in this investigation, and I'm glad whoever did it, got away with it. She shouldn't have fired me."

"So, as I understand the situation, you didn't do it, but you have no alibi?"

"Yup, that's about it, partner. Now anything else?"

"What about other people that might have had a reason to hurt or harm her? Was there anyone else that stood out that might have wanted to do her harm?"

"No, not that I know off."

Andy looked through his file until he came to her statement given at the time of the murder.

"As I look through the notes made three years ago, I see you mentioned something about Brian—about the fact he had some problems with her. Is that correct?"

"You'll have to ask him."

Andy leaned forward in his chair, and said, "Look, Amy, assuming you are innocent, which at this point I assume you are, I'm not the enemy here. I'm just trying to put away a guy that murdered someone. It shouldn't matter whether you had issues with her. That's an entirely a separate issue. I'm sorry that happened. But it shouldn't affect your desire to catch a murderer."

She looked away for a moment, then turned toward him and said, "I think you'll find in your paperwork there, that I also mentioned a guy by the name of Greg Long. You see his name anywhere on all that paperwork you have?"

"Let me look."

He quickly checked through page after page of notes.

Andy pulled out a half-sheet of paper and read the small amount of print that was on it.

"Yes, yes, here it is. It just says you mentioned they had a bit of a contentious relationship right before you left. Is that correct?"

"They did around the time she was killed, yes."

He put that in his file, as he said, "Anyone else?"

She smiled as she stood and said, "Nope that's about it. Anything else?"

He looked up at her and said, "You know, you may very well be the key to bringing a murderer to justice, Amy. You were with her all day every day during each week of her life for a long time. You are an important cog in the justice process concerning this case, and without your input, it's going to be just that much harder to figure out who really did this. Your reluctance could leave a murderer running loose. I can tell you that if whoever did it, gets away with it, that just leaves the door open for them to do it again."

"Not my problem. I don't care. I hate her. I don't care who did it, or what they do with their life. I've said all I'm going to say about her murder." She smiled. "You know where the door's at."

She turned around and walked out to the counter, pulling a tissue from the box sitting there.

He stood and walked toward her as he said, "I think you should know and understand one thing. If you are so angry after three years, that you're willing to let the person who did this go free, assuming it *wasn't you* that did it, that's fine. But remember this. If he or she kills again, *that's on you.* If you don't want to help, that's fine, but if anyone else dies and we find out later that killer also killed Susan, *that murder is at least partially, or maybe completely, on you."*

"Go. Get out."

He shoved all his notes in his file folder and walked out of the building. He knew she knew more than she let on. But he couldn't force her to tell him about any other suspects she might know of, if there really were others. She was withholding information. He would stake his reputation on that.

Andy got in his vehicle and sat there for a moment, quickly writing down the essence of his brief conversation with her. Once he had finished, he decided to drive in the direction of the home of the Jacksons at the time of the murder, just to look at the intersection where she was murdered, as it might pertain to this investigation.

He pulled up and stopped at the intersection on a red light. He was in the right lane, as he always was when he reached this point, so he could proceed forward on toward his home. That night, Susan would have also been in the right lane, stopped and ready to proceed straight ahead, to their home, which was about a mile away.

The killer would have had to drive up alongside her in the turning lane. There had been little construction yet completed beyond the intersection. Houses were being built along the roadway, but had not reached the intersection.

There were still no traffic cameras anywhere.

He drove on through the intersection and continued to drive until he reached his home. He knew she would be at work. He pulled in the driveway, sat for a moment, and wondered if this would *always* remain his way home. He was now really concerned their marriage might be on the rocks. Andy knew he needed to try a little harder—he didn't want that his marriage dissolved under any circumstances and he was willing to try harder—to try and reach that level of commitment and enjoyment that Susan and…His phone buzzed.

He noticed the caller was Amy Smith.

He accepted the call, and said, "Hi, Amy."

"You got any more time for me? I think I've made a mistake. I think I need to help you resolve this. I'm sorry. I'm sorry for how I let my feelings for her and what she did, get in the way. You're absolutely right. I don't want what happened to my boss, to happen to anyone else because I may not have done all I could to stop it. I couldn't live with myself if I did that. I'll give you the names of a few people you need to interview. The murderer may not be on the list, but if he or she isn't, at least I've done all I can do to help."

"I understand. I have an appointment in a few minutes, but what about late this afternoon—maybe around four-thirty? Does that work for you?"

"I'll be here…and this time, I promise I'll be a hell of a lot more cooperative than I was a few minutes ago. See you then."

Chapter 41

He arrived at Amy's office building shortly after four-thirty. She was at her desk, and as he approached, he said, "Sorry I'm late. I had a lot going on and…"

Not a problem. I understand." She stood. "Let's go back to the conference room."

He followed her, and as they both sat down, she said, "I think I might have some names for you that you might not have—people I knew had a problem with Susan, or just plain didn't like her. I never said anything about any of them to anyone. I don't know if anyone else did either. Let's start with me."

"Okay, that's fine, but hold on a second. First of all, what changed? What happened since we last talked? Obviously, you weren't interested in helping me then. Why now"

She looked away for a moment, and when she reengaged, she said, "Because something you said really resonated with me—something I had never considered and that no one else had ever suggested. The very idea that whoever did this might still be free to do it again because I hadn't provided all the information I might have, is more than I can handle. I'm still bitter about what Susan did, even after three years. But to think it might affect someone else because I remined silent, is more than I can handle."

"I understand. Now, let's just start with you. Where were you when this happened—let's just remove you from further consideration right now."

"Well, that's going to be a little difficult to do. I was in the process of getting pretty damn drunk that night, by myself, at home. My husband was gone for a couple of days, and I just washed away my sorrows with a good bottle of scotch. Oh, I talked to him by phone during the course of the evening, but that doesn't help in establishing where I was during that time period. I have no alibi, plain and simple."

Andy stared at her for a moment, made some notes, and said, "Guess that still leaves you in the running, doesn't it? Isn't there anyone…anyone at all that can place you somewhere, anywhere but the location of the murder around the time it happened?"

"No. So, leave me on your list and let's move on. I simply have no alibi for that time period. It very well could have been me as far as you're concerned…wasn't…but could have been for all you know."

"Okay, let's move on. Who's next?"

"Well, Susan prosecuted one guy around that time period that was more than a little contentious. His name was Hepner I believe. He was charged with burglary as I recall. I'm not sure he would have been capable of murder. But his wife was an out and out bitch. She made it very clear she was unhappy with Susan. And from what I was able to ascertain, she was capable of doing most anything."

"What about him, her husband? Was he convicted?"

"Yes, and ultimately sent to prison. I believe either he or Hepner's wife could have done this. So, you might take a look at both of them—determine if they remember where they were and what they were doing at the time of the murder."

"Anyone else?"

"Well, there was this woman, Dorothy Longmire, who was a high school friend of Susan's, and who had just recently struck up a renewed friendship with her. They hadn't seen each other for quite some time. Dorothy contacted Susan and wanted to renew the friendship. They met a few times and had coffee, but around the time Susan was murdered, they were at odds. In fact, she called the office the last time they had any contact and called Susan every name in the book. She wanted money or help or something, and Susan wasn't going to give her any of either. She was mad enough at Susan that day to hurt someone. Susan was lucky they didn't happen to be near each other on that particular day, because I truly believe the woman was at the end of her rope and was dangerous."

He wrote as he said, "Dorothy Longmire. Got it. Go on."

"You apparently know about Brian—that they had some words while they were running for office. But I think they got everything all cleared up before she died."

"Yes, I have his name. He's been interrogated a couple of times, but as I recall he had an alibi."

"Then there was a guy, a defendant by the name of Wagner who was a real scumbag. Susan prosecuted him for beating the hell out of a guy."

"Did she convict him?"

"Yes. He was sentenced to prison, but the PSI hadn't been completed and he wasn't in prison at the time of her murder. This guy was an animal. Nothing he did would have surprised me. He was a real thug."

"I know his name isn't mentioned as far as the file is concerned or I would have remembered it."

"The guy was capable of most anything. Murder for him, at least in my opinion, would not have been any more of an issue than eating supper might have been."

"Got it. Next?"

"There were a couple of guys that were friends of hers that you may want to question. One was Greg Long. He was a former lover. Once upon a time, I think they lived together. He called a number of times and wanted Susan to go out for a cup of coffee which she did, I think, twice. She told me it was just a friendship. But it appeared to me by the nature and tone of his calls, and by what I saw when he stopped in the office, with him at least, it was way more than friendship."

"Who was the other one?"

"Corey Abbott. Now, Corey was a problem. He's an attorney. I don't think he's probably worth a shit at what he does, but at one time they were really close. They lived together for a while. They split up when he beat her around one night. He tried a couple of times to get close to her again—he wanted a job if Susan won. But she was having none of it. They tried a case against each other, and she beat the shit out of him. He wasn't happy. He wasn't happy with her in any respect before the trial. The verdict in that case just exacerbated the problems between the two of them. He, as much as anyone, probably had the temperament to hurt her, based on their relationship at the time Susan died."

"And he's still practicing?

"I don't know. I heard he got himself in trouble with the bar association, but I never followed up because I just didn't care. He was a piece of shit. I didn't have to deal with him, so I just let it go."

"Got it. Who's next?"

"That's about all I got for you. Those are just people who may or may not have done something to harm her—people I figure maybe no one else but someone that was working closely with Susan, might have known about."

"Yeah, I only recognize a couple of the names you've given me. This will really help. It appears to me all the people you reference might have had a motive to do her harm. I'll contact all of them."

"I know I'm part of the that list. I hated her for what she did, but I've never hurt anyone and…Well, I've never physically harmed anyone other than the tussles my husband and I have. I could never, as disappointed in her as I was, have done anything to harm her. Deep down, I knew she was justified in what she did. I knew there was no one to blame other than myself—but sometimes that's just a little hard to accept."

Andy stood, as she did. "Thank you so much for reconsidering. I'll interview all these people and let you know what happens. I'll probably call you if something comes up that's puzzling or not clear with any of these people, if that's okay with you."

"Certainly. Not a problem."

"By the way, do you own a pistol?"

"Nope."

"Never purchased one—never had one registered in your name or your husband's name?"

She smiled. "No. You asking that question of all these people or just me?"

"Standard procedure, Amy, standard procedure."

Chapter 42

"**I**s this Janet?"

"Might be. Which Janet you looking for? In case you don't know, there's a hell of a lot of them out there. Who is this?"

"This is Andy Price with the Nashville police department. I'm looking for Janet Hepner."

"Which Janet you looking for again?"

His short temper was evident as he said, "Come on, now. Enough with the games. Is this Janet Hepner or not?"

She hesitated. "Ya got me. Yup this is who ya got. Now what the fuck do you want?"

"I need to visit with you. When would you have some time to stop by the police station?"

"What for? What's the reason that I should take time out of my busy day to stop by and see you?"

"Why I need to see you, most likely amounts to nothing, nothing at all. But I *do* need to see you. I'll tell you more about it when you get here."

"Am I considered a suspect in some crime?"

"Maybe. That's why I want to visit with you. To clear you—to clear your name."

"Sorry. I did nothing wrong and I sure as hell don't have time for you today. Good luck with your investigation."

She terminated the call, and Andy hung up.

"Shit."

Garth turned toward him and sarcastically said, "From what I just heard, that *had* to have been a really productive phone call. Who was it?"

Andy leaned back. "Oh, one of those new potential suspects in the Jackson murder case. I knew she would be tough, but that's about as much pushback as I ever got from an individual I thought might be involved in something. She's not shy, that's for sure."

"So, what's next?"

"I'm not sure. I really need to visit with her. From what Susan's secretary told me, she's definitely capable of committing a crime. A murder? Maybe, maybe not, but she's definitely in the running."

He picked up the phone and once again dialed her number.

"What?"

"Would it make a difference if I came to your house? I'll be glad to do that if you would rather not come here, to the station."

"Hell no, it won't make a difference. I didn't do it. I didn't do anything wrong—ever. Leave me alone."

Again, she hung up.

"Sounds like you're just digging yourself a deeper grave to me."

"I need to find a way to get her to talk to me. I really think she could have done this. I'll try my old dependable method and see if that works."

"You call me again, I'm calling the…I'm calling someone and making sure they know you're harassing me."

"You listen and you listen good. You figure out how to get down to my office, or find time for me to stop at your house. I'm not putting up with any more bullshit from you. If you hang up without making arrangements for an interview with me, I'm filing a charge of withholding evidence against you, and your family can figure out how to survive with you in jail. Now, ma'am, what's it going to be?"

She remained silent for a moment, then said, "You know, I don't really think you can do that, I really don't." She hesitated. "Oh, what the fuck, you guys harass everyone else whenever you please and as you wish. I guess I can join the club for one fucking interview. You be here at one. If you're a minute late you're not getting in."

She hung up.

Andy hung up, smiled at Garth, and said, "Works every time."

"You're going to get your ass in trouble doing that someday. I'm glad it worked today, but you're going to get yourself in trouble if you keep using that to get people to talk to you."

At precisely one, he parked in front of the Hepner home.

As he got out of his car, he noticed a couple of children standing near the fenced-off front yard, talking through the fence with a couple of older children. The area was full of dilapidated homes and the home of the Hepner family fit right in.

As he approached the house, the front door opened and a woman he assumed was Janet, said, "Come on in. Sorry about the condition of the house. I just haven't had time to clean it up yet today. Sit down on the couch there. I'll be right with you."

As he sat, he couldn't help but notice the condition of the furniture-the condition of the house in its totality. The furniture could only be described as early American—*way early*. He was somewhat afraid to sit on the couch, concerned something he couldn't identify might creep up between the cushions and take a bite out of his thigh.

He could hear some children arguing somewhere outside, behind the house, but couldn't see what was going on.

A few minutes later, and after the arguing between children had subsided, she walked back in the room, extended her hand and said, "I'm Janet."

He stood, shook her hand, smiled and said, "I'm Andy Price."

"You mind if I see your badge?"

"Not at all." He pulled it out and handed it to her. She looked it over, handed it back to him and said, "Have a seat."

As he did, she sat as she said, "Okay, now what the hell is this all about? Is he in trouble again?"

"Your husband? No, I don't think so but that's why I'm here—to figure out whether you or your husband might have been involved in a crime. What is he doing by the way? He apparently is out of prison."

"Yes, he's been out a while now. He finally got a job and he's working full time. He works at the grocery store down the street. What he makes is barely enough to keep us going, but at least he's got a job. It just takes a lot to keep all of us fed and in clothing. I'm glad he's not why you're here."

"Well, in part, he is."

"Okay, go on, don't make me pull each fricken detail out of you. Why are you here?"

"You didn't happen to read the story in the paper a while back, about Susan Jackson's husband committing suicide, did you?"

"Does it look like we have enough money to enjoy the luxury of a daily newspaper? Hell no, I didn't see it. And how would her husband killing himself have anything to do with us? I'm surprised he didn't kill himself while she was still living. *I would have if I lived with her.*"

"Why do you say that?"

She moved forward in her chair, looked him straight in the eyes, and said, "Because I hated her. Because…"

She stared at him for only a moment before she said, "What difference does it make how I felt about her?" She sat back and said, "Why are you here? You're not here because her poor henpecked husband killed himself, that's for sure. Why are you here, talking to me about her?"

"I've decided to take a closer look at the case. No one was ever charged with her murder. I'm looking into it."

She thought for a moment. "Now wait. You don't think I killed her, do you? Is that why you're here?"

"Did you?"

She stood. "Get out."

"Where were you that night? Who were you with? Just tell me so I can cross you off the list."

"Get out, before I call…just get out. I'm not answering any questions. You're not gonna pin this on me…or my husband."

"Either of you own a pistol?"

"Get out!"

He stood. "You know, unless you have an alibi for that night, and tell me what it is, you're always going to be considered suspects. I know all about your feelings concerning Susan Jackson, and that makes you not only a suspect, but a *prime* suspect."

"Get your ass out of here before I start screaming and draw all the neighbors over here. Now wouldn't that look good for you. You got nothin' on either of us, nor will you ever have anything on us as concerns Susan Jackson. Now, get out."

He walked to the door, turned around and said, "Do yourself a favor. If you two do have the name of someplace where you were that night, just call and let me know. A simple phone call will take both of you off the hook. Otherwise, I'll be sneaking around watching whatever you do, trying to get some idea who I might talk to in an effort to determine if it was in fact, you or your husband that murdered her. Just make it easy on yourself. I guarantee you're never going to quit hearing from me if you don't."

"You get your ass out of my house. You got nothing on either of us and never will."

He looked at her for a moment, then turned and walked out the door.

Later, as he walked toward his desk, Garth said, "Well, what did she have to say? Is she or her husband a possible suspect?"

"Hell, I don't know. I hardly got a thing out of her before she chased me out of the house—which made no difference to me. I'm just getting started anyway. We'll see what she does. I'll go talk to her husband and see what he says."

"Is he a possibility?'

"Yeah, but he's never been charged for using a weapon in any crime. She, on the other hand, has probably more of a temperament to have shot Susan than he has."

"Well, you've already, even in the short time you've been involved, come up with one more possible shooter than they had at the time of the crime. That's a good sign."

"I guess. I'm not real sure I made much headway today. We'll see what happens tomorrow."

Chapter 43

Andy had read everything he could find online concerning Dorothy Longmire. Available information didn't amount to much, but he was able to obtain somewhat of a feel for her life by reading what he found. He visited with her by phone and was to be at her home by eleven, later this morning.

Garth said, "So what were your final conclusions concerning that woman you went to see yesterday?"

"She gave me nothing to work with and then threw me out of her house. She's one tough cookie. I do however, have a meeting set up with her husband around nine today so we'll see what he has to say. He was much more receptive about setting up a meeting than she was. She's a tough woman. I would need a very good reason to live in the same house with her, I can tell you that."

"Well, you *were* trying to pin a murder on her."

"Correct. I haven't ruled her out yet either. We'll see what he has to say later this morning."

Physically, Sam Hepner amounted to little more than nothing. He was short, small boned, and Andy had no doubt his wife could beat the living shit out of him if she was of such a mind.

He was employed at a small mom and pop grocery store not far from their home. He had willingly agreed to meet with Andy, assuming he wouldn't take much time away from his job, which Andy had assured him he wouldn't.

Once there, Sam took him into a small backroom where their product was stored. They both took a seat on boxes of canned goods as they talked.

"Sam, I won't keep you. I don't want to interfere with your job responsivities. You know why I'm here? I assume Janet told you why I was in your home talking to her and why I set up an appointment with you here."

"Yes, she told me about your meeting yesterday."

Andy smiled, and said, "I'll bet that was an interesting conversation."

"She's one tough woman. Really, it's more that she's protective then tough. She'll do whatever she has to do to keep me out of prison. She's really a good wife, but I understand where you're coming from."

"Let me get right to the point. I'm looking into Susan Jackson's murder. I'm sure she already told you thar. I want to make it clear that is *all* I'm interested in. Do you remember the night she was murdered?"

"I do, yes."

"Do you remember where you were—what you were doing?"

"Yes. I was out with a couple of guys drinking beer. I only had a few weeks left before my PSI would be ready and I had no doubt I was going to prison. I was with them when I heard she was murdered. In fact, my friends and I have a favorite bar where we go to have a beer. Once we heard it on the news, we discussed it amongst the three of us and also with the bartender. He's still there at the same bar, and both my friends are still around. Any one of them will tell you exactly where I was the night she was murdered."

"Okay, good. Call my number and leave a message with the contact information for all those people. That should take care of you. Tell your friends and the bartender I'll be in touch."

"I will." He stood. "Is that it? I really need to get back to work."

"Just one more question. You know where your wife was that night around the time Susan was murdered?"

He looked away for a moment, then turned toward Andy and said, "No. In all honesty I have no idea. I know she wasn't home when I got home. What with all the issues surrounding Ms. Jackson's murder, taking care of kids, and being half drunk, I do still remember that. I never asked her where she was—she never told me. To be honest, as much as she hated Susan Jackson, I guess I didn't want to know where Janet was when she was murdered."

Andy stood, extended his hand, and said, "Thank you, Sam. Thanks for discussing everything with me. I'll check out your alibi. We'll try to figure out Janet's situation later. By the way, I assume neither of you own a weapon."

Sam smiled. "No. You know as well as I that one of the conditions of my pre-trial release, which carried through to the time I was sentenced and my probation, was there were to be no weapons in the house. Neither of us possess, nor most likely *ever will*, possess or own a weapon."

Later that morning, he pulled up in front of the Longmire home. It wasn't in much better condition than the home he just visited. It was apparent this family was having as much financial stress as was the Hepner family.

He walked to the front door, where she was already waiting for him.

"Come in, Mr. Price."

As he walked through the door, he said, "Thank you. And you can call me Andy."

"Come on in to the living room and have a seat. Now, I guess I don't fully understand why you're here. Can you explain in detail, why you needed to see me?"

As he walked through the house, he looked around. It quickly became apparent these people had nothing. All the furniture was well-used, the walls needed a fresh coat of paint, and the carpeting was nearly ruined. He carefully took a seat on the couch.

"Well, Dorothy, I'm looking into the murder of Susan Jackson. I don't know if you saw that article in the paper not long ago about her husband committing suicide, but that generated some renewed interest in who murdered her. I am looking into her case again, and your name came up as someone that might have some information in that respect."

She smiled as she said, "Is that just a diplomatic way of saying I'm a suspect?"

Andy smiled. "Not really. I'm just trying to cross people off the list that might have had issues with Susan at the time of her murder. Your name came up, but I wouldn't go so far as to say you're a suspect."

Dorothy looked away, then wiped a tear from her cheek.

As she redirected her attention toward her guest, she said, "Okay, I understand. What do you want to know?"

"Well, first of all, how did you know her?"

"We went to school together. We were best friends. I hadn't seen her in a long time and had in fact not even thought about her until I saw an article in the paper indicating she might run for district attorney general. I called her and we met for coffee. We met a couple of times after that before I made a fool of myself. That ended our time together….and I lost the friendship of one of the finest individuals…I ever…knew.”

“What created the problem between the two of you?”

“Me, plain and simple. It was all me.”

“Please explain.”

She turned away and again wiped the tears from her cheeks.

“We were broke. Financially, we were a mess.” She turned toward Andy and said, “I asked her for help. She gave me a little money one time and I asked her for more. She wanted me to get some professional help concerning money management and other things. She was willing to pay for it all…*for me*, she was willing to pay for it all. I got mad. I wanted the money without any restrictions or without going to the effort of figuring out a permanent solution to the underlying problem. I just couldn’t see the forest for the trees. I said some pretty bad things to her secretary and then never contacted her again. Since her death, there hasn’t been a week go by I haven’t punished myself for what I did.”

“Did you ever see her again?’

“No.”

“Do you or your husband have any weapons? Either of you own a pistol?”

“No.”

“Do you remember the night she was murdered?”

“As if it were yesterday.”

“Tell me about it.”

“We were just finishing supper. We had an elderly couple that lives down the street, over for supper that night. I got a phone call from one of our old classmates. She told me they had just found her body in her car. I went to the bathroom and got sick.”

“So, you have at least three witnesses that can verify you were here the evening she was killed?”

“Yes. You can ask my husband and check with the older couple down the street. My husband sent them home when we found out. I was to upset to carry on with the evening.”

He stood. “I’ll check with them and verify. That’s all I really needed to know.”

She stood. “Are you having any luck determining who did this?”

"We're just sorting through the names of some additional people that weren't interviewed at the time of the crime, like you. It's too early to know much of anything yet."

"I punish myself every day for the way our relationship ended—every day."

"I wouldn't worry about it. I'm sure she understood the pressure you were under and just accepted things the way they were. Don't beat yourself up. You just need to live your life. You're able to do that, she can't. You're the lucky one. She wasn't so lucky. Take advantage of the time you have and that she never will have." He extended his hand. "Thanks for seeing me."

"Did you make any headway today?"

"Yes, a little, Garth, a little. I eliminated one potential suspect, and I have a feeling I probably eliminated two. But I got a few more things I want to look into before I completely let go of them. As far as being able to point the finger at anyone, I'm as far away now as I was when I started. But I'm not near finished. We'll just see what tomorrow brings."

Chapter 44

A few pressing issues involving other cases had taken him away from the Susan Jackson case. They were issues he could not avoid, but taking time away from her case concerned him. It had suddenly become one of the most intriguing and compelling cases he had ever worked. Theories concerning the murder dominated his thoughts whether he was actually working the case or was involved in a completely different matter.

He called Greg Long's office and couldn't get in to see him for a couple of days. Andy told his secretary the appointment involved pending legal issues which he needed to discuss with Greg as soon as possible. He assumed if he told her the truth, he might end up on Greg's calendar six months down the road.

As he sat, waiting to see Greg, he realized the list of potential suspects was becoming shorter by the day. Only a few of those that had not really been considered viable suspects at the time, yet remained to be interviewed. Once the list was complete, if he didn't have a strong indication concerning one of those individuals being responsible, he would need to start reinterviewing those that *had* been interviewed immediately after the murder—a process which obviously had been less than successful at the time. In addition, he would, without doubt, be on an even shorter leash with his boss than he was now.

"Mr. Long will see you now."

As he walked into Greg's office, he stood and extended his hand. "Good afternoon, Mr. Price. Have a chair. My notes from my secretary indicate you are having a marital issue we need to discuss."

Andy shook his hand, sat down, and said, "Well, the truth of the matter is I *am* having a few marital issues, but that's not really why I'm here."

As Greg sat, he said, "Oh, really? Why are you here then?"

Andy pulled out his badge, and showed it to Greg, as he said, "I'm with the Nashville PD, and I'm investigating a murder that's got a little age on it. I'm reinvestigating the murder of Susan Jackson."

Greg said nothing. He looked away for a moment, cleared his throat, then turned toward Andy and said, "Any reason you are reopening the investigation?"

"Well, I never had anything to do with it at the time it happened, but the article a few weeks back about her husband's suicide, piqued my interest. There were a few people who had close contact with her within the last few weeks prior to her murder that were never interviewed. You were one of them."

"Yes, you're right. No one came to see me. And based on the last contact I had with her I can see why someone might now feel her murder should have been discussed with me."

"You have a few minutes to do that very thing?"

"I do. You and your 'marital' issues, were given about a half-hour of my time. I don't think what I can tell you will take that long, but go ahead—ask me whatever you wish."

"First, just tell me a little about your relationship. For instance, how did it all start?"

"We met shortly out of law school. I really don't remember initially where or specifically when, but we became friends and eventually we were really close. We were involved in a romantic relationship for about six months I guess."

"What happened? Why did it end?"

"Oh, I don't know. I guess we finally just grew apart. She was hell bent for leather on prosecuting and I was deeply involved in my own private practice. We just seemed to be moving in different directions. Our relationship was a little shaky anyway, but once she met Tom, I was in her rear-view mirror. I was history. And, to be honest, that was okay with me. I was involved in my practice and had started to date around anyway."

"What contact did you have with her after you split up?"

"Really, we had none, until I contacted her one day and asked her to meet me for a cup of coffee, which she agreed to do."

"What happened between the two of you after that contact?"

"We just agreed to meet and discuss business and other matters whenever one called the other."

"How did that all work out?"

Greg looked away, thought for a moment, then turned toward Andy and said, "It was good…at first. But the more time I spent with her, the more I wanted to be with her. In addition to that, I couldn't figure out for the life of me what Tom could give her that I couldn't, and that was frustrating."

"Did you continue to meet with her until the time she was killed?"

"No. When I could see I was going nowhere with her—when I found out how much she loved Tom, I was done. I could see the handwriting on the wall."

"Were you angry about it—about her not being interested in you?"

"Angry? Maybe…maybe a little. But more than that, I was embarrassed that I had even contacted her in the first place."

"It's my understanding there was at least one time when you made it very clear that you were upset with her because she wasn't involving you in her life."

"Yeah, I pretty well made a fool of myself a couple of times, which I regretted. I was going to call and apologize for what happened, but ultimately figured the less contact the better."

"Do you own a pistol?"

"No."

Greg thought for a moment. "Hold on now. You don't think I had anything to do with her murder, do you?"

"How would I know. I assume you didn't, but I'm also trying to discard the assumption and replace it with fact. Where were you that night, if you recall?"

He thought for a moment, then said, "I can't remember, I really can't. I remember the funeral. I remember the feeling of despair I felt when I heard she was murdered. But I'm not really sure where I was the night she was killed. I can check and get back to you."

Andy stood, and said, "That would be fine. The sooner the better."

Greg stood and said, "I can tell you one thing though. I didn't murder her. I may be a lot of things, but *murderer* is not one of them."

"Just provide me with the information about where you were and who you were with that night as soon as you can, so I can cross you off the list."

"I will."

"So, how did your interview go with that attorney?'

"Oh, all right. I really don't feel he was involved nor upset with her to the extent that he would kill her. He can't remember where he was that night. I told him to figure it out and call me with some names so that I could verify it wasn't him. He said he would. At this point, I really don't feel like there is even enough there to follow up. But you know how those things go. Many times, the least likely suspect ends up being the one that committed the crime. So, we'll see what he comes up with."

"You're about at the end of that list of people that weren't interviewed, aren't you?"

"I got a few to go. I also want to reinterview some of the others that *were* interviewed at the time. I just hope the boss gives me time to do all I feel I need to do before he pulls me off the case."

"Do you think Harlan should have interviewed some of those that weren't interviewed at the time of the murder—you know, some of those that you are just interviewing for the first time? Did he miss the boat there?"

"I haven't come up with anything from any one of them yet. No, I don't think so. We each have our own way of doing things. I'm sure he had a reason why he didn't contact some of them at the time. Of those, not one of them appear to have had anything to do with the murder. I'm not going to second guess how he handled the investigation. He was always a true professional in every sense of the word."

Andy thought for a moment, then said, "Besides that, all the information I am getting now is coming from Amy Smith, the former secretary that Susan fired. I had to find a way to get her to talk to me. I have no doubt most of the names she gave me were not mentioned to Harlan. I know for a fact she didn't discuss with Harlan many of those individuals I'm talking to now."

A few minutes later, Andy was on another call when Garth whispered, "Your daughter is on line four. You want me to tell her to hold, or do you want to take it?"

Andy quickly ended his call and connected with Kim as he said, "Hey, sweetheart, how are you?"

"I'm good Dad, how's everything at work?"

"Good, everything is good. Is there a problem? You don't normally call me at work. Is something wrong?"

"No, no not at all. I just haven't seen you or heard from you in a while and I wondered if you were okay."

He hesitated. "Yes, I'm fine. I'm sorry. I should have called. In fact, I should have called more than once since the last time I saw you."

"Not unusual."

"How's your mother?"

He could hear her take a deep breath, before she said, "She's fine, Dad. She misses you, as do I."

"I know, I know and I am so sorry. It's going to change. I promise you it's going to all change. Just give me a little time and…"

"You know how many times I've heard that…that mom has heard that. More times than both of us can count. I just don't understand. Don't you care? Doesn't she or me, either of us, matter more than that damn job? Surely there's something else you could do in the police department or somewhere else, that could allow you to spend time with us…to be a family…I just don't get it."

"It's going to change…I promise. I'm working on it now. I've had enough too, and…"

"I'll believe it when I see it. Believe me, it's what we both want, but I'll believe it when I see it. I gotta go. Be safe today, Dad. I love you."

"I love you. Kim…Kim…"

She terminated the call as he sat there looking at the phone.

"Sound like you need to make a change, buddy."

"I'm going to. I'm not sure what I'm going to do, but I'm going to."

"I'll believe it when I see it."

Chapter 45

He mentally reviewed the conversation he had with his daughter, off and on all night. He woke up repeatedly, as he normally did anyway, but instead of thinking about an appropriate sentence for a crook, tonight he thought about how to mend relationships ignored for years.

It was much easier to resolve the crook issues than it had been to resolve his relationship issues. But this time he was certain—it was time he stopped ignoring those relationships and make things right. As he prepared to go to work, he figured for the first time in a long time, he now had his priorities and goals properly in mind. He just needed to determine how to reach them.

"So, who you seeing today in the Jackson case…anyone, or are you finished?"

"A guy by the name of Corey Abbott, if I can find him. I think I know where his office is located, but I haven't had a chance to call him—I can't come up with a cell number for him. I'm not sure he even has a phone."

"He must be dead then. Everyone alive has a phone."

"I *think* I finally tied down his location, but I'll know for sure later this morning. I can cross one guy off the list as of this morning, at least as concerns interrogating him,"

"Oh yeah, who's that."

"A guy by the name of Jim Wagner. He was one of those that Susan had prosecuted and was a good suspect. Not long after Susan's murder, he was shot and killed. According to people that knew him he was a definite suspect, but we'll never know now…he's dead. So, I scratched him off my list and I'll just move on with the people that are still here and still alive. But he was a viable suspect for sure."

Andy sat in his car looking at what was apparently the office of Corey Abbott. It was located in a strip mall south of Nashville. He had been observing a couple of hours and had watched an array of characters march in and out of his office, none of which he would have wanted to meet in a dark alley.

Corey was an attorney, but from what he had observed so far, the guy must have fallen on hard times. The sign above the door indicated he was now a private investigator. Andy had no idea if that was in addition to his profession, or whether he had given up practicing law and changed professions completely. But he was about to find out.

He walked in the front door and into a one room office. Seated at a desk near the back wall, some twenty feet away, was apparently Corey Abbott. A few chairs were scattered throughout the office, but other than that, there wasn't another piece of furniture in the room.

The individual near the back wall stood and said, "Come in, come in. Come on up here."

Andy slowly walked forward until he reached the desk, stuck out his hand, and said, "Hi. I'm Andy Price. I'm with the Nashville PD."

"Morning. I'm Corey Abbott." He shook Andy's hand and as he did, he said, "Have a chair."

As Corey sat, he said, "How can I help you?"

"Well, I guess first off, are you an attorney or a private eye or both?"

Corey smiled and said, "I'm a private detective. I no longer practice law. I gave it up. It wasn't what I wanted to do the rest of my life. Now, how can I help you?"

"Well, actually, I'm not sure you can. I'm investigating the murder of Susan Jackson. I don't know if you saw the article in the paper a while back about her husband's suicide, but his death has regenerated some new interest because her murderer was never apprehended."

"I saw the article. Sad situation. Susan and I weren't close at the time of her death, but it was still sad to see such a promising career come to such a tragic end. Now, that being said, what do you want from me?"

"First of all, how did you know her?"

"Well, I, or rather we…Wait a minute. Do you consider me a suspect in her murder? Is that why you're here?"

"Nope. I am just trying to put all the facts together from people who were close to her at one time or another. You are one of those individuals."

"So, I'm not a suspect?"

"No, not really. I have no idea what your answers might be to the questions I'm going to ask you. I mean, I suppose if you told me you were in the same car with her the night she was murdered, I would then consider you a suspect. But all I know about you is that the two of you were friends. I'm just trying to figure out what happened and why she was murdered. If you can shed some light on that issue, I would be thankful."

He thought for a moment, then smiled and said, "Okay, okay I understand. I'll work with you until I feel uncomfortable about your questions. If it reaches that point, I'm done and you can go through my attorney. Now, start again."

"Let's change directions. I thought you practiced law. I thought someone told me you knew her and you practiced with her or something like that. Do you practice law now?"

"Not really. Oh, I try to advise people that come in here concerning the mess they might be in, but other than that, no, I don't. I don't like the courtroom. I just got tired of all the drama, so I changed my profession."

"Now Corey, you know I can check the record with no effort at all. *Were you disbarred?"*

"What's the difference? I don't practice law anymore, end of story. What else do you want to know? I got a lot going on today."

"How did you get to know Susan?"

"Oh hell, I don't remember. We were practicing law at the same time and somehow we became acquainted."

"Did you become involved?"

"How?"

"Now come on. You really going to make this whole process that difficult? You know what I mean. Answer the question."

"Well, yeah, we fell in love if that's what you're getting at."

"Did you live together?"

"Yes, for a while we did."

"Why did you separate?"

"Oh, you know how those things go. We just grew apart."

"I notice a couple of domestic abuse charges filed against you by a couple of other women, that were dismissed before they were processed. Did you assault Susan?"

"No, I…No, I didn't hit her."

"There have been charges filed against you for that though haven't there—other women, other charges?"

"Yes, a time or two, I guess. But the reason they were never completed is because they were bogus. They amounted to nothing."

"What happened to the relationship after you two split up?"

"Oh, we saw each other now and then, but nothing ever happened involving the two of us as a couple."

"By the way, do you own a pistol?"

"Yes, certainly. I wouldn't be in this line of work without one."

"What caliber?"

"Twenty-two."

"Is that the only one you own?"

"Sure is."

"You own nothing more powerful than a twenty-two?"

"No. No need to."

"To be honest, that's a little hard to believe, but I'll accept your answer for now. How were you getting along with Susan at the time of her death?"

"Fine…no, really good. We were good."

"Did you try a case against her not long before her death—one in which you lost?"

"Oh yeah, I did. No problem there. She should have won. The guy was guilty. I told her I was glad she won that case."

"Really? You told her you were glad you lost?"

"Yup, sure did."

"Did you ask her for a job in her office if she won the election?"

Corey hesitated. "Who told you that?"

"What's the difference? True or false?"

He thought for a moment, then said, "Yes, I did. She said she'd let me know. That decision had not been made at the time of her death."

"Anything about that issue that pissed you off?"

"No, no not at all. There was still time for her to consider hiring me and it was all conditioned on her winning anyway."

Andy quickly reviewed his notes. "Where were you the night she was murdered?"

Corey never said anything, as he continued to stare at his interrogator. "You know, I'll have to check on that. It's been a while. Someone should have checked with me right after she was murdered and I could have told them right off. But I've heard from no one concerning her death, and a lot of water has gone under the bridge since then. Let me get back to you on that."

"As I understand the situation, you were in a hell of an argument about losing that case to her and about her not hiring you if she won. Is that information correct or not?"

"Not really. We were good at the time she was killed. There were no issues between the two of us at that time."

Andy closed his notepad, stood and said, "That about does it. Now I need to know where you were and who you were with that night, by the hour. If you can't remember, you better figure out a way to *try* and remember, because at this point in time, you are high on the list of possible suspects. Do we understand each other?"

Corey stood and said, "You mean just based on what I told you today—*because of that I'm a prime suspect? You must be kidding?*"

"I'm *not* kidding. I would never *kid* about such an important matter. Get back to me soon, Corey. I need to know what you were doing that night. Thanks for your time."

Chapter 46

"**M**orning, Andy. Where the hell you been?

"Am I late? I don't think so…*Garth*. Are you my keeper now, are you?"

"Okay, you're not technically late, but you're always here before I am."

"Not that I'm under any obligation to explain why I've arrived at work a little later than I normally do, but I took all my notes home with me last night and went through them—on the Jackson case. I wanted a chance to look everything over without the phone ringing and people walking up to my desk bothering me for one thing or another. I just needed to study where I've been and where I still need to go."

"So, where *are* you on the case? What happened with that appointment yesterday? I left before you got back here yesterday afternoon. Did it look like it might amount to anything?"

"You know, the guy I talked to, Corey Abbott is his name, is the most likely of all I've talked to so far."

"Does he have an alibi?"

"Not yet. From what I can tell he's a real loser. He was an attorney, but he has been disbarred. He's working now as a PI, but I saw no one walk in his office while I was waiting to see him, nor while I sat there watching his office for a couple of hours after I walked out. I could tell through the dialog I had with him, that he had issues involving Susan. I told him to provide me with information concerning where he was that night, and what he was doing. I wouldn't trust the guy as far as I could throw him."

"He got a record of any kind?"

"Just as an idiot—nothing legally."

They continued to visit about the case, along with other cases involving both of them until Garth said, "You seem upbeat today. That's unusual for you. What's going on? You just excited about finally finding someone that may have been involved in the case?"

Andy remained silent.

"Hey. You gone deaf? You hear what I said?"

"Yes." Again, he hesitated, until he finally said, "I got a date tonight."

"Really? Mind if I ask with whom?"

"My wife."

"You call that a date? I'd call it an obligation."

"Actually, it's a privilege. I've asked her out to dinner a number of times since we've been separated—this is the first time she agreed to go."

"Well, it's nice to see you so upbeat about it. Good luck."

"Thanks. I'm sure I'll need it."

They were to meet at seven. He was there by 6:45, she finally arrived at 7:15. He stood and reached out for her chair, pulling it out for her as she reached the table.

"Thanks. You haven't done that for a while."

As he sat, he said, "I haven't been with you for a while. I asked them to bring you a glass of the house red when you arrived. You all right with that?"

"Certainly."

They both remained quiet, until she said, "Andy, why are we here? What are we doing here? What do you want that you couldn't have asked me about over the phone?"

The waiter brought menus along with her wine.

He started to look at the menu.

"You know, there's no sense in looking at the menu yet. Let's just enjoy our wine and go from there. I want to know why you wanted to meet me, here tonight. What's the reason?"

He hesitated, then said, "To talk, just to talk."

"About us?"

"Yes, about you and I. About turning this marriage around. We've been heading in the wrong direction to long Jess, and I want it to stop."

"I'm not sure that's possible. I'm just afraid…"

"Wait, wait…let's just talk for a bit here and if you think the conversation isn't worth your time, you're welcome to leave whenever you wish."

She took a sip of wine, and said, "Go on. This is your party, lead the way."

"I want to be a family again."

"I've heard that maybe twenty times before. Never has worked. What's changed to make you think it will this time?"

"Because this time, I'm ready."

"I've heard that twenty times before too. That hasn't worked out yet either. What's changed?"

"I have."

"How's that? What's changed in you?"

"I want a marriage. I want a family. I want…what they had."

"What who had, Andy?"

He looked away for a moment, cleared his throat, turned toward her and said, "I want what Susan and Tom Jackson had."

"What the hell did they have?"

"An unbelievable love. An unbelievable relationship. I want what they had."

She thought for a moment. "Okay, just tell me, Andy, how are you going to get there? I mean, for anyone to say we have either of those things to any extent would be a joke. You can't just say you want it and expect it to happen. You have to work at a marriage and a family. You know that. You've *always* known that. You've never, ever been willing to take the time necessary to make a marriage *or* a family work."

"I'm willing to start. You know, for the first time in our married lives, I think I finally understand, and I'm willing to do about anything to make this work."

"Think of all those things you're going to have to change. Let's take a look at the list. First and foremost, you're never home. You say it's your job that keeps you out of the house and out of our lives in the evenings, on weekends, and on holidays. How are you going to handle that? You have a new job, do you?"

"I'm working on that."

"You know, you've never even tried. For instance, you're never there for Kim's birthday. Many times, you've stayed home Christmas morning just long enough to open gifts and then you're off to the office. You're never there after one of Kim's dates to ask her how everything went, to see that look of joy and excitement when she tells you how it went."

"That's all going to change, I promise."

"Really? You know, you haven't, since we've been married, ever once done something for me, or for your daughter, just because we're special to you. Never once have you sent flowers to Kim for a special day she's had, or come home during the day just to say hi…never once have you performed even one random act of kindness for either of us. You're telling me that's all going to change?"

He sat back, and said, "Yes. *I want what they had.* I want my family back. I'm willing to make whatever changes you feel I need to make, to get us all back together again as one family."

"Okay, Andy, let's say I buy into this. How are you going to make this plan work?"

"Well, I haven't figured it all out yet. I needed to know what your position was before I went any further. Now, that I know you're good with it, that you're on board, I'll start figuring that out."

She stood. "Tell you what Andy. You talk a good story. You show me *how* you're going to work this through to fruition, and we'll talk again. All I've heard so far of any consequence is, 'I want what they had.' That's nice, but talk's cheap, and that's all I got to take home with me from this meeting. Figure it out. Give me some specifics that will send all three of us in the right direction, and I'm on board. Until then, I got a daughter to raise…on my own."

Andy stood. "Wait, Jess. Let's at least eat together. Please don't go."

She looked away. When she reengaged, she wiped a tear away, and said, "Let me know when and if you're in the process of making the changes we both know have to be made to save this marriage. Otherwise, don't bother me. I'm not going much further, Andy. I love you—I still do. But I can't take living this way. I didn't marry you to live this kind of life and I'm not going to much longer."

Later that evening, as he downed the second of a couple of scotches, he looked around his two-room-dive, and thought about how that meeting he was so looking forward too, fell completely apart.

She was right. She was always right, and tonight was no exception. It was now imperative that he come up with a plan to change his life in a manner which incorporated his wife and daughter. Otherwise, even the small amount of family he now enjoyed, was, no doubt, going to end permanently.

As he evaluated his position, it was clear there was one major factor that he needed to change in some manner, as soon as possible—his job. It clearly was sucking the life out of his marriage.

Maybe he needed to talk to his boss and determine if there was some other type of job available within the department. He had previously asked his boss about just such a position, but only in passing. Maybe if he impressed upon Arthur that he needed to make a change, and make it soon, he would find something for him. He had little doubt Jess meant what she said. He had little doubt if he didn't do something, and soon, his marriage to the only woman he had ever loved, was about to come to an end.

Chapter 47

As Andy sat down at his desk, Garth said, "You got a call on line one."

"Take a number. I'll call them back. I just got here. You *know* it always takes me a little time to get organized before I start my day."

"You may want to take this one. It's your daughter."

He picked up immediately.

"Hi, Kim. How are you?"

"I'm good, Dad. Sounds like you and mom had a good talk the other night."

He leaned back, and said, "Oh, I guess. There were some things I needed to tell her, so in that respect it was a good night *for me*. But I don't think the conversation we had meant much to your mother. At least that was the impression she left me with."

"Well…okay…but I'm just calling to tell you it *did* have an effect on her. She was upbeat when she got home and she did mention maybe there was just a sliver of hope all would turn out okay."

"I actually didn't come to that same conclusion, but I'm sure at this point you're better at reading her than I am."

She hesitated, took a deep breath, and said, "Don't stop."

"I'm sorry? Don't stop what?"

"Don't stop doing what you're doing. Don't stop trying to patch things up with her. Don't stop making that effort to come home—to turn us back into a family again, Dad. Don't stop…please."

Her comments caught him completely off guard. He leaned forward and said, "I won't, Kim. Not this time. I'll find a way. I'll find a way to make this work, believe me."

"I hope so. I love both of you so much it hurts and to see you separated and both unhappily living your lives this way, is awful. Figure it out Dad…for me, for Mom, and for you."

"I will sweetheart. I will, I promise."

"Gotta go. Love you. Talk to you later."

As he terminated the call, Garth said, "That sounded pretty serious. Everything okay?"

"You know, there's something inherently wrong with you being able to listen in on all my personal calls. Yes, everything is fine. I need to find a new desk, somewhere else, somewhere away from you."

"I was only trying to help."

"Whatever."

"What did she want? Sounded pretty serious. Is there anything I..."

Andy's phone rang, stopping his coworker in mid-sentence.

"Price."

"Is this the cop that came to my office to see me yesterday?"

"Little hard to tell whether it is or isn't if you don't give me your name."

"Name's Corey Abbott."

"Then yes, this is the cop that came to see you yesterday."

"Okay, good. You told me I needed to figure out who I was with the night Susan Jackson was killed and where I was when it happened. Then I was supposed to contact you."

"I remember our conversation. It really wasn't that long ago. What did you figure out?"

"Nothing."

"What do you mean 'nothing?'"

"Just what I said. I've asked around, I've tried to find an old calendar or something that might tell me where I was that night, but I got nothing. I remember her getting killed, but at that time she meant so little to me, I just didn't care. I still have no idea where I was or who I was with when it happened."

"So, you have no alibi for that night at all?"

"Guess not."

"Did I ask you if you own a weapon?"

"You did. Remember, I told you I just had a twenty-two?"

Andy remembered—he was just hoping for a different answer than Corey gave to the question the first time he answered. "Oh yeah, sure, now I remember. You still living where you've lived for the past few years? That address still the same?"

"Yes, why?"

"Anyone living with you?"

"Yeah, I got someone living with me. Why?"

"How long has that individual lived with you? Was anyone living with you at the time of Susan's murder?"

"She's been living with me about a year. And no, no one was living with me at that time—no one was."

"Okay, thanks. I'll get back to you."

"If you're going to have a search warrant issued for my home, don't bother. The only thing there is the twenty-two. You'll find nothing as concerns Susan Jackson, I can assure you of that."

"Thanks for the additional information. I'll be in touch."

Andy terminated the call.

"Who was that? Was that the guy you though might be a pretty good suspect when you got back to the office yesterday?"

"Yes. He now tells me he doesn't have an alibi. I'm going to get a search warrant issued for his house. He's by far the best suspect I've had yet."

"If he's an attorney, you really think issuing a search warrant for the house will be worth the effort? You know he'll have anything and everything that might pertain to Susan's murder out of there by the time the warrant is served. That's a waste of time if you ask me."

"You may be right, but I'm doing it anyway. I want to put just a little heat on him. We'll see what happens when I do. I may follow him a while, see where he goes during his evenings and who his close friends are, just to see where it all leads."

As Andy reviewed his notes, Arthur indicated he needed to see him in his office when he had a moment.

"Hey, boss. What's going on?"

"Have a chair, Andy."

As he sat down, Arthur said, "Where are we on this Jackson case? You've been working on it quite a while now. I know you mentioned you had some people that you hadn't talked to yet, but where do you stand right now?"

"Well, I've talked to a number of people and actually yesterday I talked to a guy who I think might have been involved. I'm going to search his house and follow him a day or two…see where that all leads."

"You devoting all your time to that one case?"

"Well, I guess I…"

"That's what I thought. You've become wrapped up in that one case to the detriment of all the others you have pending."

"Well, I really don't think that's completely the case, Art. I'm spending some of my time on other cases, but yes, this one is taking a good bit of my time as you can imagine. A lot of water's gone under the bridge since the crime occurred."

"But to be honest, even with all the time you've spent on it, you're not really close to making an arrest, are you?"

"No. But, I do a have a few people that have a motive and no alibi. I'd like the opportunity to interview them again, and also finish off all those that I haven't even had a chance to talk to yet."

Art looked away, then leaned back in his chair, clearly deep in thought.

"Well, Andy I know how involved you are in the case, but I really need you on current issues, rather than spending all your time on this damn cold case that's been sitting here for three years and most likely never will be solved. Two weeks. That's it. You got two more weeks, and I'm pulling you off it."

"Okay. I understand. I'll do what I can during that time frame and stop at the end of two weeks, as you wish."

Arthur leaned forward, and said, "I'm not kidding about the time you're working this case. You got two weeks and don't even think about asking me for one more day. Thanks for coming in. That's all I really needed."

Andy never moved. After a couple of seconds of uncomfortable silence, Arthur said, "We got more to talk about? Something else on your mind?"

"I need to talk to you about my job."

"What about it?"

"I probably need to make a change."

"You mean quit? You're surely not thinking of quitting, are you? What are you talking about when you say 'a change?'"

"I don't want to quit, no. But I do need to alter my responsibilities to something that's a little more defined in terms of time spent on the job. I need to start working at a job that has defined hours and allows me to have a life outside of this building."

Arthur leaned back in his chair, and folded his hands in his lap. He started to smile and said, "Is it time for family, Andy? I wondered how long it would take for you to figure out what you considered *were* your priorities, and what *should* be your priorities."

"Yes, it's time. And it's also reached the point where it really matters to me. It's not just her, it's not just Jess—it has become important to me too."

"I understand. No, I don't have anything along those lines available right now. You're thinking desk job, right?"

"Yes. Something that's eight to five, and that's comparable in pay. I know the jobs exist, and I need one. Otherwise, I may have to leave the department, and move on to something else—take a job some place where I can work and have a home life like so many other men in this world seem to have."

'I understand. Let me see what I can do. No promises, but let me see what I can do."

He stood. "Thanks, Art. Let me know if you come up with something. I don't want to wait too long. If there's nothing here, I need to start looking around."

"I'll get right on it. I really don't want to lose your experience. I'll see what I can do."

Chapter 48

He finished another beer, and carefully placed his notes concerning Corey Abbott on his apartment floor, in its appropriate location amongst his notes involving all the other potential suspects.

Andy had left the office, grabbed a bite to eat, then went to his apartment, where for the last two hours, he sat on the floor, reviewed his notes and drank a couple of beers. He was short on time. He needed to figure this puzzle out now, before Arthur yanked the rug out from under him—before he became the final individual to unsuccessfully review all the facts and ascertain the killer.

He had no doubt that if he came up with nothing concerning Susan's killer, the crime would most likely remain forever unsolved.

As he mentally reviewed those he had interviewed and those he hadn't, he considered Sally. He hadn't interviewed her yet, but he would tomorrow morning. He was sure she could provide information, but not as a suspect. Of all the potential suspects, she had absolutely the least to gain from Susan's death. Hopefully, however, she might shed some light on who might have benefited the most, or who hated Susan enough to kill her.

Then there was Jim Wagner. Andy had taken the time to review the court file and also Susan's office file concerning Mr. Wagner. He appeared to have one of the strongest motives, along with a personality to physically carry out his act of revenge against Susan. But there would never be an opportunity to discuss her murder with him—he was dead. There were other suspects that might just as well have committed the crime—luckily, *they* were still alive.

The one he was really interested in was Corey Abbott. He had considered the conversations he had with Corey in the last few days, and concluded he was the most likely to have harmed Susan of all those he had interviewed so far. He was ready to take the next step today as concerned additional evidence involving Corey.

Andy hadn't set up an appointment with Brian yet. He was near the end of his first full term as district attorney general. Andy would visit with him, but as was the case with Sally, it was only to glean any information from him that he might have concerning the case. He didn't believe Brian to be an actual suspect.

Then there was Amy and Janet Hepner. He seriously doubted Amy was capable of murdering someone, but he couldn't rule her out. Neither Janet nor her husband had contacted him concerning an alibi for that night. Tomorrow morning, he would contact one of them to determine what they were doing the night Susan was killed, and whether either of them had an alibi.

As he crawled into bed, near midnight, he could now understand why his predecessor had never been able to come to a conclusion concerning a possible murderer. Even with the additional possibilities given him by Amy, he was still not much closer to determining Susan's murderer than he was when he started his investigation. Something needed to happen soon, or he had no doubt his boss was going to terminate his investigation in a case in which Andy had now become personally involved. There were others to consider, but he would consider them another day—his eyes were just to tired to move on tonight.

Sally McHorton and Andy sat down after he had closed the conference room door.

"Thanks for coming in today, Sally."

"Glad to do it. I would do anything to help solve Susan's murder. I cooperated at the time, and as I have told you, just let me know what you need or what I can help you with and I'll be glad to do it."

"Why don't you start out by telling me about your relationship with her—things like how it all started and how you two got along."

"Well, she decided she wanted to run for office, and she gave me a call. She just initially asked about the process, which she knew I was familiar with, then she asked if I would help her through it all."

"Had she decided to run when she first called you, or was she still on the fence?"

"She asked a lot of questions, but I could tell all the way through that first conversation I had with her, that she was going to run."

"How were you involved in that process?"

"I guided her through it. I told her what to expect while the process was playing out. I introduced her to people I already knew and that I felt would help her financially. I set up all the fundraisers for her. We were close—we were…" She hesitated, cleared her throat, and said, "Sorry. Even as long ago as it's been, I still get a little choked up when I talk about it."

"I understand. That's happened a lot while I've been involved with this investigation. People really liked her. Apparently, someone didn't, but by and large she was really well-liked."

"As the campaign moved forward, she made friends and supporters all over the city. The polls just kept showing her gaining more and more support. I have little doubt she would have been the first female district attorney general this county ever had if she would have survived."

"I have been interviewing those who were interviewed at the time along with a number of other people who weren't interviewed. But as of today, I'm afraid I'm not much further along than the last guy that tried this. What were your observations concerning people that might not have liked her, or that might have held a grudge against her?"

She thought for a moment, then said, "First, let me ask you—are you considering me as part of the group that might have not liked her or that might have had a grudge against her? Am I a suspect? Do I need an attorney?"

Andy smiled and said, "No, you're not and no you don't. I am looking at you solely for the purpose of trying to determine who might have committed the crime—solely for information concerning the crime from your point of view, nothing more, nothing less."

"Okay, let me think."

"Take your time."

"Let's see, I know she had a problem with a former boyfriend—maybe a Corey something."

"Yes, he was and still is a suspect."

"I know there was a problem with that secretary of hers also. Her name was Amy something. I always got along with her, but Susan told me one day she had let her go, and she was sure she wouldn't be voting for her. So, I assumed by that, she had a problem with her."

"What about the guy she was running against? Any problems there?"

"Yes, at least initially. But they cleared all that up. He, of course, won the election, and from what I hear is doing really well. To be honest, I don't know much about anyone else she might have had issues with."

"Do you remember that night?"

"Like it was yesterday."

"Do you remember where you were?"

"Yes. I was home with my husband." She smiled. "Just can't let that cop thing go, can you? Even though you told me I wasn't a suspect, you're still just making sure I couldn't have done it, right?"

"I'm sorry…yes… I'm sorry."

"Not a problem, I understand. Yes, I was home when I heard about it. I was with my husband and our three teenage boys."

"Do you own a weapon?"

"Nope."

"Is there anything else you might be able to tell me about her murder or about her that might help in the investigation?"

"Not that I can think of, but if I do think of something, I'll give you a call."

"To bad about her husband, Tom."

She looked away. When she reengaged, she wiped away a tear, and said, "What a tragedy. What a horrible tragedy. They were so close. What a loss to all of us that knew them."

Later that day, he concluded one way or the other, he had to either let the Hepner couple go as suspects, or step up his investigation concerning both of them. He had a phone number for Sam at his place of employment—time to use it.

After he punched in the number, and had asked to speak to him, he was on hold for almost five minutes.

Finally, someone said, "Yeah, this is Hepner. Who's this?"

"Hi Sam, this is Andy Price from the Nashville PD. You got a minute?"

He hesitated. "You the one that contacted us about that prosecutor that was murdered?"

"Yes, I am. I thought maybe one of you might get back to me concerning an alibi for that night, but I've heard from neither of you."

"Yeah, neither of us are much into conversations. Now I gotta go."

"Do you have an alibi for that night—the night she was murdered?"

"Nope. I don't remember where I was, and she don't neither. Does that help?"

"So, either one of you might have killed her, is that what you're telling me?"

"That's about right. Either one of us might have killed her. Now let's see you prove it. Listen, I got in trouble taking time to talk to you the last time I saw you. Now, I gotta get off the phone."

"Either one of you own a weapon?'

"Do you honestly think I'm going to tell you if I own or possess a weapon? If I told you I did, you *know t*hat would be a violation of my parole and could send me back to prison. What are you, an idiot?"

"With those kinds of answers, I'm going to investigate every move you and your wife made back then. You know this isn't going to end until I figure out who killed her, so just be prepared to hear from me one way or the other, damn near every week for the rest of your life, unless you cooperate."

"Go to hell. Don't stop here to talk to me again, or call me here at work. I'll file a harassment charge against you if you do. Good luck with your three-year-old investigation, you piece of shit."

He hung up. As Andy put his phone down, Garth said, "That sounded a little confrontational. Is he part of the Susan Jackson investigation?"

"Yeah. As you just heard, he's no longer a *voluntary 'part'*, but he's a possibility for sure."

Chapter 49

Andy had spent most of his morning working on office work he had been neglecting. Those matters he had neglected could no longer be finished up 'some day when he had time.' They needed to be handled today.

As his mind wandered, he figured it was only a matter of days before he walked into his boss's office and said, 'Here are my notes concerning Susan Jackson. I'm done. I'm also defeated. I got nothing for you to pass on to the next guy.'

Without doubt, the truth of the matter was that there would most likely be no 'next guy.'

As he continued to finish up, his phone rang.

"Yeah."

"Hello. This is Andy Price, correct?"

"Yes, it is. Who's this?"

"Greg Long."

He sat up as he said, "Greg, good to hear from you. You got some information for me or are you without an alibi?"

Greg laughed, and said, "Sorry, Andy. I *do* have an alibi."

"Okay, well I guess that's good for you and bad for me. Where were you when it happened and who were you with?"

"Okay, I'm going to email you three names, and three phone numbers. I was out drinking that night. I had just won a pretty big case. I along with these three guys, were once upon a time, part of the same law firm. They were good friends then, and still are. They convinced me, as the day came to an end, to go out for a drink. We were at that bar until it closed. They took me home. I was too drunk to drive. That's why the event and the night didn't match up. I remember nothing about that night from about eight on. I heard about her murder the next day when I got to the office. They will verify all of that."

Andy took notes until Greg finished. He then put his pen down, and said, "I guess maybe that clears you then, doesn't it?"

"I think it might, yes. Sorry I took so long to get back to you, but it was only when I casually told one of my friends you had contacted me, that he told me where I was and what I was doing that night."

"Thanks, Greg. I'll put the information in her folder."

"Any leads yet?"

"No. In fact, I'm beginning to wonder if it was just a random shooting. I have very little to go on—much like the prior officer that investigated her murder at the time it happened."

"I'll keep my ears open. Certainly, if I hear anything, I'll let you know."

"Thanks. Before I cross you off my list, I'll go ahead and call these guys. Be sure and forewarn them that I'll be calling so they don't put my call off. Thanks for your help."

As he shoved the information concerning Greg in the file, he looked at his watch. He grabbed the file and walked toward the door. He was to meet with Brian Jenkins in ten minutes and he didn't want to be late. His secretary had a hell of a time fitting him in as it was. Andy didn't want to reschedule.

He had been waiting almost an hour. Just as he reached the point where he concluded he had waited long enough—he would leave and reschedule—his secretary said, "Brien will see you now. Go on in."

He walked through Brien's office door, into a large, well-decorated office. Brien stood as Andy approached his desk and said, "Andy Price, I assume?"

"Yes sir, I am. Nice meeting you, Mr. Jenkins."

They shook hands as Brien said, "Have a seat. How can I help you?"

As Andy sat, he said, "I'm looking into the Susan Jackson murder. I've interviewed a number of people about the incident and felt I needed to visit with you, at least for a moment, about your relationship with her—both the good and the bad."

Brien smiled and said, "Yes, there was a little of both for sure."

"Tell me about your relationship, would you?"

"Certainly, I'll be glad to. But first, tell me why you're here. That crime happened years ago and was thoroughly investigated at the time. What's happened to bring it all up and start the investigation over again?"

"Tom's suicide. I read about it in the paper and asked if I could look into it. I was given the go ahead, and that's what I'm doing."

"Yeah, that suicide note was so sad. And they were both such good people. So, are you here to discuss the case with me as a co-worker or as a suspect in her murder?"

"I'm just trying to tie all the facts down once and for all. You're not a suspect, by any means. I just wanted your thoughts on her, on the situation and perhaps any ideas you might have as concerned who might have done this."

"Got it. Well, first of all, we worked together for almost five years. We were close. By that, I don't mean romantically or anything like that. We were just good friends and working associates. I tried a lot of cases with her. She was a hard worker and one of the smartest attorneys I ever met."

"What was your personal relationship with her—I mean outside the office?"

"We both had our own set of friends. She had hers—I had mine. We seldom saw each other outside the office, which worked out well for both of us."

"What about enemies? Did she have any that you know of?"

"Not one. Not one in this office nor in her personal life of which I am aware."

"Had any complaints been filed against her as a prosecutor?"

"Oh sure, but they were filed by people she had convicted. Nothing of any consequence, and at the time she was murdered, none of them were pending. Most of the people that filed a complaint were in prison. There is no one I know of that exhibited any type of rage to the extent they might harm her."

"How'd you get along with Tom? Wait, let me rephrase that. How did Tom get along in the office?"

"Great. He was far from the lawyer she was, but everyone liked Tom. He was a hard worker and had no enemies that I know of."

"Were you aware of anyone outside the office that had an issue with her?"

"No."

"How did the two of you get along?"

Brien smiled, as he said, "It just depends on the time frame. Initially, we got along great. We tried cases together, we worked together on a number of cases, and even socialized together. But through the years, that changed, at least to some extent."

"Why was that? Why did it change?"

"Oh, I don't know. We ended up working on different types of cases for one thing. And our personal interests changed. Just life, I guess. While we were never competitors, we both ended up going a slightly different direction."

"Did you have issues with her, or she you?"

"No. We just went our own way."

"What about both of you running for the same office? How did that work out?"

"Well to be honest, initially it worked out well. It really didn't matter to me who I ran against. But as time went by, I think the competitive juices started to flow for both of us. There was a time for a while, I'd say a couple of weeks, that we didn't talk to each other. But, one day I woke up and realized what was happening. I walked into her office and told her I was a fool. After that we had no problems whatsoever."

"So, on the night she was murdered, you were both getting along?"

"Absolutely."

"Where were you the night she was murdered?"

Brian hesitated. "I didn't think I was a suspect."

"You aren't and the answer to this question will further support my decision not to list you as one. Now, where were you?"

"Home, with my wife. I left the office early, and we were both at home when the newsflash indicated she was murdered."

"You own any weapons?"

"Oh, I got an old twenty-gauge shotgun I use to hunt with, but nothing else."

"You don't own a pistol?"

"No. What need would I have for a pistol? No, I don't."

As he drove back to the office a few minutes later, almost everyone he had interviewed seemed to have an alibi. Few had a motive to murder. He was really beginning to think this shooting might have been nothing more than a random act of violence. Maybe it wasn't planned. Maybe it didn't matter to the shooter who the victim might have been.

He was near the end of his list of possible suspects. If something didn't turn up soon as concerned his few remaining possibilities, he was afraid he was going to be forced to conclude the shooting might well have been at random and the crime unsolvable.

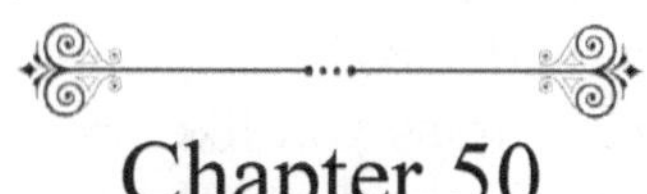

Chapter 50

“So, what direction are you taking today concerning Jackson? You're about at the end of your list of new subjects, aren't you? What's the plan today?”

“I don't know where the hell I'm going today, Garth. I don't have much time left. As I told you, Arthur told me this was about it—if I didn't turn up something soon, he was pulling me off the case. He's told me that a couple of times, but always extended the deadline. I don't have much doubt this time they will be no extension.”

“You've still got a couple of those people from the new list of suspects that could be the killer, don't you?”

“Yeah, I got a couple, but even with them, all I have is a lack of alibi. As of yet anyway, I can't tie any of them to the crime. I think I'll start interviewing some of those other individuals that were interviewed at the time of her murder, and see if I might be able to pull something out of them that they didn't mention the first time they were interviewed.”

As Andy considered his remaining options, his phone buzzed.

“Hey sweetheart, how are you? What's going on?”

“Nothing Dad, mostly nothing.”

“Is everything all right?”

“Yes, everything's fine. I just wondered how you were—how work was going. I miss hearing you talk about cases you're working on. How's that case you said you were working on with that woman that was murdered a long time ago? Anything new on it?"

He leaned back and said, "No, not really. I've run into a bit of a wall right now. But that's not unusual in cases like this. You just keep working them and working them, hoping something turns up. I'm having a little trouble making any headway at the present time, but I'm still hopeful. What's going on in your life?”

“Not too much today. It's been a good summer though. I go to work at three, so I probably won't do much between now and then.”

She remained quiet, until she said, "I miss you, Dad. It would have been a lot better summer if you'd been living here. Seems like my time with you is less and less."

"I know. I understand. I miss you like crazy. But I'm working on it. What about your mom? Everything okay with her? Oh, and how's whatshisname—that   boyfriend of yours? How's everything going with you two?"

"We've both moved on. I'm not dating anyone right now."

He hesitated before he said, "Is that a good thing or a bad thing? How do you feel about that?"

"It's fine. I broke it off. I'm fine with it. Dad, I need to talk to you about mom."

He leaned forward, as he said, "Is she okay? She got a problem? What's going on?"

"No, no she's fine. But…I think that talk you two had the other night made a difference. She's talked about you a lot since then. I think she really misses you. It just sounds to me like you need to see her…to talk a little more like you did the other night. Can you do that? Do you have time to stop by and see her? I think if you came over and told her you're working on some of the changes you've discussed, it might be all you need to do."

"Certainly. I'll go see her today. I'll call her first, then drive out."

"Thanks. I'll keep my fingers crossed."

"So will I."

Garth said, "That was Kim? How's she getting along?"

"Good, good. It was an enlightening conversation. She thinks maybe Jess is coming around. Good God, maybe I still have a chance of saving what's left of our marriage."

He stood, and said, "I need to go see her. While I'm driving, I'll give her a call and tell her I'm coming." As he walked away, he said, "Wish me luck."

Garth said, "I do. I wish you luck, but I also know your track record with her. I'm not holding my breath."

Andy called Jess on the way to the house. She said she wasn't busy and looked forward to seeing him.

As he walked through the front door, she said, "Hey, good morning. What are you doing here so early? Something wrong? Something going on?"

"Nothing special. I just wanted to see you. I figured right now was best, as opposed to later in the morning when I might be tied up in some case or another."

"Come on in. Let's sit at the kitchen table. Kim is still upstairs, sleeping I assume. You got time for a cup of coffee?"

As she walked to the counter, he caught up with her, grabbed her arm, turned her around and kissed her.

"What was that for?"

"It's been too long. I've missed you. I've really, really missed you."

She smiled and said, "Sit down. I got some coffee still hot from earlier this morning. Want a cup?"

Over the next half-hour, their conversation covered a myriad of subjects, from old friends to new, from her job to his, from cases solved to cases that remained open. He reached out about halfway through the conversation and took her hand, which she didn't resist.

Finally, he simply said, "Jess, what about moving back in? What about making this family whole again? Don't you think it's time? Didn't I explain away most of the issues that involved us when we met for supper a while back?"

She pulled her hand away, as she said, "I agree you have resolved most of the issues I initially had. But, Andy, you know the major issue was, and still is, your job. And to be honest, I don't think that issue is resolved nor is it resolvable. You like what you do, you're committed to what you do, and you're good at what you do. I just see it getting in the way again and again as it has in the past. I really think if you could resolve that one issue, we'd have a chance, I really do."

She stood. "I need to get ready to go to work."

He stood, took her in his arms and kissed her. "I love you. Always have. I've tried to make all those changes I needed to make to put this family back together again. I'm not sure there's much else I can do."

"You know, Andy, I'd let you move back in the blink of an eye, but until we get that one problem fixed, for good, I'm so afraid we'll just end up like we are today. I'm sorry, but until you can at least resolve that issue to *some* extent, we need to keep seeing each other this way. I just can't see resolving our problems in any other manner. Your job is extremely important to you. You've shown me time after time it comes before us, and until that ends we need to either stay the way we are or dissolve the marriage."

A few minutes later, he sat down in his office chair, and started to go through phone messages, hoping there might be one there that would help take his mind off the conversation he had just had with his wife.

As Garth walked up to his own desk and sat down, he said, "So, did you resolve anything with her?"

"Mind your own business."

"Hmm. Guess that probably told me all I need to know."

A few minutes later, after he had reviewed his messages he said, "This job keeps getting in the way. I'm afraid I'm going to have to start looking somewhere else. I hate to. I love what I do. I hate to end my career in law enforcement, but I'm afraid that's the only way she'll let me back in."

"All a matter of priorities, buddy. I'm thinking you're about to get yours in the proper order for the first time in your life. It's about time."

Chapter 51

Andy cupped his hands behind his head and leaned back in his chair. He wasn't sure he would start or finish much of anything today. Sleep was a nonfactor last night. Today he would pay for it.

He went through scenario after scenario, hour after hour, but unfortunately always came to the same conclusion. She had made her point and made it crystal clear. Unless something changed in Andy's professional life, there was little chance of resolving their issues.

The suicide note had started it all. As he read and reread the note, the way Tom Jackson described *his* married life was what *he* wanted. But reading it, and wanting it was the easy part—actually getting there, now seemed almost impossible.

"Hey buddy. How's your day look today? How are those marital issues coming along? Sort anything out overnight?"

"Ha, I wish. Nope, still struggling."

"You want some advice?"

"Nope. I've told you before I'm not taking advice from someone that's been through multiple divorces already in his young life. I'm good, but thanks."

"Well, I got a good education from both those marriages, and…"

His lecture was cut short by the buzzing of Andy's phone.

"Price here."

"Andy, this is Amy Smith. How are you?"

He sat up, and said, "Amy, I'm good, how are you?"

"Oh, fine. How is the investigation going? I think of you often. I haven't seen you since the first time we met, but I've wondered a number of times how you were getting along."

"Oh, as well as might be expected, I guess. I have not had a breakthrough of any kind and I've about gone through that list of names you gave me. Of course, no one is overly excited about even visiting with me. They've all mostly made her murder just a distant memory and tried to forget it. Oh course, none of them know anything specifically about the facts. Only Corey ever indicated he owned a pistol. None of them…well you get the idea."

"I was afraid that would be the case. I'm really sorry to hear that. What's next? Are you going to reinterview any of them? Are you going to reinterview those that were interviewed the first time around? Is there anything I can do to help?"

"No, there's really no more you can do. Initially, you helped immensely. I would have never known anything about all those people I interviewed if it hadn't been for you. I'm just not sure where to go from here. As soon as I figure out which direction I'm taking with the investigation I'll let you know."

"I'll be glad to do whatever I can to help."

"One of the major issues is that I'm running out of time. Since this was a dead file, my boss gave me a limited amount of time to work on it. I'm about at the end of my rope I'm afraid. I'll stay in touch though, Amy. Thanks for calling."

As he terminated the call, Garth said, "I think the boss wants to see you. He looked over here a time or two, then kind of pointed your way. I *think* he motioned for me to tell you he wanted to see you. I'm not real sure, but I'm guessing he wants to see you."

"Thanks."

Andy stood and slowly sauntered toward Arthur's door. He had no doubt what the subject matter of this conversation would entail.

"Morning., have a seat."

"Thanks. I haven't seen you in a bit, Art. Everything ok?"

"Everything's fine. I haven't seen you around either Andy, but I really figured you were intentionally avoiding me."

"Might have been, boss. Might have been just a little."

"You ready to give up the ship on the Jackson case?"

Andy hesitated. "Oh, not really. I know what our agreement was, and to be honest, I have little to show for the time I've spent investigating. But I'm really not ready to give it up. Susan and Tom were the best, both of them. They basically were both victims of the same murder and they deserve justice as concerns what happened to both of them. But I know what our agreement was, and I'll stand by it."

"You know, Harlan Anderson was one of the best detectives we ever had and he came to the same conclusion you did. He came up with nothing. That's why I was reluctant to assign more manpower to the case…again. Not that you weren't as good as he is, but he's as good as I ever knew, and he came up with absolutely nothing."

"I know, and I understand. That's was our deal—I was to use only the time you gave me to solve the case. I didn't get it done. You want me to stop?"

"Yes. I really think you're going to need the extra time anyway—you know, to get use to your job and your office."

Andy smiled and said, "By now Art, I'm pretty much used to my office and have become pretty well acquainted with…"

He moved forward in his chair. "What…I'm sorry…what job? I don't understand."

He smiled. "You said you wanted a new job. With a new job comes a new office. I thought that was what you wanted."

Andy stood. "Are you kidding? Desk job? Defined hours? Are you kidding me?"

"Nope. One opened up. I'm not sure you're going to like it, but you got it if you want it."

"Is the pay…"

"Pay and benefits are comparable."

"Oh my god, Arthur. Thank you. Thank you so much."

He reached out and shook his hand. "I got someone I got to tell. I'll see you later today…maybe…and then maybe not, but whenever I see you, I'll tell you thanks again. Thanks again, Art."

Andy sat down at his desk, as he tried to figure out what to do next.

"What did Art want? You done on Jackson?"

"Yes, I think I am. We didn't really discuss that issue. I need to consider everything he just said and figure out where to go from here."

"Did he have issues to discuss with you other than Jackson?"

"He did yes, he certainly did."

He smiled and said, "I suppose he finally did what's right and fired your lazy ass. Is that what he did?"

"Nope. Here's what he did. He found me a desk job—*that's* what he did."

Garth sat quietly as he processed the news. "Well, I guess you got just what you wanted. Are you going to an office?"

"I have no idea where he's going to put me. I don't care. I just know that what I do is going to have defined hours and it just very well might put the pieces of my marriage back together again."

Garth thought for a moment then smiled. "I hope it does buddy I really do."

"I got to call her."

He quickly punched in her number.

"Morning, Andy."

"Jess, I got some news for you."

"What's that?"

"Oh, no, I'm not doing this over the phone. I'm coming to see you. I need to tell you in person."

"Well, okay, that's fine, I guess. Good news, bad news?"

"Good news, Jess…really good news. You home tonight?"

She laughed. "No, I got a hot date. Yes, certainly. We're both home tonight."

"I've got a few problems here that I need to take care of, but I'll be home as soon as I can get out of here. I love you."

"Well, this is all kind of strange, but I'll see you tonight. Love you too."

Andy started looking through case files and making notes. Someone would be taking over all his cases and he wanted to make sure everything was up to date. He wasn't certain yet what his new job might be, but it made no difference to him. He got what he wanted, and hopefully, it would change his life—hopefully it would change all three lives in a positive manner from here on.

Late in the day, just as he was getting ready to leave, his phone buzzed.

"Amy, what's going on? Two calls in the same day. You forget to tell me something?"

"No not really. But something you said kind of bothered me. As concerned all those you interviewed, did you ask the same question about whether or not they owned a pistol?"

"Yes. I got the same answer from all of them, which I expected. Only one of them, Corey, admitted owning one."

"Well, as you know at the time of the murder, I completely distanced myself from all of that. I didn't care, I was mad, and I absolutely was not going to be involved in the investigation, in any respect."

"Yes, I know, and I understand why you felt that way."

"Now that I have become involved, after your conversation this morning, I got to thinking. Not long before Susan was murdered, I had some paperwork to take down to Brian's office. I walked in and his secretary, whom I was good friends with at the time, just told me to take the paper work in to him—he was alone and available. I opened his door, and he had a pistol in his hands. He was surprised I walked in unannounced. He apparently had just purchased it, because the box it came in was sitting on his desk. He put it in the box, put the box in a desk drawer, and took the paperwork from me."

Andy sat up, and said, "He lied to me."

"Sounds that way to me."

"And certainly, if he just purchased it, it would seem logical to assume he would have kept it for at least a few weeks. He lied to me."

"That's why I called you. What you told me and what I know to be a fact, aren't consistent at all. Now, maybe he forgot. Maybe he didn't have it at the time she was murdered. But I'm thinking he did."

"Thanks, Amy. I'll go see him yet today."

Andy tried to reach Brian the remainder of the afternoon, with no success. He called his office three times and had not received a call back. It was now after six, and he had no doubt Brien was no longer at his office.

He knew he needed to follow up on Amy's information today. As a result of his change in jobs, he wasn't sure how much longer he would be investigating any of his current cases. It was imperative he bring his files up to date, prior to starting a new position. Arthur had given him a couple of days to tie together all those loose ends.

Andy had told Jess he would be home tonight to explain what happened, and he would. In addition, for the first time in longer than he could remember, tonight Jess and Kim would come *first* not last. No matter when or where he found Brian, his confrontation with him would take place *after* his conversation with his family.

His phone buzzed.

"Price here."

"Mr. Price, this is Brian. I understand you have been trying to reach me."

"I have, yes I have. Where are you?"

"I'm home now. Can this wait until tomorrow?"

"No, it can't."

"Oh, come on. Is it really that important?"

"I want to see you tonight, end of discussion."

"Whatever." He hesitated. "Okay, where do you want to get together?"

"I'll come to your home. I'm about ready to leave here. I need to stop at home for a moment, but it's on the way to your house. I'm leaving right now. Probably be about an hour before I get there. Your house is east at the intersection of 117th and Cedar, right?"

"Yes. Can I ask what this involves?"

"Same thing as before—Susan Jackson's murder."

"You got something new we need to discuss or is this just a follow-up concerning something we've already discussed?"

"I'll tell you all about it when I get there. I'll see you in about an hour."

Once he had terminated the call, he finished up with the most immediate issues lying on his desk, concluding he would finish off the rest of the files he needed to review, tomorrow morning.

He finished up a couple of mindless tasks he had started before his discussion with Brian, then started his drive home with hope in his heart, for the first-time in a long time. He wouldn't be able to spend much time with Jess and Kim tonight. But hopefully after he finished all he needed to finish up with his files tomorrow, he could move to his new desk… his new office, and life would change. For the first time, his life with his wife and daughter would become what it should have been years ago. He couldn't drive fast enough.

As he approached the red light at 117th and Cedar, he couldn't help but consider what started this change, this transformation of his life. If it hadn't been for Susan, if it hadn't been for Tom, he most likely would never have found his way.

In the darkness, as a car beside and slightly behind him slowed for the light, he noticed the front seat passenger window was rolling down. As he turned to see if it was someone he knew, or was someone wishing information, the last thing he saw was a slender ray of light as it reflected off the silver barrel of a pistol.

Chapter 52

A few days later

A   She was expecting him. The knock on the door came as no surprise. She opened it as she said, "Officer Graf, I assume."

"Yes ma' am."

"Come on in."

As he walked in, he said, "I'm so very sorry to meet you under these circumstances. But…

She led him to the living room and said, "Have a seat."

As he sat, Kim, her eyes red and with tissue in hand, walked in the room.

"Officer, this is my daughter, Kim. She wanted to sit in with us. Based on what we're about to discuss, is there any reason she shouldn't sit with us?"

"No ma'am, no not at all. She's welcome."

Jessica sat down, and said, "Quite a funeral. I never saw so many people at one funeral."

"Andy was well liked by everyone in the department that knew him. They all turned out with their families, along with a large number of private citizens."

"Why are you here? What did you want to tell us?"

"Well, I just…actually my boss wanted me to come just to explain what happened after Andy was killed—what we did, what we found out. He couldn't be here today or he would have come himself. He sent me, not wanting to wait any longer in providing you with this additional information. He knew you were left in the dark concerning what was actually going on and felt you should know what we now know."

Jessica looked away and dabbed at her eyes. When she reengaged in conversation, she said, "Thanks for thinking of us. What have you found out?"

Well, first of all, I'm sure you already know, but the shooter was Brian Jenkins."

"You're sure he's the one—the district attorney general of our county is a murderer?"

"We're sure, yes. There's no doubt."

"And was what happened somehow a result of Andy's involvement in the Jackson case?"

"Yes. If it hadn't been for him, the murder of Susan Jackson would have never been solved."

"What was the timeline on all that? How did it come to happen as it did?"

"Andy got a call from one of the potential suspects who was helping him try to solve Ms. Jackson's murder. She told him that even though Brian had told Andy he didn't own a pistol the day Susan Jackson was murdered, she was pretty sure he actually *did* own one. Andy called Jenkins and told him he wanted to come to the house to talk to him about the case. He explained that he needed to make a short stop at his home first, but then he would drive to Brian's home from there. Brien went crazy knowing something had come up that would most likely tie him into the case."

"So, Brian's home isn't far from ours?"

"No. In fact Andy had *told* him your home wasn't far from his. So, he accessed records he had at his disposal and determined Andy would be going through the same interaction Susan did. He took the chance he would be stopped there at that stoplight because he knew traffic from that direction always stopped there...you can never go right through the intersection when coming from the direction Andy was coming from because of the setting of stoplights on that stretch of roadway. He had driven that road many times. A left turn at that intersection took him home He then did exactly what he did that worked so well the first time at that intersection—he shot his victim while he was stopped for the light. He figured it worked once, it would work again."

"And why *didn't* it work this time—why didn't he get away with it the second time?"

"Well, first of all, a couple of us knew where Andy was going and they also knew why. So, we had an idea that Brian very well could have been involved in the Jackson murder. As I mentioned, it was easy for him to access a few records he had at his disposal and determine Andy lived on the same street as Susan and that he would need to come through that same intersection. There was absolutely no traffic at the time of the shooting, but there *was* a guy sitting in his driveway, car off, waiting for his wife to come to the car so they could go out for supper. Even though the house was a distance from the intersection, he heard the shot and could describe the vehicle that took off at a high rate of speed. The description fit the car Brian drove perfectly."

"Did you confront him at that time?"

"We did. We confronted him with what we then knew, and he admitted everything. He admitted Susan's murder and admitted killing Andy."

"But I thought he had an alibi for the Jackson murder. I thought somebody told me that."

"It was his wife that provided his alibi. His wife told us Brian was home all evening. She lied. She's now admitted that."

"Why did he kill Susan? What was his reasoning?"

"He simply didn't want to lose. When their boss decided to back Susan, and he started to see polls indicating Susan was beginning to run away with it, he felt he needed to take care of the problem and eliminate her as a candidate. She had previously told him he might not even have a job with the District Attorney General's office at all if she won and he lost. He was desperate. He felt he just couldn't chance losing. So, he eliminated the problem."

Jessica sat back and thought for a moment, before she said, "Well, that's good to know. At least, Andy's death wasn't in vain. He solved a murder of a highly regarded public servant and put a corrupt one behind bars. That's good, I guess."

She looked away and remained quiet.

He stood and said, "I better go. Do you have any more questions?"

She stood, hesitated, then said, "You know, Andy had something he was going to tell me—something he wanted me to know, and he was really excited about it—really excited about what he wanted to tell us. Do you have any idea what that might have been?"

"No, ma'am, I don't, I really don't. I didn't work that closely with him"

She looked at Kim and dabbed at her eyes. "Oh well, I guess it doesn't matter now." She looked away. "Something…something must have seemed so important to him…I only wish he could have told me what…" She wiped away the tears again, as she whispered, "I guess I'll never know."

About the Author

JB Millhollin resides near Nashville, Tennessee. He has published a number of novels and continues to write, using the city and surrounding area as a backdrop for his stories. If you enjoy his style of writing, stay in touch through his Facebook author page, on twitter (@jbmillhollin), and through his website at www.jbmillhollin.com.

www.ingramcontent.com/pod-product-compliance
Lightning Source LLC
Chambersburg PA
CBHW021313190726
48288CB00003B/821